M000191427

After the Sun

Book Two of the *Coming Back to Cornwall* series

Katharine E. Smith

HEDDON PUBLISHING

First edition published in 2018 by Heddon Publishing.

Copyright © Katharine E. Smith, all rights reserved.

No part of this book may be reproduced, adapted, stored in a retrieval
system or transmitted by any means, electronic, photocopying, or otherwise
without prior permission of the author.

ISBN 978-1-9997027-9-3

Cover design by Catherine Clarke

This is a work of fiction. Names, characters, businesses, places, events and
incidents are either the products of the author's imagination or used in a
fictitious manner. Any resemblance to actual persons, living or dead, or actual
events is purely coincidental.

www.heddonpublishing.com
www.facebook.com/heddonpublishing
@PublishHeddon

Katharine E. Smith is a writer, editor and publisher.

An avid reader of contemporary writers such as Kate Atkinson, David Nicholls and Anne Tyler, Katharine's aim is to write books she would like to read herself. Katharine has written and published eight novels to date, with bestselling *A Second Chance Summer* marking the start of the Coming Back to Cornwall series.

She also runs Heddon Publishing; working with other independent authors all over the world.

Katharine lives in Shropshire, with her husband and their two children. She hopes she will be able to add '(and their dog)' to this very soon.

O, wind, if winter comes, can spring be far behind?

- Percy Bysshe Shelley

After the Sun

It is a late summer day when Sam and I head off to the college to pick up his exam results. He drives while I gaze out of the window, greedily consuming the various views and vistas, first of sea then of moorland – sparsely populated, with the occasional crumbling old tin mine cropping up here and there – then glimpses of deep, dark sea once more as we approach the other side of the Cornish coast.

I still can't believe my luck. Not six months ago, I was catching crowded, too-hot buses; windows coated with condensation, then trudging through the tail end of winter, in a litter-strewn town, back and forth to my job at the World of Stationery offices, returning each day to an empty flat. Not that my life was awful. Far from it. I was happy, or content at the very least. But now when I look back, it seems somehow devoid of colour. I feel ungrateful and disloyal to the place where I grew up, and the people I grew up with, but it just can't compare to being here, by the sea, in the glorious sunshine, with the beautiful man I have been in love with for ten years. To top it all off, I've found a job I love, taking over the reins of a great hotel. I have not felt this happy for years, if ever.

Sam is quiet as we pull into the car park. I know how much today means to him and I can feel his nerves, emanating from him, seeping into me so that my stomach performs cartwheels on his behalf.

He's been working towards these exams for two years, squeezing in lessons and study time whenever and wherever he can, between work and looking after Sophie, his daughter. This, now, is his chance to really do something for himself.

I realise his hands are shaking on the steering wheel. I reach out, placing my fingers over his. "You'll have done great, you know," I tell him. "You've worked so hard for this, and you know all your stuff."

He turns and smiles at me, and I lean over to kiss him. It still feels novel, and exciting, but at the same time just… right.

"I hope so," he says, unsure of himself, kissing me back.

"Come on," I say, feeling his reluctance to leave the safety of the car and the not knowing how he's done. Right now, for all he knows, he could have got the best marks of any student, ever. They might want him to teach the courses himself from now on. Or he could have failed abysmally. "Let's just get in there and find out, shall we?"

Sam takes a deep breath. "OK." He opens his car door.

We walk hand-in-hand through the car park, passing other students, some of whom Sam says hello to. There are a mixture of younger A-Level-age students and older, mature students like Sam. The younger ones gather in gaggles, giggling and shrieking, girls holding each other's hands as they group together before going in to find out their fate. Boys walking in pretend-nonchalantly. Like it doesn't really matter either way. I smile at Sam as we pass one such group. These kids are the age we were when we first met. A lot has happened since but I don't feel much older than them. I'm aware that to them I probably look ancient, though.

As we pass from the warmth of the day into the cool

entrance hall of the college, we can hear excited chatter and an occasional exclamation. The clamour grows in intensity as Sam leads me along a corridor towards the main hall. As we go to walk through the double doors, a teenage girl pushes past us, sobbing. Close behind her is another girl, calling, "Lindsey, what's happened?"

Lindsey calls back, "I didn't get in, I didn't make it." Her voice is stifled by sobs but she waits for her friend, who catches her up and puts her arms around her. I am surprised to find tears in my own eyes at this emotional scene. I feel Lindsey's disappointment and I also love the display of friendship. It makes me think of Julie.

Sam looks at me and I squeeze his hand. We walk into the hall together, ready to meet the future.

When we get back to David's, there is a bottle of champagne in an ice bucket, waiting in the hallway, and a helium balloon with the word 'Congratulations' in large letters bobbing about in the breeze which comes in with us.

"There's a card there!" I say to Sam. I pick it up and give it to him.

"You read it," he says, so I open the envelope and slide out a card. I smile as I read the words out loud:

"Dear Sam, and Alice too,

These are for you – to say congratulations to Sam because I don't even need to know what your exam results are. I already know you'll have excelled. And for both of you, to say well done for sorting it out and getting together. Maybe I'm going soft now I'm about to be a married man but we have to take these opportunities for happiness when we can.

Wishing Sam the very best for what I know is going to be a hugely successful future, and both of you lots of love for a very happy life together (I can say that even though you've only been back together a few weeks).

"With much love from David and Martin xxx"

"Wow!" Sam says. "That's so cool. I hardly know David, really."

"He is just great, he's one of the most lovely and generous people I know."

"Well, he obviously thinks the world of you," Sam says, moving towards me and slipping his arms around my waist. "And he's not the only one."

He kisses me and we stand for a few moments in the cool, dark hallway, taking our time to enjoy the feeling of being together again.

"Come on," Sam says, pulling back gently. "I'm in the mood to celebrate!" He takes the balloon and hands it to me, then he takes the ice bucket from its stand, and ushers me in front of him. We head upstairs.

1

It's just a couple of weeks now until Bea leaves for America and we have so much to go through. She always made running the Sail Loft look so effortless. I knew it must be harder than it appeared but it's only since she started her handover to me that I have appreciated quite how complicated running this business is. There is maintenance of the building; keeping insurance up-to-date; making sure all soft furnishings, bedding, etc., are in excellent condition or else replaced; paying staff; finding cover in case of illness or annual leave; advertising and marketing; networking with other local businesses; negotiating with suppliers; making sure Health & Safety regulations are followed and risk assessments up-to-date… the list really does go on. And on.

"We'll leave it for today, shall we?" Bea smiles at me from behind her desk. "I don't want to overload you. I know it seems daunting but you know I am also always at the end of the phone, or email, or whatever."

"You'll be too busy trekking through the National Parks with Bob, wrestling bears," I grin.

"Don't mention the bears," Bea grimaces. "Now go on, get out there and get some sunshine. It's the last you'll see of the outdoors for some time!"

As she says this, my phone starts to ring. I reach into my pocket.

"Bet it's Sam," is Bea's parting shot. I glance at the screen.

She's right.

I smile. "Hang on," I say into the handset, "I'm just leaving, I'll call you right back."

I reach behind the reception desk for my bag and I head out through the gleaming glass door at the front of the Sail Loft, to be greeted by a wide open view of the town and the sea. I breathe it all in, just for a moment, before I speak again. "Sorry about that, I was just grabbing my bag. How are you?"

"I'm OK." Something in his voice immediately puts me slightly on edge.

"What's up?" I ask.

"Nothing… nothing, really," he says. "Well, that's not quite true. Can I meet you for lunch?"

"Yes, of course you can, I'm just heading back to David's. I'll drop off my stuff and come down to town."

David's house is soon to be mine and Julie's – or at least we will be renting it from him when he moves over to Martin's, just around the bay. I want to ask again if Sam is OK but something stops me.

"Great, I'll see you at Joe's in about twenty minutes, if that's OK? Love you."

He's hung up before I have had a chance to say anything more. I hurry along through the streets, all thoughts of the Sail Loft now out of my head, as I wonder what it is that Sam wants to say. Images of Sophie and Kate float through my head. It's been tough with them, or with Kate at least, since Sam and I got together. Sophie seems OK with the situation.

What else could it be? I wonder. I hope I am worrying about nothing but there is just a very slight niggling feeling in me; things have been almost too good lately, with Sam and me, and my new job and beautiful place to live, then

Sam exceeding all expectations with his exam results. I have wanted to take it all at face value and I have been overwhelmed by how wonderful life has become. The only downside is that Sam will be studying in Plymouth so we will have less time together but as I'll be busy learning the ropes at the Sail Loft, this may not be a bad thing. I take a deep breath when I get to the little flat at the top of the stairs and tell myself to stop being paranoid. I am probably worrying about nothing.

***

"Oh." I feel like my stomach has dropped to the floor. I try to look happy. "But that is brilliant, isn't it? It's an amazing opportunity, it's perfect for you."

"Alice," Sam says quietly and I look at him. "It's not perfect, is it? Because it would mean being away from you."

He's been offered sponsorship through university, including a year's practical experience partway through the course, and guaranteed employment afterwards. His exam results were some of the best in the country for his chosen course, Applied Marine Biology, and he's actually been head-hunted by a brilliant conservation society. It's more wonderful news, on top of everything else. Only the course they want him to do isn't at Plymouth, it's at Bangor, in North Wales.

414 miles away via the quickest route (seven hours, ten minutes). 389 miles via the A30 (seven hours, thirty-two minutes), five changes on the train (eight hours, fifty-eight minutes).

"You have to do it," I say, "you have to. It's too good an opportunity to turn down."

I am saying the right words but I am willing him to say

no, he won't, he doesn't want to. We have been apart for ten years, and back together again for a matter of weeks. I can't bear the thought that we will be separated again. But I know that this decision needs to be his. He looks at me, his blue eyes serious and holding my gaze. I look away first, scared that I might cry.

"I don't know," he says. "I don't know."

"Number fifty-three!" The lady behind the counter calls out cheerfully.

"This is us," I say, "I'll go and get it." I am grateful for the opportunity to break this moment. "Do you want any sauce?" I ask, trying to match the cafe lady's tone.

"Alice…" Sam says but I am on my feet, walking towards the counter with a smile on my face while inside my heart is breaking. I know that he has to go.

2

After the initial shock, Sam and I spend the day together and talk through all the options but I know that realistically, there is only one. Anything else could leave Sam years in the future wondering what might have been. He could even end up blaming me for denying him the opportunity to do something he loves and has been working towards all these years.

"I don't want to leave you, Alice."

With those words, I know that he will be doing just that. We are sitting up on the coastal path, burrowing down in between the sun-warmed rocks. He is looking out to sea, the sun directly behind him, a slight glow outlining his profile. Behind him, long, dry grasses sway gently in the sea breeze, their seed heads a sign that summer is on its way out.

Sam turns to me, his expression serious and his eyes seeking mine, as if trying to read my thoughts. I try to look neutral. He can't think I don't care but I can't emotionally blackmail him into staying.

"You have to do what's right, Sam. I know that is such an easy thing to say. And I know you don't want to leave me but if we've managed to make it ten years down the line and still feel this way about each other, then a few more years won't make a difference." I smile at him, wanting to see him smile back, but he doesn't.

"You're thinking about Sophie, aren't you?"

"No. Well, yes, I am, I'm thinking about both of you."

"She'll understand," I say, but I think back to being nine years old and wonder if that's true. "Well, she may not, but you will make it work. You just need to tell her, as soon as you can, so she has time to adjust to the idea before you go. Which will be… what? Another four weeks or so?"

"Yes," he sighs, "it's only about four weeks away. If I decide to go," he adds.

"Sam, you have to. You know you do. Now you just need to make things here as good as you can beforehand. I am going to be here, and Sophie will be, too. Maybe we can travel up together to see you some weekends." I already know Kate will hate that idea, and I'm not sure if it's a realistic prospect given I am about to take on management of the Sail Loft. I can tell how nervous he is about all this, though, and I can't help wanting to comfort him.

"I don't know how to do it, what to say to her. I left her once already, when I left Kate."

"But you didn't really leave her. OK, you no longer lived together, but you know you've always been there for Sophie, and she knows it, too."

"Hmm." He doesn't look convinced and I feel, as I have ever since finding out Sam had a daughter, that he is in on something I can only partially guess at. I am not a parent; I have no idea what it feels like to be one. And even though Sam is not Sophie's biological father, I know he is still her dad. And she has no idea that he is not her biological father, which I guess might make this even harder.

We concoct a plan. We will go back to my place and he will phone Kate; explain the situation to her and ask if he can take Sophie out tonight.

"Why don't you book a table at the Cross-Section?" I suggest. "You know she loves it there. Make it a nice occasion, too."

"But won't she then associate the Cross-Section with something negative?"

"It doesn't have to be negative!" I say. "Tell her as soon as you can, so she knows you're being open with her. Tell her you don't want to leave her. See if she has any ideas about how you might make this work: Skype calls; visits to Bangor for her, back home for you; meeting up halfway for a weekend. Somewhere like Bristol. You could halve your travel time. I can travel with her, if you like. I can go on up to Mum and Dad's."

All these suggestions are things which have already whizzed into my head as to how he and I might make this work. But I think he has to work things out with Sophie as a priority. I can't try to push myself forwards, I've only been back in his life a few weeks. And I'm getting on for thirty (well, I'll be twenty-nine in a few days) while Sophie is not even ten yet. I have to be the grown-up here and I have to let Sam see that.

I am aware of the emotional pressure which Kate has applied to Sam over the years. I cannot behave that same way. If we are going to be together, then we have to be able to do it fairly and squarely, and support each other.

I am surprised from these thoughts by Sam planting a firm kiss on my mouth, then taking me into a full-on hug.

"What was that for?" I laugh.

"For being bloody brilliant," he says. "For being brilliant."

"Well, it just comes naturally, to be honest."

He laughs now, and kisses me again. "Thank you, Alice."

I can't say anything back as it's just hit me properly that it's taken me ten years to find Sam and now I am about to lose him again. I put my head on his shoulder and take a moment to compose myself. Tears can come later.

Kate is angry. I can hear her voice, make out most of her words, from the tiny kitchen in my flat while Sam speaks to her on the phone from my bedroom.

"What am I meant to do?" I hear and, I'm pretty sure, "You're shirking your responsibilities."

I also hear my name, more than once, and I hear Sam's reply, "Don't be ridiculous. You know I've been working towards this for the last few years and anyway, Alice is staying here. She's going to be managing the Sail Loft. I thought you knew that." He goes quiet, and I have a sneaky peek at him through the doorway. He is biting his lip, almost as if he's trying to stop himself saying the wrong thing. He listens, then says, "That doesn't make any sense, does it? Come on, Kate, I know this isn't ideal but this is something I really have to do. I will not be abandoning you... yes, we might have to look at finances, but you could probably do a few more hours now Sophie's a bit bigger. Find something..."

From the furore at the other end of the phone, I suspect that this suggestion hasn't gone down too well.

When Sam comes through to see me, post-call, his face is red.

"You managed to stay very calm," I say. "Well done."

"You could hear her?"

"Yes, I suspect most of the town could!" I do feel a bit bad for Kate; in fact, I would feel really sorry for her if her behaviour didn't impact on Sam, and me, and of course Sophie. Before I knew she was Sam's ex, Kate and I had become friends and although she had been a bit full-on, I know she's a nice person really. Just very insecure and quite needy. Sophie, however, is a lovely girl and I know much of that is due to Kate being a great mum.

"She's just upset," I say. "She's going to miss you, too. And she's probably worried about Sophie."

"Alice, stop being so fucking understanding, would you?" Sam laughs, putting his hands on my waist and pulling me close so that I tingle with excitement despite the emotions of the day. He kisses me slowly, taking his time, moving his mouth from mine towards my ear, and my neck. I sigh as his tongue gently touches the skin on my collarbone. Kate is not the only person who will miss him.

We lie curled together on my bed for some time, the flimsy curtains blowing slowly to and fro in the breeze. The town is in the throes of the last week or two of the high season. It's almost palpable, as people try to squeeze as much as they can from these last days of summer and freedom. That was me ten years ago, inseparable from Sam, who I knew I was going to have to leave. I had a place at university to go to; now it is his turn.

Soon enough, though, it is time for Sam to go to his daughter, tell her his news. He looks sad as he gets dressed and I want to reach out to him, tell him it's going to be OK. But I also want some time to myself now, to let the day's events sink in.

"Call me after you've seen Sophie, will you?"

"I was hoping I could come back here, actually."

"Of course you can. Julie should be back by then, too, so don't worry if you're not feeling sociable and change your mind."

"It's nothing to do with feeling sociable," he says, taking my hands in his. "I just want to be with you as much as possible."

"You've got another call to make, you know." He looks puzzled. "You need to accept that offer, you idiot!

13

Otherwise all of this will be for nothing."

"Oh yeah, good job one of us has got a brain, isn't it?"

"Yep."

When he's gone I think half-jokingly to myself that maybe I shouldn't have reminded him. But I am pleased to realise that alongside all my sadness about him leaving, I really am happy for him that he's done so well and he's going to do something he really cares about.

3

"Hi honey, I'm home!"

I'm not sure when I've been so glad to hear Julie's voice. Since Sam left this afternoon, I have been in the flat on my own. I know I should go for a run, or at least a walk; clear my head, let the sea air work its magic, but somehow I just can't summon up the energy.

My overwhelming feeling now is of flatness, tinged with fear.

"Good luck!" I had waved Sam off with a smile, trying to maintain a cheerful attitude for his sake. Kate will not have made this easy for him, I'm sure of it, but worse than that, Sophie is going to be devastated. She loves Sam so much and at the moment they see each other three or four times a week. A horrible thought keeps crossing my mind, that there is no way he is going to have time for his studies, his daughter, and me. And I feel like it's last in, first out – and also that any other way would be wrong. Sophie has to be number one, but Sam has been working so hard for years to get to this point, and I only arrived back on the scene a matter of weeks ago. Still, I push this thought down when it appears; like Whack-a-Mole at a fairground. It's not helpful but it keeps popping back into my head.

Julie bounds up the stairs, and I come to the top of the banister to greet her.

"Missed me?" she asks, out of breath, thrusting a bottle of wine into my hands. "Here, Luke sent me back with this."

I look at the bottle, reluctant for a moment to tell her my news, which will only make it more real.

"What's up?" she asks, clocking my expression for the first time. Those two words are enough to bring the tears which I had been expecting earlier flooding in. Julie takes me by the hand and leads me through to her room, goes to the kitchen and returns with a bottle opener and a couple of glasses. Expertly, she unwraps the top of the wine bottle and extracts the cork, pouring a generous glass for us both.

"Here, you look like you need it."

"Thanks, Julie. You are brilliant." I take a sip of the dark red liquid; it is soothing, I must admit.

"So, what's happened? No, let me guess… it's something to do with Casey, I mean Kate…"

When I first met Kate (initials KC) there had been some confusion and I'd thought she was called Casey. Julie hadn't really taken to her even then, although I'm not sure they had met in person. While Julie and Luke were beginning to spend all their time together, I did go out with Kate a couple of times. Julie is not the jealous type, but I don't think she was all that happy about my new friendship.

"What? No. Nothing to do with Kate, well not directly."

I explain to Julie about what has happened and how in a matter of weeks Sam will be in Bangor and I will be here, a minimum of seven hours and ten minutes away, in his home town.

"Oh no, Alice, I am sorry. Really, I am. But it's good for Sam, isn't it?"

"Yes," I sniff, "really good."

"And you two, well you've loved each other for years, even when you hadn't seen each other. Now, you're at an advantage. This course is four years, right? And one of them could be here, in Cornwall, when he's doing his work

16

placement or whatever it's called?"

I nod.

"And, best of all, you know you love each other now, don't you? You can talk and visit, and have wild phone sex. But not too loud because don't forget I'm in the next room."

I can't help but laugh.

"I know, it's not easy," she says. "I'm already finding that with Luke and he's here every second week, plus London isn't as far away as North Wales. But it's hard, especially so early in a relationship." She stops and thinks. "But look at us, we're living here in this amazing place, and about to have full use of this beautiful house. I've got loads of agency work lined up and you – well you're about to become manager of a fantastic hotel. You won't have time to miss Sam!"

This, I think, is partly true. I am, despite everything, really looking forward to this new challenge, and it is going to be extremely time-consuming. I am just going to have to find a way to make the long-distance thing with Sam work, for now. I know I'm at the Sail Loft until at least May and then, who knows? A few months ago this uncertainty would have bothered me greatly but I am trying to shrink that steady, predictable side of me, and grow into somebody who doesn't need to have a plan for everything.

"Thank you, Julie," I manage a small smile. "You're right."

"Course I am!" she grins.

We both take a sip of our wine at the same time and let out a co-ordinated "Aahhhh."

I smile and lean against my friend. Sam may be leaving but luckily for me I still have this brilliant person by my side.

***

At about 9.30, the front door bell goes. By this time, Julie and I have finished the bottle of wine and I feel kind of warm and fuzzy. There is still a niggling feeling at the back of my mind, and I am not happy that Sam is going – of course I'm not – but Julie's right that I have lots of good things going on as well. And I really do want to make this thing work at the Sail Loft so perhaps not having Sam around to distract me will be a blessing from that point of view.

"Hi," I say, as I open the front door to reveal him standing in the moonlight. Just a couple of weeks ago it was still light at this time of night. "How are you?"

"I'm OK," he says, but he doesn't really look it.

"How did Sophie take it?" I ask, ushering him in.

"Oh, not too bad, I suppose. Better than expected. She did cry a bit when I told her but we came up with a plan together, how we can make it work."

This makes me smile. I love the way Sam and Sophie are together. They seem to have an understanding of each other, they laugh a lot, and Sophie shares her dad's love of the natural world. Sam follows me upstairs. "When I told her about my course, what I'd be studying and what I'll be doing – hopefully – when I've graduated, her little face lit up." Sam looks sad as he says this. "Bloody hell, that was worse than her getting mad at me, I think. I just thought how much I love her and how much I'll miss her."

"I hope you told her that?" I take his hand and pull him gently into my room, sitting him on the bed and placing myself carefully next to him.

"Of course I did. And I'll keep telling her. And I'll keep telling you, too, how much I'll bloody miss you. God, Alice, am I totally mental doing this?"

"No, you're not. You're very brave."

He kisses me with such conviction that I feel light-headed. "I love you, you know," he says, looking me straight in the eye. "I wouldn't have said that for a long time, if I wasn't going away. Even though I know it's true. You're not meant to say it too soon, though, are you? In case you sound desperate or something."

I smile. "No, you're not, and you're right, now I just think you're a saddo."

He laughs. "Is Julie back?"

"Yep, she's in her room. I'm pretty sure she'll be snoring away in there soon, it sounds like she and Luke have been living it up in London."

"Doesn't surprise me," Sam laughs. "Luke's having the best time. Julie's just what he needs with everything that's happened this year."

"I know, I can't believe I ever doubted them." I kiss him, feeling his stubble against my cheek. "Oh, I had something to tell you."

"Oh yeah?" Sam raises his eyebrows.

"I love you, too."

"Saddo."

4

The weeks have whizzed by since that day. There's been so much going on. First, my birthday – the last one beginning with '2', as people like to remind me. I went to work at the Sail Loft, suddenly appreciating the simplicity of my current role as breakfast waitress/receptionist – the nerves I have about stepping into Bea's shoes and actually running the place are never far away - and then Sam picked me up and whisked me away along the coast to a beautiful little beach I haven't been to before, which can only be reached by a long, steep set of steps. We shared the sand and the sea with a small family and their dog, and Sam had packed enough food and drink to keep us going till midnight. There were small bottles of Prosecco, a bottle of freshly squeezed orange juice, a baguette, sweet-smelling tomatoes, and three French cheeses already going runny and ripe in the sun; some onion chutney, a brown paper bag of apples, and a tub of olives. Then there were doughnuts and brownies, and some proper Cornish fudge to finish, along with a flask of coffee.

"Wow!" I'd laughed as he'd spread it all out on the picnic blanket; he'd insisted that I lie back on my beach towel while he did all this but it felt weird, being waited on. I sat up and watched him as he laid out all these beautiful things he had bought. He caught me looking at him and smiled, almost shyly. I wanted to kiss him then and there but he was already standing up. "Wait there," he commanded me.

He dashed back up the steps and came back red-faced and panting, with a beach umbrella and a couple of chairs. "Come on, it's your birthday, got to do this properly!"

"Sam, you are just too good to be true," I said. "I can't believe you've done this."

"Wait till later," he said.

"Oh yeah?" I'd smiled.

"That too," he grinned. "But that's not what I meant."

It turned out that what he did mean was he had bought me a present for each of the birthdays I'd had since we had been apart. There was a hardback book about Cornish wildlife, a photo album with pictures from that first golden summer (as Julie and I have always called it) and some from this summer, too. Three CDs he'd bought for himself and listened to in the years since we had been apart, and found himself thinking about me when he did so. A soft stripy sweater ("To keep you warm when I can't"), a beach bag, a painting of the town by an artist who had been a friend of Luke's mum, a bottle of perfume, and a new smartphone.

"Sam!" I had been almost moved to tears by all of this. "You really shouldn't have got me all these things. You're meant to be saving your money to see you through your student days."

He'd shrugged and looked a bit embarrassed. "I just wanted to spoil you, show you how much you mean to me. How much I've missed you, and how much I'm going to miss you."

He had also organised a meal out with Julie and Luke, Sophie, Bea, David and Martin, at the Cross-Section. Sophie had led me in by the hand; in honesty I knew something was up because she had been far too excited and kept putting her hand over her mouth as if physically trying to hold the words back. But I was still surprised to see all of these people; my oldest friend, and people I have known only vaguely for years, who are becoming increasingly important to me.

We stayed late, taking our time over the delicious tapas menu, and wine, and dessert, and coffee, then nightcaps. Luke and Sam were driving so the rest of us all got a bit merry; in honesty I don't think I'd recovered from the afternoon's combination of sunshine and Prosecco. I embarrassingly got a bit teary – at first with happiness, quickly turning to a brief spell of melancholy at the thought of Sam going, which was just as quickly washed away by my friends deciding that was the moment for the enormous pecan cake to be produced, along with twenty-nine candles and a resounding round of *Happy Birthday*.

A few days later, David officially moved in with Martin. Having decided there was no need for a removal van, as Martin lives so close by, but still having half a house's worth of furniture, clothing, soft furnishings, CDs, DVDs, and other assorted belongings which he couldn't live without, David had us all carting his stuff to the other side of the estuary whenever we had a spare moment.

"The sooner it's gone, the sooner you two get this place to yourselves!" he'd sung at Julie and me. We had looked at each other, shrugged, picked up some of his boxes, and followed him out of the door.

Now we have David's house to ourselves and I still haven't got used to coming in and not running up to our little flat in the attic. I have David's room now; it's roughly the same size as half the first storey of the house. Julie's, just behind mine, is not much smaller. We also have the reception rooms downstairs, a full-sized kitchen – which Julie is most excited about – and a luxurious bathroom. The house is still David's, of course, but he's not planning to move back any time soon – or indeed, ever. I imagine he might want to sell it one day, or he could make a bomb renting it as a holiday home but he says he has no interest in doing so. "I'd much rather it was used by locals," he'd said, and Julie and I had both laughed.

"We've only lived here three months," I reminded him.

"Ah, but you've lived here before. You've returned to us. And you feel local to me. You decide if that's a compliment or not!"

It has been lovely seeing David so happy, and already I miss him – the house feels strange without his cheerful presence but, as he always tells me, he is never far away. He'd put framed photos of himself on Julie's and my bedside tables as "a special treat" for when we moved downstairs.

After we'd settled into life 'downstairs', there were roughly two weeks left before Sam's departure and as he'd saved a lot of his annual leave, he was now free to spend his time as he chose, which was mostly with Sophie, or me, or Sophie and me, and with Luke and Julie when they were around. He had a big night out with those of his mates who still live nearby, and turned up at David's – I must get used to calling it 'my' – house at some ungodly hour, stinking of booze and declaring his undying love for me. "C'mon, Alice, lez gotubed," he said, and I humoured him, letting him kiss me in a less than seductive way before sliding between the sheets and promptly falling asleep.

Two hours later, when my alarm went off for me to go to work and I switched my light on briefly, two red and tired eyes looked at me from somewhere under the sheets. "What did I do?" he groaned.

"Don't think about it, just go back to sleep." I tiptoed from the room and got dressed in the bathroom, then tiptoed back in and left a glass of water and some paracetamol on my bedside table. The curtains in David's − my − room are thick and luxurious, in contrast with the thin, insubstantial ones in the room I'd had upstairs. This is great if you want a lie-in, which apparently Sam did as at 11.57am I received a text saying:

Just got up. You are an angel xxxx

I smiled and replied,

Yes, I am. And you are a pisshead xxxx

Then came Bea's leaving do. This was an emotional affair, even though her plan is to leave for only a few months. David has been taking it quite hard.

"What am I going to do without my big sister?" He had decided to make an impromptu speech. "She has saved me from myself more than once, as kids and as adults. I just love her so much."

"What you are going to do," Bea had said, standing up and putting her arm around him, "is wish me well and have the best time of your life, moving in with Martin and planning your wedding together. But I will miss you, too. And I love you so much as well."

As a reasonable amount of wine and champagne had been consumed by this point − Bea doesn't do things by halves − many of us were in tears at this display of sibling affection.

Bea flew off two days later. As I walked around the Sail Loft on the first morning after she had gone, trying to feel convincingly like I was in charge, I realised that ever since I moved down to Cornwall, the people I cared about had either left (even though David is only a few miles away) or were in the process of leaving. It's enough to make anyone paranoid.

And now… now it is time for Sam to go. I can't bear those words, or that thought. I can't believe he is going and there have been times I've felt angry at him for it but I know that is selfish, and defensive. He's not leaving because of me, and he has even said he would stay if I asked him to.

I could never do that.

5

"Please don't go!"

Oh no. I know I've drunk too much. I know my mascara is smudged because I rarely wear it and I've rubbed my eyes without thinking about it.

"Alice…"

"I know, I know," I struggle against a sob, "you have to, and I told you to. But, you know, I thought of a wise old saying: If you don't ask, you don't get."

Sam smiles and pulls me to him. "It's going to be OK, you know. You'll be so busy with work you'll hardly notice I'm gone."

"But it's a whole month till I see you!"

Sam will be coming back here for a week for the study break, the university equivalent of half-term. He hasn't even gone yet but I am already counting the days. Before then, in two weeks' time, Sophie will be going to visit him. Kate has insisted she be the person to take her up there and I do appreciate that at not-quite-ten, Sophie is too young to travel alone on a journey she's never done before. But, despite knowing that there is really nothing between Kate and Sam anymore, I can't help feeling jealous.

"A month is nothing; we just have to keep reminding ourselves we spent ten years apart. One month… a year… four years… it's all doable."

"What if all the fresher girls fancy you? Who am I kidding? They're bound to."

"I am not going to university to chase eighteen-year-old girls," Sam tells me sternly. "Now come on, I really should go back in to *my* leaving party. We'll have a proper night together tomorrow."

Tomorrow. My heart sinks at the word. It's his last day before he goes up to North Wales. We are having a night in at my place, in fact Sam has been living there for the last week as his landlord found a new tenant who needed to move in quickly. Julie is cooking us an amazing meal then, in her words: "Getting the fuck out of there." She will stay with Luke and his dad for the night.

"You've already had a leaving party," I say childishly but I smile, swallowing back any more undignified pleading. "You're right, I shouldn't be taking you away from your mates."

We leave the cool fresh air, which is creeping through the streets from the harbourside, and I follow Sam back into the Black Horse, watching his broad shoulders and admiring the back of his neck, where his freshly-cut hair sits close to the skin. I want to kiss him there, right now, but I manage to refrain. A resounding cheer greets us, and we are engulfed in an impromptu round of the Hokey Cokey. I can't help but laugh, though it's strange to think that after tomorrow it will just be me here in this town, with these people. Sam's friends, although friendly and welcoming, are unlikely to socialise with me in his absence. As Sam says, they are all busy working, and settling down; he only sees most of them every couple of months – they probably won't even notice his absence.

Amongst the well-wishers are Julie and Luke. They are sitting facing each other on bar stools, and apparently can't keep their hands off each other.

"You two are soooo lucky," I slur at them. "You've got

27

no… what's the word… *baggage* to worry about."

"Apart from my ex-fiancé, and having to cancel my wedding, Alice," Julie reminds me, and I know she's half-joking. Luke, kindly, doesn't remind me that it is a matter of mere weeks since his mum died.

"Ha, sorry," I say, "I'm just so gutted he's going."

"We know, mate, we know." Luke and Julie gather me into a huge hug from both sides. "But don't worry, you've got us. And David. And an amazing new job."

"And," Luke adds, "Sammie ain't going to forget you, you know. He'll be back as much as he can. And you can get up there."

"I suppose," I half agree, although I know it won't be easy to get time away from the Sail Loft – particularly at weekends, when the hotel will be at its out-of-season busiest.

"It'll fly by," Luke assures me. "Think back to when you were at uni. With the long summers off and the regular study breaks, plus Christmas and Easter, you were hardly there. That's what it seems like to me now, anyway."

"I suppose," I agree.

"And," Julie adds, "no distractions from Sam means that you can do an amazing job at the hotel and you and I can start making plans for our own business here."

I smile. Julie is temping as a chef for an agency, which means she could be pretty much anywhere in the county. She is finding it hard because each place she works is different, but she is determined to stick at it until she lands her perfect job and in the meantime she's convinced that she and I will be able to set up an amazing business – 'fully catered self-catering', she calls it. "That way, people can look after themselves but we give them that little bit extra – delicious meals, a cleaning service, booking taxis and days out, that kind of thing."

"We'll see," is generally how I respond.

I am cheered by the thought of my new job, though. I had become highly competent but also highly bored in my previous role at World of Stationery. Jason, my old boss, still drops me a line from time to time, saying he would still welcome me back, but I am in no doubt that that stage of my life is over. Whatever happens with Sam – and I can't tell you how much I hope we will make it work between us – I am determined to do the best job possible looking after the Sail Loft in Bea's absence and, from there, who knows?

I take a seat next to Julie, ask the barman for a glass of tap water, and watch Sam saying his goodbyes to people, who are beginning to drift away. By and by, we are the only four customers left in the bar so we thank the barman and the four of us head back home together.

6

Despite the sad reason for this occasion, I can't help feeling a little bit excited about my evening with Sam. Julie has outdone herself, preparing a few new dishes for us to sample and giving them silly names: Amazing Avocado Appetizers; Stunning Stem Ginger and Perfect Pak Choi with Naked Noodles; Crazy Cauliflower with Popping Pomegranate Salad and Super Sourdough; followed by Blow-your-mind Baked Cheesecake and Plum Purée.

Delicious aromas fill the house but Julie has banned me from the kitchen, instead insisting that I prepare the dining room and then have a long, hot bath; maybe even a nap. I am too wound up to sleep but as I lie on my bed in David's cool, airy bedroom (when will I start calling it mine?) I let my mind wander and every now and then I catch myself just before dropping off; I am too alert, it seems, there is something in me which won't allow me to relax enough to sleep.

Sam is spending the day with Sophie, taking her down the coast to her favourite beach, at Sennen, then for tea at a pub on the way back.

"You'd better not fill up on chips," I say.

"Oh come on, you know me – I could put away a full pub meal and then come back for more."

"You'd better not," Julie had chipped in, "I'm going to be working my arse off for you two."

"OK, OK," Sam had laughed. "But only because I'm

scared of you, Julie."

"You should be."

Sam had kissed me on the way out and I had shut the door on the self-pitying thoughts which were trying to push their way in. Instead, I went straight to the kitchen to make coffee then I picked up my phone to call Stefan, the new night manager at the Sail Loft.

Bea and I had interviewed Stefan together before she'd left for the States. He seems perfect. He is Swedish and highly experienced in the hospitality trade. He's come over to England to be with his girlfriend, April, and their baby, Reuben. He says that he's used to being up in the night from years of working nights and that the hours work for him as he can give April a rest during the day while he looks after Reuben.

"When do you sleep?" I asked him.

"Well, of course if I can I'll sleep at the hotel. If I have to be up and I miss out on a few hours, it's no problem, I've been up forty-eight hours at a time before, I'm used to it."

"OK," I said, entirely convinced by his earnest demeanour. And he's right; as long as there is nothing going on at the hotel: customer emergency, leaking ceiling, guest losing or forgetting their key to get back in - that kind of thing - then just as long as he is present and able to respond to an emergency he can get a few hours' rest, and get paid for it.

We do alternate weekends of being on duty full-time, and we have Jonathan, the chef, on call if there is an emergency with either one of us. It's pretty full-on but I have to remind myself that Bea has done all of this almost single-handedly until now. Luckily, Sam's last weekend here coincides with my weekend off.

"Everything OK?" I asked Stefan when he picked up.

"Hi Alice, everything is absolutely fine, no problems at all," he assured me. "Now didn't I tell you not to ring? I will let you know if there is a problem, I promise."

"OK," I laughed. I've already filled him in on the situation with Sam. He's a very easy person to talk to. As soon as he started at the Sail Loft, I felt at ease. I think we're going to work well together.

"Now have a great time."

"Thank you, Stefan, I will. I promise."

Mind at rest over work, I turned it to all the things I would have to do to make this evening perfect.

After coffee and a shower, I headed out in the car, on a mission. First stop, the Cross-Section, where Christian had promised me a few bottles of Sam's favourite beer and 'something special' in the wine department.

The wide, open sky - fresh and blue overhead - and the road weaving in and out of view of a glittering sea kept my spirits high as I drove, windows down and radio turned up.

Christian was waiting in the sunshine on the parking lot, sitting on a great big chopped-off tree trunk, a mug in his hand. "Catching the last of the summer," he said, smiling at me. "Though autumn's been pretty warm these last few years, too. Come on in, do you want a cuppa?"

"I won't today thanks, Christian. Lots to do!"

"Oh yeah, last day before Sammie leaves. My head's still sore from his leaving bash. Sorry I couldn't make it last night. Tell him good luck from me, will you? There's a table for you and him, and Soph, here, next time he's back."

"Thank you, that's ace," I grinned. "I'll make sure I tell him."

Christian fetched a box for me from the kitchen. "There's those beers he likes, BrewMonkey – watch the dark one, it's dead strong – and a bottle of local champagne, though I think you're only allowed to call it sparkling wine - and a couple of nice bottles of white and red. Julie told me what she was making and I've tried to pick some good ones to go with it. She's a great chef, isn't she? I wish we could have her here."

"I'll pass on that message, too. You should definitely let her know if you ever do need somebody; she'd bite your arm off, I'm sure."

"Not sure I want her if she's going to maim me." Christian grinned and I laughed, moving to pick up the box. "I'll carry that," he said gallantly and so I followed him out to the little red car and opened the boot. He put the box in, gave me a hug, and sloped off back to his tree trunk, waving at me as I drove away, the wheels sending up clouds of dust from the dry car park.

Next stop, Truro. I wanted to find something new to wear. I felt like I should get some work things, too, now I'm the manager and all. It was already nearly eleven and, knowing me, shopping would take hours out of my day. I hate it, and I become extremely indecisive. I don't like to be ripped off but I don't like to buy from shops which I think use dodgy third-world factories, so I have to find reasonably-priced and hopefully responsibly-sourced clothing.

After an hour or so, I had managed to find a dress that I liked, except I don't really like wearing dresses, so I had a little argument with myself about it. I still needed to find some workwear as well and there was a small part of me suggesting I should also get some new underwear, seeing as I was shopping for a special occasion. Instead of the dress, I settled for a knee-length denim skirt, and a strappy top, which are now both hanging on my bedroom door.

I trawled the charity shops for a while, managing to find two nice pairs of trousers and three tops, which will do for work, then it was off to good old Marks and Spencer for some underwear.

I bought a sandwich at M&S, which I hurriedly ate on the way back to the car, then I headed for home. As soon as I got there, Julie insisted that I hand the alcohol over to her, and then banished me upstairs for that bath.

Since then, I've been doing as I'm told by Julie, who has turned into quite the romantic since being with Luke. It's still early days but they are obviously so happy together – almost sickeningly so. I voice this to Julie as she pushes me out of the kitchen.

"I keep telling you, I've got it covered!" she says. "Anyway, yes I am very happy, thank you – and you would be too if you were being whisked off to Ibiza for a week."

"Luke's taking you to Ibiza?"

"Yeah, well, I wanted to pay but he won't hear of it, not till I've got a more stable job. What a man!"

"He is," I agreed, "but then you're quite a lady. Well, 'lady' might be stretching the truth somewhat. You're definitely female. At least, I assume you are."

"Thanks for the vote of confidence," Julie says, blocking the kitchen doorway and darting about to make sure I can't see past her. "To be honest, I genuinely don't feel that comfortable with him paying. I need to sort my work out so I can pay my way. I don't want him or anyone else thinking I'm with him for his money."

"I don't think Luke will ever think that, and if anybody else does, well, that's their problem, isn't it?"

"Yep, it is, but I still don't like the idea of it. Luke's worked really hard to get where he is, and I've worked really hard to get… well, nowhere right now, but I just need to find the right place for me. It's coming, I can feel it."

"I'm sure it is, really. I just wish I could get you back in at the Sail Loft."

"Thank you, Alice, but really, with no offence to the Sail Loft, Bea, or you – or Jonathan, for that matter – I think I need to be doing something a bit different. I want to get on *Masterchef*. I want to run my own place."

"And I really am certain that you will. When are you off to Ibiza?"

"A week on Wednesday. Luke's got to get back to London tomorrow then we're meeting in Bristol and flying from there."

I experience a tiny tweak of envy at the thought of them jetting off for a romantic week together but I cast the thought aside. Luke deserves a break after all he's been through lately and Julie probably does, too – I was a bit hard on her about the situation with Gabe, her ex, but it can't have been easy for her.

"Now shoo! I need to get on," she wafts me away with a tea towel and I head upstairs, where I lie on my bed, attempting to read my book and stop myself from checking the time every five minutes.

At 6.40pm exactly; the earliest time Sam had estimated he'd be able to get to me, there is a knock at the door. Julie had told him he wasn't allowed to use his key this evening; he had to treat this as a proper date. I run down and open the door, to be greeted by a huge bunch of flowers behind which, presumably, is Sam.

"Wow!" I laugh. "Is that you?"

"Yes, get me out of here, I'm being eaten alive by gypsophilia."

I take the flowers from him, a few stray fronds tickling my nose. "They're beautiful, thank you. Come in."

Julie steps out from the dining room. "Please be seated in the main reception room," she gestures towards the downstairs living room, "where drinks will be served."

Sam and I giggle.

"This is not an occasion for mirth," Julie says with a straight face, leading us into the living room, where there are two dark-red cocktails and bowls of olives and deep-fried broad beans on the small table by the window. "Drinks will be served now, and dinner shall begin at seven prompt. At which point I shall take my leave." She bows low and backs out of the room.

Sam turns to me, his eyes bright. He kisses me.

"How was your day with Sophie?" I ask. "How's Sophie?"

"It was great; she's great. I definitely feel more sad than she does; she just keeps going on about coming to visit, and the train journey. I think she's been enjoying showing off to her friends about it all."

"And how are you?"

"Oh, I'm fine… well, you know… OK. Sad. But happy to see you. But then sad again, and nervous. And a bit excited."

He looks at me as he says this, as if to check it's OK.

"Good!" I say. "If we were doing all this and you weren't excited, it would be pointless."

"God, I love you!" He pulls me in towards him and kisses me deeply, just as Julie enters the room.

"No canoodling before dinner."

I turn my gaze on her, giving her my best Paddington Hard Stare.

"OK, OK, do what you want. I've just brought you

36

these." She places on the table a platter of tiny flatbreads topped with avocado, chilli and garlic, a drizzle of balsamic vinegar over the top.

"Now, these are your appetisers, as you'll see." She pulls out a printed menu from her back pocket. I can't believe she's gone to so much trouble. "On here are the list of courses, plus any instructions for what to do with them once I've gone. I've got to cut the apron strings sometime, you know. Everything is ready for you, whenever you're ready for it. Champagne's in the ice bucket, red wine's breathing on the sideboard. I'm off now, to Luke's. I hope you have a lovely evening and I will see you soon, young Sam."

"Julie, thank you!" I hug her and Sam echoes my thanks, kissing her on the cheek.

"Look after Luke for me," he says.

"I'll do my best."

She leaves, closing the front door securely behind her, and now it is just me and Sam.

7

It's quite a funny situation; semi-formal, yet in my own home – which I have yet to really feel is my own home. And it has the potential to be an emotional night. But I want it to be fun, too. Memorable for all the right reasons.

"Come on," I say, "let's try these drinks."

We pick up the cocktails and clink glasses, toasting each other, then both take a sip.

"Bloody hell, what's she put in that?" Sam exclaims.

"I've got no idea!" I laugh, "but she definitely doesn't do things by half."

The drink is delicious but heavy on the booze. We nibble on the appetisers, try to balance things out. Sam tells me about his day with Sophie and how Kate was when he brought their daughter back. "She wasn't as frosty as she has been, she even said she hoped we have a good time tonight."

"Really?" Before any of this happened with Sam, when she and I knew nothing of each other's significance in his life, Kate had confided in me that she drinks every night. I wonder if she's doing so now. I feel sorry for her, but I don't think there is anything I can do to help; she would not want my help, I'm sure of it. Then I smile to think of Sophie bragging to her friends about her trip to glamorous North Wales.

"I am going to miss you so much, Alice Griffiths," Sam draws me close and kisses me again.

"You sure that's not the drink talking?"

"Most definitely not." Sam runs his fingers down my back, then up again, softly strokes the skin of my arms, his fingers trailing goose pimples in their wake.

I kiss him back fervently, trying to take in every detail, to remember when he's gone. He presses himself against me and lets out a low, soft groan. "Can we go upstairs now? Please?"

"I want to, I'd love to," I say, "but Julie's gone to so much trouble. I think we need to do the grown-up thing and enjoy our lovely meal."

"You're right, I know you're right. I have a feeling you're always right."

"Then you're a clever man. Come on," I kiss his cheek, take his hand in mine. "Let's eat, drink and be merry."

***

As our stomachs fill, the combination of cocktails, champagne (sparkling wine) to accompany the starter, and the red wine which we have with our main course (which Julie has described as a vegan steak), takes its toll on our mood, and our conversation. I am starting to feel a bit emotional again; I am so happy to be with Sam, and so grateful to Julie for making this evening special, but at the same time so sad that this time tomorrow, my one true love (see, I told you I'm feeling drunk... I mean, emotional) will be miles away, in deepest, darkest North Wales.

While Sam is otherwise occupied in the bathroom, I allow a small tear of self-pity to slide down my face. What am I going to do without him, and can our relationship really stay the course? Four years is a long time and even if he, as he hopes, is able to have his third year – while he will be working – in Cornwall, that is still two years away. I hear his footsteps bounding back down the stairs and I wipe the tear away but he's quicker than I think and he catches me.

"Alice?" he asks gently.

I turn, trying to fix a bright smile to my face. "Yep?"

"Are you crying?"

"Nope." But my face collapses and before I know it, he is crouching next to me, his arms around me as I lean into him, his face buried in my hair.

"I just… can't believe… you're going."

I know my nose is starting to run now and it will be turning red, along with the rims around my eyes. Not my most flattering look.

"I'll be back in a few weeks," he soothes. "Just four weeks. It's not long."

I sniff but I meet his eyes.

"Come on," he says, "it'll fly by. And that's not to say I won't miss you, because I will. Probably too much. But I'm going to be so hard at work, and so are you – by the time my week off comes round, we'll both deserve a proper break. I was going to suggest that you see if Stefan will swap a couple of days with you – maybe me and you can get away somewhere."

"Really?" I feel immediately brighter, but slightly ashamed of myself, like I'm a small child being promised a new toy if I stop making a fuss.

"Yes," he laughs. "I mean, it won't be Ibiza… my finances don't compare to Luke's, I'm afraid, and of course I'll need to spend time with Soph during that week, too. But maybe a night or two somewhere nice… a spa hotel or something?"

"You hate spa hotels!"

Sam laughs. "I don't, not really. I've never been to one,

40

so how can I? I bet they're very… relaxing…"

Now it's my turn to laugh. "I think that is the general idea, yes. That would be lovely." I feel like pulling myself together now. I blow my nose, and wipe my eyes, thinking I really should have done those things in the opposite order. "Really lovely. Something to look forward to."

"Alice, we've got loads to look forward to, I promise."

Sam kisses me and I try to concentrate on the moment. His soft skin; his warmth, and his familiar smell. I determine that there will be no more tears. We will enjoy this evening, and our time together in a few weeks will be all the more special for being apart.

"Shall we have a coffee, and some cheesecake?" I suggest. "Maybe out in the garden?" I can see through the French doors that the daylight has faded but I know it's still warm out. A bit of fresh air and caffeine should help to see off the melancholy. Not to mention a slice of Julie's amazing cheesecake.

"That sounds perfect," Sam says and, taking my hand, he pulls me to my feet. "Come on, let's make the most of tonight."

"We will, I'm sorry for getting upset."

"Hey, no need to apologise. I'm the one messing things up!"

We help ourselves to some generous slices of cheesecake and Sam makes coffee, insisting that I go and sit down. "Let me look after you now," he says.

"Julie's been looking after me all day!" I protest.

"Well, you deserve it. You can look after me when I come back; I'll be a poor, malnourished student by then, I'll need feeding up."

"It's a deal," I say. I head out into the small garden, which

41

is a sun trap by day. The scent of some of the flowers David has planted tints the still air. Jasmine, or something, I think. It's delicious.

The sky is a generous dark blue, and clear so that the nearly-full moon provides plenty of light. When Sam comes out, I switch off the lamps in the dining room and we sit together on the blue bench with the chipped paint, in the semi-darkness, eating delicious cheesecake and sipping our coffee; companionably quiet, each occupied for a while with our own thoughts.

"Will you see Sophie while I'm away?" Sam asks suddenly.

"Well, yes, of course I'll be happy to but would Kate want me to?"

"I don't know," Sam admits. "But I want you to. And Sophie's my daughter as much as Kate's. It might be awkward, I guess."

"Well, if you speak to Kate about it, then I'll do it. But I don't want to have that argument myself. More importantly though, are you sure that Sophie would like to see me too?"

"She loves you!" says Sam. "And it's not like she thinks Kate and me will get back together. We talked about it all today, you know, at the pub. She's so grown-up for her age!" Sam smiles in the moonlight and I can see pride etched on his face. "I can't believe it's only five years since she started school. She was so tiny. Now she's got her own taste in clothes, and in music, and a bunch of mates."

It is Sam's turn to look sad now and I am struck by something which I knew already, in my heart of hearts. While Sam might be sad to leave me, leaving his daughter is something else altogether. I am going to have to be grown up about it, and accept it. He is a parent, and I have to support him, try to understand how he feels.

"She is great," I say. "I don't remember being half that mature when I was her age. And I will go and see her – take her to the beach or the shops or whatever – as long as she and Kate are happy about it."

I am rewarded with a huge smile from Sam. "I don't know if I can possibly love you more," he says, and he puts his arm around me, leaning in to kiss me. He tastes sweet, of cheesecake and coffee. Gently, he manoeuvres me so that I am sitting on his knee. I feel his hands move in under my top and I shiver at his touch, and the cold of his skin.

"Sorry!" he laughs but he shivers too.

I kiss him now, taking my time and letting my hair fall into his face. I move my mouth from his and kiss along his jawline, letting my tongue flick out as I approach the top of his neck, just below his earlobe. He gasps and I breathe onto him, softly, warming his skin there. His hands move up under my top and he finds my new M&S bra, unfastening it slightly clumsily. My turn to gasp now as those cold fingers reach under the soft material, stroking the warmth of my skin.

"Shall we... go in?" he asks.

"Yes," I say, "in a minute. I love it out here, let's stay a little bit longer." I kiss him again, and lose myself in the moment. I can just hear the sea, not far away, down the hill, and there are other sounds: people calling to each other; a car door slamming; a motorbike speeding somewhere up near the top of town. Here, in the garden, it is just me and Sam. Even the seagulls are nowhere to be seen; at night, a great cloud of them comes together on the headland between two of the beaches, where the white of their feathers glows against the darkness. If disturbed, they rise into the air, like a flock of small ghosts.

Sam's hands are warming up, becoming more eager. I

pull back and look at him, smiling.

"What?" he asks, smiling shyly back.

"Just this… Us. Being here. It's just perfect."

"Come on," Sam says, "it's getting cold out here. Let's get these things inside and go up to bed. We can clear up in the morning."

I don't need to be asked twice. I cast a half-guilty glance at the array of dirty plates and dishes but Julie won't be coming back tonight so I don't need to worry.

"I can tidy up after you've gone," I say, "I want to make the most of every last minute with you."

I move into the hallway, Sam close behind me. He puts his hand on my waist and I turn to find him right in front of me, his hand moving gently to the back of my neck as his mouth moves in to kiss me again and his body presses me against the wooden panelling below the staircase. I feel the cool paint under my skin as Sam tenderly pulls the straps of my top from my shoulders, kissing the skin there.

"You are… so… beautiful," he murmurs and I close my eyes, feeling his hands on my hips and his kiss sliding along my right shoulder then back again and up my neck.

His right hand moves down slowly, plays with the hem of my skirt. He pulls it up a little, his fingers stroking my thigh. I can't think of anything but him.

"Sam…" I sigh. "Sam…" and at that moment his phone starts to ring.

"Ignore it," he half-growls into my ear. "Who cares?" I feel his body press against mine and I can't help agreeing. Who cares? But then the phone goes again and I sense a small shift in Sam; just a tiny drop in his focus on me. It rings off but starts again and this time, Sam's face falls. "I'll have to get it," he says apologetically. "I'll be right back. Don't go anywhere." He kisses me firmly.

He is not right back, though; not in the same way, at least. I hear his end of the phone call, going from annoyed to concerned to determined. "What? You know I'm… Alright, I'm listening… she's OK, though? Is she? Are you sure it's not just… no, sorry… I can't, I've been drinking too. OK, I'll sort it. I'll see you in a bit."

With each of the words he utters, my heart sinks a little further, and I move towards him. When he turns around, he looks a bit pale.

"Is everything OK?" I ask, knowing full well that it isn't. Just wishing it was.

"That was Kate," he says; which of course I also already knew. "Sophie's not well. Got really bad stomach pains, Kate's worried it might be appendicitis. We need to get her to A&E."

A&E is miles away, this being one of the problems of living somewhere like this.

"Can't Kate call an ambulance?" I ask, and I think I see a momentary flicker of annoyance cross Sam's face but he stifles it. "No, the sooner we get her to hospital, the better. I'm going to have to get a taxi. I'll call it now, and pick them up on the way."

"OK," I say, realising there is no way this situation can be rescued now but also feeling bad for being so selfish when there's a little girl out there who could be really poorly – and not just any little girl but Sophie. It looks like my skills at being understanding and supportive are going to be tested sooner than I'd anticipated. "You get your stuff together, I'll call a taxi for you. I've got an emergency number for Brian, to use for hotel guests. He'll come out, I'm sure of it."

It's not that late but this is a small town and cabs are few and far between. I ring Brian and Sam gets his coat and wallet and keys, then stands next to me, watching keenly as I speak to Brian who, luckily, is available to come right away.

"Thank you, Alice," Sam says. "I'm so sorry our evening's been ruined." But I can see his mind is really on his daughter, as it should be.

"It's OK," I reassure him. "Just as long as Sophie's OK. Keep me posted, and I'll see you when you get back, assuming she's alright."

"I hope so, I hope she's alright, and I hope I can get back here to see you. Fucking typical, on my last night. I'm so sorry."

The passion evaporated, we stand together in the hallway awkwardly, like we hardly know each other, just waiting for Brian. It is only a matter of minutes until we hear his car drawing up outside. Sam kisses me and rushes out, desperate to get to his little girl.

I watch as the car disappears down the street then I close the door and head into the kitchen to tidy up.

8

The day after Sam has gone, I am back at work and I have to admit, I am glad to be here.

Sophie was fine, as it turned out. After a forty-minute taxi journey, and an hour or two in the children's assessment unit, the pain seemed to have died down, and it was blamed on a mixture of over-eating, trapped wind, and possibly constipation.

After the initial relief, during the taxi ride home, Kate suggested that it was Sam's fault for giving Sophie too many treats on their day out, and letting her talk him into buying a huge pudding at the pub.

Sam said he bit back, saying that Kate was too obsessed with her diet and he was happy to let Sophie enjoy a day where she didn't have somebody watching what she was eating all the time.

Sophie sat between them, small and sad, and as soon as Sam and Kate realised this, they both apologised to her.

"We're just a bit stressed, love," Kate had said, "We were worried about you."

"I ruined your night with Alice," Sophie said to Sam.

"Don't worry about that," he said, "Alice understands."

He relayed all this to me when he finally came back at about three in the morning. He had promised Sophie he'd settle her down in her bed back at the flat, and then she had become clingy. He said he'd held her hand until she fell asleep but it took quite some time for her to do so.

He walked back down the hill to my house, and let himself in. I was on the settee, dozing, knowing Sophie was OK and he was on his way. I woke as soon as I heard him.

I made us both a hot chocolate and we took them to bed with us. Although we kissed a little, we were both too tired, Sam too exhausted from worry, to do anything more than that, and we fell asleep in each other's arms at about 4am.

Just a handful of hours later, awake again, I made Sam a coffee and brought it to him in bed, along with a croissant smothered in butter and jam.

"I'm sorry about last night," he said, rubbing his eyes.

"It's fine," I said, "It can't be helped."

"No, but it's not fine. That was meant to be our time. I will make it up to you, I promise. I'm going to book us that spa hotel as soon as you sort out a couple of days off with Stefan."

"That sounds perfect," I said, sliding into bed next to him. My feet were cold and I pushed them next to his legs, making him jump.

"Oi!" he laughed, and put his coffee and plate on the bedside table. "Come here, you." He put his arm around me, turning so that he could kiss me, and laid me down on the bed, moving his body over mine.

When it could be delayed no longer, I helped Sam put his bags in the car. The duvet and pillows fill the back seat, and various items press themselves against the back window. "Don't try and open the boot until you get to your flat," I laugh, "you'll never get it all back in."

"I didn't know I had so much stuff!" he lamented.

"Give me a ring when you get there," I said. I was actually keen for him to leave; not because I wanted him gone but I knew it was inevitable and I just wanted to get on with it.

What would be the point in delaying things any further?

"Of course I will," he kissed me, then kissed me again. "I'm going to miss you so much. And I'm bloody nervous!"

"You will be fine, I promise. Better than fine, you'll be brilliant. And you'll love it."

"I hope so. Or you might see me back here within a week!"

My heart leapt a little at this even though I knew that would never really happen. I just couldn't quite stop myself from imagining if it did.

So now here I am; on my own in Cornwall – well, with Julie, while she's here. And I have David and Martin just a few miles round the coast, and Stefan and Jonathan at work. These are my friends and family here right now. I am happy to be at work, with something to focus on.

I must admit, I love Bea's office. Although it is still very much 'her' space, she very thoughtfully took down all her personal things, telling me to make the place my own. So my first job was working out which of my pictures to put up; which books to put on the shelves. I've also bought a digital radio to keep me company.

When I came in this morning, the first thing I did was put the radio on, then I popped into the kitchen to get some of the coffee left over from breakfast.

"Here, I'll make a fresh lot," said Jonathan.

"Wow, this is just like Lorelai and Sooki in *Gilmore Girls*," I said but he looked blank. "Never mind!"

"How are you?" he asked, once he'd put a beautifully dark coffee into my hands. "Cream?"

"Yes, please," I said and, "I'm OK, really. Just got to get on with things. And this place is going to give me plenty to get my teeth stuck into."

"Have you spoken to Bea yet about the theme cuisine nights?"

This is one of Jonathan's ideas. He is a very keen chef, a few years younger than me, eager to get established and introduce some new ideas. Not long back from travelling, he is staying with his parents at the moment but has plans to get his own place sometime soon. It's not easy round here; it's so expensive.

Jonathan is really keen to develop the restaurant side of the Sail Loft and he has got a good point; out of season, when we have fewer residential customers, it could be a great way to boost our income. However, right now I am trying to plan for Christmas and New Year – and I need him to work on a menu for both, while I design the perfect packages to tempt people to come and stay with us. I have never spent New Year's Eve down here but by all accounts it's a hugely popular event, with thousands of people on the streets in fancy dress. It's something which the town is really proud of, and which I am quite excited about – although I'm going to be on duty rather than partying in the street. I want to make it a spectacular night for our guests and ensure they have somewhere great to come back to once they're cold, or if it's pissing it down with rain.

For Christmas, I am aiming for something traditional, where we take care of everything so that our guests can relax completely. I feel like this might appeal to people who have spent previous years cooking for huge numbers of family, dealing with the inevitable arguments, tantrums, etc. which are as much a part of Christmas as Santa Claus and mince pies.

"Once we've got Christmas and New Year sorted, I promise I will mention it to Bea. Nudge, nudge…" I say. I have never really had to manage people before. At World of Stationery, I was often a mentor to newcomers, and I was always happy to lend a hand, but I'm finding that actually having to get people to do things is a different matter. Really, I only have to manage Jonathan, the ever-reliable cleaners, and waiting staff from the agency, but of all of them, it is my chef who is turning out to be a handful. He is so enthusiastic about his craft (as he calls it), which is excellent, but it means that he does tend to forget that the main business of a hotel is, well, being a hotel.

"OK," he sighs, "I will get something back to you this week, I promise."

"Promise, promise?" I rest my chin on my hands and flash him a smile.

"Promise, promise," he agrees.

The only problem is, he promised last week, and the menu didn't materialise. I am trying the cajoling tack for the moment but I know that if he doesn't sort it out soon, I am going to have to try something else. He is the son of some of Bea's friends but I can hardly threaten to tell his mum and dad. I also don't want to go crying to Bea about it.

"Great, because I have to start advertising next week," I say. "It may be only September but we're already quite late. People who are going away for Christmas will already be booking their breaks. I don't want to miss the boat. We'll probably have the Christmas tree up in November, you know, as soon as Bonfire Night is out of the way."

"Well, I think that's ridiculous," Jonathan huffs, his good-looking face becoming more boyish as he scowls.

"Ridiculous it may be, but it's how it works and it's what people expect. It's exactly the same in the restaurant trade, you know."

"I know," Jonathan flashes me a smile, which I expect he

is used to doing to get his own way; he is almost too good looking, if you ask me. He gets up to leave.

"Friday by the latest," I say sternly, "then I can work on the literature over the weekend."

"Wow, wild," he teases.

"Wait till you're my age, young man," I find myself smiling at him despite my misgivings.

"Let me know when you need your Zimmer frame," he says, and dodges out of the door before I have a chance to respond.

I sit in the office, swivelling around in Bea's big comfy chair. It's leather, which I shouldn't really like, being a committed vegetarian and against animal products wherever possible, but I have to admit it's very comfy. And great when you spill things, too; something I do fairly often.

My mind turns to Sam and I wonder what he is doing at this precise moment. Meeting lecturers, getting timetables together, that kind of thing. Since the disappointment of our last night together, I've turned events over and over again in my mind until I've started to suspect Kate of deliberately sabotaging our evening. I tell myself I'm paranoid but from what I know of her behaviour towards Sam when they were together, and the way she behaved during our brief friendship – very forward, to the point of being pushy – I can see she is very keen on getting her own way. It must have been a real blow to her when she realised that Sam and I were seeing each other, but I really had no clue about their history.

However, I know that no good can come of this line of thought and I banish it from my mind. It can be easy to let these things spiral out of control and, having been in a relationship with Geoff, who was really jealous amongst other things, I do not ever want to go down that route. Instead, I turn to a blank page on my notepad and begin jotting down ideas for the Christmas and New Year celebrations.

***

The day flies by and I'm really excited to take a week-long booking from a touring company from the West Midlands, which is and always will be my neck of the woods, even if I manage to stay down here for good. I am surprised to experience a little pang at the familiar twang of the accent, and I keep the agent on the phone possibly longer than he had anticipated. It's usually the other way around.

By the time we've finished, I've managed to discuss a possible discount for our Seasonal Celebrations, without mentioning that these are yet to be arranged. I'm so excited. This is the first real chance I've had to sell the business I am responsible for running, and it seems that my time at World of Stationery was not wasted. All those tedious sales courses were now paying off: how it's good to smile when you're on the phone as your potential client can 'hear' the smile; how you should remember important details about your client so they know you matter to them – in this case I'd never spoken to the guy – Chris – before, but once I'd established that he was a similar age to me, I was able to talk about things we'd both have experienced growing up in the West Midlands. School trips to the Black Country Museum ("Every year!" Chris had laughed), being allowed to go into Birmingham without your parents for the first time. By the end of our conversation, I knew that we had clicked and I promised to phone Chris back with the details of some special Christmas and New Year offers.

When I got off the phone to him, I was smiling for real.

***

We have twelve rooms here at the Sail Loft and can cater for private parties so I've decided that this year over the festive season, I will offer exclusive hire of the hotel – to include dinner, bed and breakfast, for a minimum of three nights at a time. Christmas Day lunch will also be provided. I can tailor the prices so that they are more reasonable between Christmas and New Year, but I think this is something people will really go for. Who wants to go to a hotel and share these special occasions with people they don't know; or at least sit in a dining room feeling self-conscious, or like they are required to be sociable? I'm thinking large groups of family and friends, or even tour groups like those which Chris organises – I could envisage that working well over New Year, but perhaps less well over Christmas. Who knows, though – those tours tend to include people who are feeling lonely, maybe bereaved or long-term single, who want to go away but don't want to go on their own. Maybe a fantastic Christmas in a beautiful place, with knock-out food and organised entertainment would be perfect for them.

One downside is how much I will have to work over that time of year; and when Sam is back from uni, too. But we will just have to be flexible with each other, and he will need to be with Sophie a lot, anyway. I don't feel I can speak to him about Christmas yet; it just seems so far away, a full three months. If it wasn't essential for work, I wouldn't be thinking about it either. I also need to see my parents during that time. I will have to work it out later. If I let too many thoughts and considerations crowd my head, I start to feel anxious. When I took on this job, I knew that it would take over my life and if I want to make a success of it, I have to give it my all. I just hope that people will understand.

I also worry that part of the reason Jonathan is so reluctant to come up with the goods for Christmas and New Year is because he actually doesn't want to work then. I can understand that; he is young, and only just back from his travels, so he wants to spend time with his mates, and his family. But, just like me, he has chosen to work in a field which requires unsociable hours, and which is all about ensuring our guests and customers have the best possible experience staying and/or dining at the Sail Loft. Unfortunately for Jonathan, he is just going to have to get stuck in.

***

On Wednesday, Julie and Luke jet off to Ibiza. I can't help but feel a tiny bit jealous. Still, I have plenty to keep me busy. As well as starting to put my stamp on things at the Sail Loft, I am also determined to make David's house feel like mine and Julie's. On Wednesday evening, however, he turns up unannounced.

"I come bearing pizza," he says when I answer the door, "but no intentions of being a nosy landlord. If you want me to go, you can just take this enormous mozzarella-and-vegetable-laden monstrosity out of my hands and shut the door in my face!"

"As if I'd do that," I say, the smell of the takeaway pizza wafting through its box. "Is that from the Smokehouse?"

"Hm-hmm."

"You'd better come in, then! There's no way I can put away a whole one of their pizzas. Well, actually, I probably could – but I definitely shouldn't."

"That is exactly what I wanted to hear."

I step back so that David can come through. "Is it a bit weird, knocking on your own front door?"

"No, not as weird as getting used to living at Martin's. He's being brill but he's been on his own there for seven years – and of course I've been on my own here for even longer. We both have our own ways of doing things. And even though I spent so much time there before I moved in, it's different, somehow. He keeps telling me off for asking if I can do things."

"Well, that's good, isn't it?"

"It is, it's great. He is perfect," David pretend-swoons, but I know that he and Martin really are perfect for each other.

"Shall I get plates?" I ask.

"No, let's eat out of the box, save on the washing up."

"Don't get any greasy fingerprints on the furniture, though," I warn, "my landlord'll go mad."

"I've heard about him," David says, "he's very handsome, isn't he?"

"Hmm…" I pretend to think, "No, not so's you'd notice."

David pushes me on the arm. "Rent can go up, you know."

I laugh, then we talk work. He tells me as much as he's allowed about the case he's working on at the moment and I fill him on goings-on at the Sail Loft.

"Sounds like Jonathan needs taking in hand," he winks mock-saucily.

"He needs more than that," I say. "If he wants his own restaurant, he'd better buy one, or ask Mummy and Daddy for one for Christmas. We need to make sure things go well – better than well – so that Bea knows she's done the right thing in trusting us; well, me in particular."

"She knows," David says. "And she knows what Jonathan's like. Basically, he's a twenty-three-year-old man-boy, who hasn't really had to work very hard yet for anything. He's a great chef, though."

"He is that," I agree. "Have you spoken to Bea?"

"Just briefly, earlier today. I had to run a couple of things past her for the wedding. Martin and I both want a winter wedding, and with Bea away it looks like we're going to have to hang on till next year. I can't possibly get married without her there."

"No – for one thing, she would kill you and Martin!"

"That's true. But seriously, I want her to be my Best Woman. Martin's mum will be there, and Bea, and that's the pitiful extent of our families, save for cousins and the odd uncle and aunt who we rarely see. I've realised how much a wedding is about getting people together, as much as it is about the two people getting wed." David's eyes fill with tears as he continues. "I know it sounds soppy, but I want this wedding to be like Christmas… you know, over-sentimental, with all the people we love most in the world there to share it with us."

"I don't think it sounds soppy, I think it sounds absolutely lovely," I say, taking a huge bite of pizza and feeling its warmth ooze through me. "This is delicious, thank you so much for thinking of me!"

"Well, I knew from what Bea said that you've been working your arse off and I also knew that with Julie away you'd probably be ripping the lid off a Pot Noodle and getting the kettle on – as I have surmised that's pretty much your full cooking repertoire."

"Oi, you cheeky bugger! I'll have you know I make an excellent beans on toast."

"Of course, I'd forgotten about that particular delicacy. I

take it all back."

I am really glad to have David's company. I am more than used to time to myself, having lived alone for years before coming down here, but I am missing Sam very badly right now and with Julie swanning off to Ibiza, I had thought that tonight was going to be a bit hollow. With David about, however, the evening is filled with laughter, amidst talk of wedding plans, and harmless idle gossip. A few weeks back, I wouldn't have known any of the people David is talking about but now I know Sue the local artist and her husband Mike, famed for their open marriage and open bed; regularly sharing it with willing third parties, or so David says. Then there is Tom, who grows the veg which eventually makes its way through to the Sail Loft, who David reckons is having an affair with one of the barmaids from the Mainbrace, because his wife is cold and horrible and just wanted him to produce children. I listen, and tut, and laugh, and hope very much that Sam and I are not being talked about in a similar vein elsewhere in town.

"Oh, you're bound to be!" David says when I voice this concern. "What else have people got to talk about? My god, when I came out and when Martin and I got together, I could practically hear the voices bubbling out of people's chimneys, it was such hot news. There's no harm meant by it, you know, at least not usually. This is what it's like to live in a small town. You're going to have to get used to it if you want to make a life here. It has its upsides as well, you know. Whenever there have been real troublemakers, the good townsfolk have gathered their pitchforks and driven the trouble out of town."

"Moving the problem somewhere else," I smile.

"Ah, but if you live here, there *is* nowhere else! Haven't you realised that yet?"

David is only half-joking, I know. I feel like no matter how long I live here, I will never really be considered a local and I don't mind that. I have split loyalties anyway, still loving the place I grew up, where Mum and Dad still live. But now that I am here, I am loath to leave. And if that means putting up with a bit of gossip, so be it. I do also like the idea of living somewhere that people feel protective of, to the point that they will – to some extent – take the law into their own hands, to keep the place and people that they love safe.

After David has headed off to his new home and fiancé, I get ready for bed, wondering what people made of Julie and me when we came back here. Probably they took little notice at first; we were just another couple of seasonal workers. But then Julie got together with Luke; somebody people would be proud to call a son of the town, even though he moved to London some years back. With his mum being ill as well, I can imagine there may have been much to occupy people's coffee break conversation. Then there came the situation with Casey and Sophie, and Sam and me. I am sure that's still good for a bit of chat, seeing as Sam has now left town and I am still here… as are his ex and his daughter. Ah well, let them talk, I think. Like David says, it's not meant in a malicious way and although I tend towards a preference for privacy, there may very well be some benefits to living in a place where anonymity is hard to come by.

***

Friday comes around and I feel slightly on edge, hoping that Jonathan is going to deliver those menus as he has promised. Not just because I want to put the finishing touches to my marketing literature but because if he doesn't,

I know I am going to have to take action. The problem is – what action? Do I come across as a hard-nosed, take-no-bullshit kind of boss? I seriously doubt that I could pull that off. And besides, I really do want this to be a happy place to work, where we can have fun. There are so few of us who work here that any ill feeling would be hard to dilute, and I am sure that guests would be able to pick up on it, too.

I decide to give him till lunchtime, when he'll be knocking off for the afternoon, and then I will go and ask him. All morning long, as I look through orders and inventories, I am waiting for him to knock on the door. The knock doesn't come.

At ten past twelve, I stand up and head for the kitchen. I push the door open to find Margaret, the lady who does our cleaning over the weekend.

"Oh hi, love," she says, smiling. "How are you?"

"I'm fine, thanks, Margaret, are you OK?"

"Oh yes, great, thank you."

"Good," I say absent-mindedly, "have you seen Jonathan anywhere?"

"Oh, he's just left, bless him. I said I'd finish up in here. He was looking tired. And he's got to come back tonight, hasn't he? I don't know how he does it, I'm sure."

"Oh," I smile through gritted teeth, "well, it's his job, and he must like it or he wouldn't have chosen to be a chef."

"You're quite right, I'm sure," Margaret is looking at me curiously. I mustn't let her see I'm annoyed.

"Well, hopefully he'll have a chance to rest this afternoon and come back refreshed tonight!" I say brightly. I stalk back into my office and shut the door, finally allowing my face and my body language to express how I am feeling.

Now I'm stuck. I've already been lenient with him over this but he promised me faithfully he'd have those menus with me today. So what do I do now?

I pick up my phone and ring Julie. I know she's on holiday but she won't mind if I rant to her for a few minutes.

"He's obviously used to charming people into letting him have his own way," she says. "You're going to have to show him it won't work with you."

Jonathan strikes me as one of those people who rely on their good looks to get them through tricky situations. I suspect that lots of girls his age and younger fancy him, and older women find his boyish charm engaging, and want to mother him. I, just a handful of years older than him, fall into neither of these categories; in fact, right now I want to throttle him.

"What would you do?" I ask.

"Well, it's a bit different for me 'cos I'm a chef, too. I'd just design the menu myself and tell him that's what he's doing. He's had his chance."

"Oh," I say. "There's an idea…"

"What?" Julie sounds suspicious.

"Well, just say I had, like, the best friend in the world, who could design a menu for me…"

"I'd say you were remarkably lucky."

"Would you? Please? Pretty please? I'll be your best friend."

"You already are, you idiot."

"OK, I'll stop using your lovely fluffy towels."

"You shouldn't be using them anyway. I'm not sure your negotiation technique is that good," Julie laughs. "But go on then. I'd love to. Let me see if I can get something together while I'm lying by the pool this afternoon."

"Rub it in, why don't you?" I listen to her chuckle. "Thanks, Julie. I owe you one. Give my love to Luke, will you?"

"Of course. I'll drop you a line later."

True to her word, before I leave work late in the afternoon, I have an email from Julie with a detailed menu for Christmas, another for New Year, and another for in between. She's even done some work on our breakfast offerings, including a Bucks Fizz brunch one day, and a 'hair-of-the-dog' Bloody Mary on the New Year's Day menu.

I hand over to Stefan but mention nothing of what has gone on. I am going to be on from tomorrow morning until Monday, which will give me plenty of time to speak to Jonathan – but for tonight I'll allow myself some time to think about exactly what it is that I want to say.

9

I tell Sam all about what's happened – or not happened – with Jonathan.

"It just goes to show," he says.

"What?"

"You should never trust somebody so good looking."

"Do you fancy him?" I tease.

"Yeah, of course I do. I'm only with you to get closer to him. You're probably equal in terms of looks but he's got the upper hand when it comes to cooking."

"You cheeky bugger," I say. "Anyway, you're pretty good looking. Does that mean I can't trust you?"

"Alice, I absolutely swear you can trust me."

"I know that, I'm just winding you up. You're not that good looking, anyway."

Sam tells me about his first week at uni, and all the amazing modules he's doing. He's so enthusiastic, I can't help but be happy for him. And what he said about being trustworthy – well, I don't doubt that for one minute. I know he is loyal and honest; my concern is really whether we can keep things going over a long distance, over such a long time. Especially when he will have split loyalties when he's back, between Sophie and me.

"How's Sophie?" I ask. "Did she get over that stomach thing?"

"She seems to have done. She was back at school on Monday."

Was she? I think, that tiny seed of suspicion about Kate lodging itself firmly in my mind. At the same time, I tell myself that Kate wouldn't use her daughter in such a way; dragging her out at that time of night. Plus, Sophie isn't stupid. She knows if she's ill or not. Kate couldn't make her think she had stomach ache. But what, I wonder, if Kate gave Sophie something dodgy to eat or drink after she got back from her day out with Sam? This is ridiculous, I tell myself sternly. Kate wouldn't deliberately make her daughter ill, even if she is pissed off about me and Sam being together.

"What do you think, then?" I realise Sam is asking me a question but I have no clue as to its meaning.

"What's that?" I ask.

"Sophie!" he says, as if it's obvious. "Would you be able to look after her for an hour on Monday? I'm sorry to ask, I don't think Kate really wanted me to. But you said you wouldn't mind and to be honest I just really love the idea of you and Soph spending some time together while I'm here. If you can't do it, no worries, it's just it will save her from having to hang out at the Pilates class."

"Monday?" I say, "Yes of course, that's fine. I'll be happy to." And I will. I really do like Sophie, and I want to make sure that the bond I have with her doesn't break in Sam's absence. It is new, and delicate, and I know it is going to need some nurturing. Some people could think cynically that I just want to spend time with Sophie to keep Sam happy – and if I'm honest, there is an element of that – but I also like the girl a lot and I enjoy being reminded of what it's like being a kid.

"You are brilliant. Have I mentioned that before?"

"I think you have, or something to that effect."

"I miss you," he says.

"I miss you too," I think of him in his little studio flat. He's sent me some pictures. There is a huge bay window in the main room, which houses both his bed and his living area. In the corner is a poky kitchen, not sectioned off from the main space in any way, and behind the wall where his bed is there's a tiny bathroom which just fits a shower and a toilet. Sam says there is no heating save for an electric radiator: "It's fine for now, but I'm a bit worried about the winter." It's not far from the sea – which is why his course fits so well there, I suppose – but he says it's quite different to here. The island of Anglesey is just across a very narrow strip of water, and Sam says the sea itself seems different; its colour, its temperament – even on a clear, still day, he says it feels like it's angry, as though it's lying in wait for something. I like the way he gives the sea a personality, and emotions.

When we say goodbye, I wander around the house aimlessly for a while. I need to eat, and I fancy a glass of wine, but I also feel like just going to bed. It is defeatist, and a bit sad on a Friday night, but it also reminds me very much of not so long ago when I lived alone and I worked at World of Stationery. If I didn't take up my colleagues' offer of a few drinks in town then I'd be home alone by seven, and often in bed by nine. The difference now, I suppose, is that although I am on my own right now, Julie will be back in a week, and Sam will be here in just four weeks. I should make the most of this time to myself; I used to love my own space, but somehow I just don't feel the same now. I want Sam, and I feel very sorry for myself. I make toast with butter and Marmite, and a large cup of tea, and I take it on a tray up to bed. As soon as I slide between the sheets I realise how tired I am. I eat my toast, drink my tea while it's just the right temperature, and watch TV for a bit but by half-past-nine I am ready for sleep so that is just what I do.

***

After that night, the first weekend without Sam here passes quickly. On Saturday morning I have my overnight bag packed and it's off to the Sail Loft.

Jonathan is in the midst of preparing breakfast.

"Can we have a chat, when you're done in here?" I ask sweetly.

"Oh, yeah, sure," I am convinced he looks half guilty and half defensive.

"Great, thanks," I turn on my heel and leave the kitchen, popping into the dining room to say hello to the guests before I head into my office.

Stefan is in there, at the second desk which we've put in for him. I said we should share but he thinks it makes more sense to have one each and I guess he's right but I feel a bit guilty, having Bea's great polished wooden desk and leather chair while he has a distinctly smaller and clearly IKEA set. However, he doesn't really seem to mind and to be fair, I do most of the administrative work.

"I've remade the bed in the flat," he tells me cheerily, "I was up early to see Mr Fairhead off. He said he'd very much enjoyed his stay, by the way. I sent him off with a packed breakfast even though he said he didn't want anything. I'm sure he'll be glad of it on his way home."

"Great thinking," I said. Mr Fairhead was visiting the area on business. He usually stays in Penzance but his trip was a last-minute one and his secretary had happened across our details. "Hopefully he'll consider coming back here. Maybe we should look at trying to attract more business customers out of season," I ponder. "Thanks for doing the bed, by the way, you didn't need to do that."

66

"It's the least I can do seeing as you're letting me have the weekend off!"

"Well you let me have last weekend off," I remind him. "And I'm really happy that you're going to get to spend some time with April and Reuben. What are your plans?"

Stefan reels off a list of fun-filled activities and I smile, trying to push back the lonely feeling which is bugging me. I don't want to be that person; lost without my partner. It's a good job I'm working this weekend, I think. I have plenty to do here and on Monday I will get to see Sophie, which is not the same as seeing Sam but she's a solid link to him, and will be good company. Then it's only two more days until Julie's back.

***

When Jonathan knocks on the door, I feel nervous, then I feel annoyed with myself for feeling nervous. I grit my teeth. "Come in."

"Hi," he smiles as his head pokes round the door, and in he comes with two cups of coffee. "I warmed some milk for yours, and added a sugar," he says. I refuse to be won over by this attention to detail, though I have to admit he does make good coffee. Before I have a chance to draw breath, he begins. "I'm really sorry, Alice, about the Christmas and New Year thing. I know I said I'd have it ready for you yesterday, and it nearly is, I promise. But I had to go, and I thought that another day wouldn't make a difference."

"You've got it for me today, then?" I ask, impressed with my coolness.

"Oh, erm, not quite… well, nearly. I'll put the finishing touches to it after lunch."

"Jonathan," I sigh, not really wanting to do the whole

angry-boss thing, and feeling a bit like I need to look after him. Which is probably something he counts on; I think of him leaving Margaret to clean up after him yesterday… he's probably got all the women in his life eating out of his hand. "You're already days late with it. You know I needed it this week at the very latest, to get all the literature done. We've been moved down the queue at the printers now," I lie.

"No way!" he says. "I'll speak to Dad. Bob's an old friend of his, I'm sure Dad can pull some strings."

Damn. Of course Jonathan would know somebody who knows the printer. "No, it's fine, I'll sort it," I say and I think I see a little concern on Jonathan's face.

"I really am sorry, Alice, I'll get it done this afternoon. Or tomorrow, at the latest."

"No," I say, "don't bother. It's too late. I've had to get somebody else to do it."

"You've got somebody else to do my menu?" Now he looks outraged.

"Yes," I say, feeling like I am talking to a little kid as I continue, "You had your chance to do it yourself – more than one chance, actually. But you didn't do it. And you can't just expect me to wait around forever."

Jonathan's face takes on a petulant look, confirming my feeling. "Great. First I have to work Christmas and New Year. Now I have to cook somebody else's menu."

"Sorry," I say, though I don't feel it. He looks like he wants to stamp his foot. It makes me want to laugh. "But if we don't have a menu then there's a strong chance that neither you or I will be working: Christmas, New Year, or at all."

"Fine," he flounces out of the room. I lean back in my chair, swivelling it round so that I can see the view of the town. I am suddenly overcome by giggles, so much so that

I don't hear him come back in.

"Can I at least..." he starts, then stops. "Are you OK, Alice?"

I realise that my shoulders are shaking. I try to compose myself as I turn the chair back towards him, wiping my eyes.

"Are you crying?" he asks, his voice full of concern.

"What? No," I begin but before I know it, Jonathan has his arm round me and is holding me. I can't help notice that he smells nice; kind of spicy.

I don't know what to do so I let him hold me for a while then I pull back. "I'm OK now," I smile and he holds my hand for a moment.

"I should have done the menu," he says, "I'm really sorry I messed things up. If you let me have this other menu, I'll take a look at it. Maybe it won't be so bad."

It's bloody brilliant, I think, marvelling at his chef's ego, but I just say, "I'll get a copy to you later."

"Thanks, Alice," he says and he gives me a sympathetic smile before turning and leaving the room. This time I wait a few moments before I allow my mirth to return. I feel much better about everything, somehow.

***

Work takes over for the rest of the weekend. Because I am sleeping at the Sail Loft, and on call, I hardly notice the absence of Sam, or of Julie. I have to get up in the middle of Sunday night to call a doctor for one of our guests who injured their ankle during the day and thought it was just sprained but on waking in pain at about 2am realised that their leg was swelling, and looking exceedingly bruised. The doctor says that it may be a broken ankle so the next thing I have to do is to call a taxi; Mrs Brewster and her husband

69

have been drinking so are over the alcohol limit for the drive to hospital. As we wait, drinking hot, sweet tea, for the ever-reliable Brian, I think of Sam's recent journey to hospital with Sophie and Kate – *his family*, I taunt myself. I imagine how worried he must have been and wonder whether he would feel as concerned for me in that situation. Don't be stupid, I tell myself sternly. I really do know that I mustn't compare Sam's feelings for me to those he has for Sophie. We occupy two different positions in his life and he must feel protective of Sophie in a way which he couldn't possibly – and which I wouldn't want him to – feel for me.

After Mr and Mrs Brewster are dispatched, with sandwiches and a flask of coffee, I find I cannot sleep and so when Jonathan arrives just before six, I have been awake for hours.

"You look knackered!" he says cheerfully.

"Thanks," I say, and he laughs. I have to say, it's hard to stay annoyed at him. And he does make an excellent breakfast, as he proves now, whipping up some avocados on toast for me, a perfectly poached egg placed on top. As the yolk breaks gently with the touch of my fork, my stomach rumbles and I smile gratefully at Jonathan as he places a fresh coffee in front of me.

"Missing Steve?" he asks.

"Sam," I remind him.

"Oh yeah, sorry! Sam."

"I've been up since two," I say, dodging the subject and filling him in on Mrs Brewster's misfortune as he begins to make the kitchen ready for breakfast.

In minutes, Lydia is with us. She's a student at the sixth-form college and I've half-reluctantly agreed to take her on; the reluctance only because I worry these early starts will make her days at college hard, but she says she can cope, and she is supporting herself through her studies. Her parents are out of work, and she has three younger brothers so money is tight.

Besides which, she is friendly and bright and the guests will love her. Since I've changed position, we've been relying on a mixture of agency staff and, occasionally, me, to keep things going. Lydia works one weekend of every two, and all week days. It's a lot for her.

"Morning!" Lydia says cheerfully and I am sure that her eyes linger slightly longer on Jonathan than on me. I can't say I'm surprised. He barely gives her the time of day, though, and I feel sorry for her. In honesty I can't believe he hasn't noticed her; she is tall and willowy, with long red hair tied neatly at the nape of her neck. Maybe she seems too young to him.

"Hi Lydia," I say, "I hope you had a good weekend?"

"The best!" she says, turning to Jonathan. "Did you have a good weekend, Jon?"

Jon. I wonder fleetingly if these two know each other better than I'd thought.

"Yeah, well it was mostly spent working, of course," he says gruffly, and I wonder at the difference in his tone addressing Lydia – offhand, even abrupt – and the one he uses with me – almost eager-to-please, although unfortunately that attitude doesn't stretch as far as his actual actions. Lydia doesn't seem fazed, though.

"I'll go and get the dining room set up," she says to me, and scarpers through the swing door before I even have a chance to thank her.

"Right, I'm off to my office," I say to Jonathan. "If you don't see me again before ten please can you come and check I haven't nodded off?"

"Of course, I'll bring you a coffee," he says smoothly.

71

"Great," I flash him a smile and wander off into my own space, swearing as I bump my thigh into the corner of Bea's huge desk, my tired state making me clumsier than usual.

I wait until 7.30 then I phone Sam.

"Hi Alice," he says and I can hear the sound of traffic nearby. "I'm just at the bus stop. Heading in early to get a few books out of the library when it opens."

"Swot," I say. "Have you remembered your apple for the teacher?"

"You may mock but you'll be laughing on the other side of your face when I'm a world-famous millionaire marine biologist."

"Do marine biologists become millionaires?"

"No," he admits, "at least not from marine biology. To be honest, I couldn't sleep. I haven't slept well since I've been here. It's not the most comfy bed, and I... I'm really missing you."

I smile. "I miss you, too." I wonder if he can hear the smile down the phone, as per my sales training. "But it's just three weeks now till you're back."

"Yes," he says, "I'm counting the days. It is OK to stay with you, isn't it?"

"Of course!" I say. "I'd be bloody offended if you didn't."

"Have you sorted out that time off?" he asks. "I've been looking at places we can go for a couple of days."

"Spa hotels?" I tease.

"Yes, and I think I've found the perfect one. Glades Manor. It's just over the Devon border, far enough away to be completely out of town."

I like the sound of this; being a couple of hours' drive away makes it hard for Kate, or work, to interrupt our time together. I make a note to speak to Stefan.

"OK," Sam says, "the bus is coming. I'll ring you later."

"I'll be with Sophie later," I remind him.

"Great, then I'll try and catch you both together. I love the thought of you spending time with her, Alice."

"I'm looking forward to it," I say, although in truth the thought of an evening to myself, and an early night, is now very appealing.

"I love you," he says.

"I love you, too."

10

Kate opens the door when I go to collect Sophie. She looks at me as though she is slightly unsure of how I am going to act, whilst I am feeling much the same about her. When we have been in the same vicinity as each other lately, we've done a great job of not talking or even acknowledging the other's presence, without it seeming too hostile. However, face-to-face, at the entrance to her home, we have no choice.

"Hi," I say.

"Hi."

"How are you…" I begin but she is already calling Sophie.

"What time do you want her back?" I ask.

"I'll be back from Pilates by half seven so by eight would be good."

"No problem. Hi Sophie!" I exclaim, as the nine-year-old appears in the doorway. "How are you?"

Sophie hugs me, which is unexpected but very welcome. Kate watches her daughter, with an unreadable expression. I think it's a shame it's come to this between us. We had got on quite well; we are certainly two very different people but Kate is nice enough, and what I feel worst about is the fact that she opened up to me quite a lot before we realised that we had Sam in common. It made me feel like I had been dishonest, tricking her into confiding in me, but it really wasn't like that. Now, though, I have this personal knowledge about Sam's ex, and his daughter's mum, which I wish I didn't. The fact that she drinks every night – Sam might or might not know about that, but Kate told me in confidence and I don't think I can betray that. Besides which, it's not like she's neglectful of Sophie. Just lonely, more than anything.

I smile at her as I hug Sophie back, hoping that I am getting my expression right. I am going for friendly and unthreatening but what if I actually look smug, like I'm trying to steal her daughter's affections?

"Have fun, Sophie," Kate says, shutting the door as her daughter steps outside.

"Where to, then, Miss? The world is our lobster."

"Don't you mean oyster?" Sophie giggles and I am overcome with a warmth for her.

"Do I?" I pull a confused expression, which has her laughing more.

"Can we go to the beach, Alice?"

"Yes, of course we can. Which would you like to go to?"

It is still a novelty to me to be able to just go to the beach at the end of a long day. And now autumn is well and truly here, the dark nights are coming decidedly quicker. We are just weeks away from having to change the clocks, losing another valuable hour of daylight at this end of the day. I want to make the most of the light evenings while I still can.

"The surf one?" Sophie asks hopefully.

"Yeah, sure… why not?"

"Mum doesn't like that one so much, now the weather's not as good. She says it's too windy and it messes her hair up."

"Well, she's got a point," I say, keen not to contradict Sophie's mother, but her face starts to fall. "But hey, my hair's a mess already so it doesn't really matter!" I grin and take her hand. "Come on, we'll stop at my place and pick up some buckets and spades, shall we?"

"Yay!" Sophie exclaims and we skip hand-in-hand down the hill.

Despite the cooler weather, the sea is still rammed full of surfers; looking broody and moody in their wetsuits, against the grey sky. I just love rounding the corner to this beach; there is a point where the buildings end and you are suddenly exposed to the elements; the powerful wind coming straight from the sea, hitting you full-on, with salt and sand and stinging freshness. I hold on tighter to Sophie's hand; she feels so small that I worry the wind today could blow her over. But she is strong, and nimble, and quickly loosens her grip so she can start pulling her shoes off, hopping first on one foot and then the other, even though we are still a couple of metres from the slope down to the sand.

"Steady on!" I say, laughing.

"I just can't wait to get down there, Alice," she says earnestly and something about the way she says my name pulls at me.

"Well, we'd better get a move on, then!" I start pulling off my shoes too, as an elderly couple walking towards us look and smile. They are fully wrapped up in long coats, the man wearing a hat and the lady a headscarf. This is that strange time of year when some people are still happy to traipse about in shorts, as though they can't bear to let the summer go just yet, and others are already prepared and wrapped up for winter. I fall somewhere in between so I roll up the legs of my jeans, put my shoes and Sophie's in my bag, and join Sophie in a headlong run down the slope to the beach, both of us laughing and calling out to each other as we hit the sand and keep on going.

Sophie seems like she may be able to carry on running the full length of the sand – which is quite some distance. I, meanwhile, am panting and puffed-out after a few metres. "Sophie!" I call her between deep intakes of breath. "Soph!" I yell, and she turns round, coming back to me.

"Don't run off like that," I say.

"Sorry, I was just…"

"Excited, I know. And that's great. It's just that your mum and dad won't trust me to look after you again if I lose you on our first outing."

Sophie grins.

"Look," I say, "I am really tired, can we stop and get a coffee, and I can get you a hot chocolate if you like..?"

"Yes please, that would be lovely."

We walk past the Beach Bar and I wave at Andrew, the owner, noting the seat where Sam and I sat on our first date this summer, now home to three young lads. The wide glass doors are closed now, protecting customers, staff and furniture from the elements. At the café, we go to the hatch and I ask for our drinks. Sophie is eyeing the cakes up, too. "Do you know what?" I say. "I fancy a cake, how about you?"

"Yes!" Sophie says. "The Rocky Road is awesome. Can I have a piece of that please, Alice?"

"Sure," I say, and ask the lady behind the counter for two pieces of Rocky Road.

Sophie carries the cake and I take the hot drinks, heading for the little outcrop of rocks where I met Sophie for the first time, when she spilled a bucket of cold sea water over me. I remind her of that now. She can't help giggling.

"Funny, is it?" I grin at her.

"Yep." She looks happy, and I watch her determined stride across the sand, thinking that Sam should be with us.

"Have you spoken to your dad much since he's been in Wales?" I ask once we are settled on our hard, uneven seats, both facing out to sea, hair blowing this way and that. I pull a strand from my eyes.

"Yes, every day, we speak on Skype," Sophie says proudly. "Dad got me a tablet before he went."

I know all this already but I wanted to find a way to introduce Sam into the conversation. To make sure things are easy between us all.

"I think he is missing you loads," I say, hoping that this is not out of my remit. "He can't wait for you to go and visit."

"I know, it's only four days till I go now!" Sophie looks so uncomplicatedly happy, I want to hug her.

"It sounds like he's working very hard," I say, "it's a great course. I could imagine you doing something similar one day."

"Yeah, I'd like that," she says, "I think. But I would quite like to be a rock star."

"Maybe you can do both," I smile.

We sip our drinks and I ask about her friends at school. Soon, I am getting the lowdown on who has a crush on whom, and which friends have fallen out and then made up again.

"Have you got a best friend?" I ask her.

"No, not really," she says.

"That's not a bad thing – better to have loads of friends."

"You've got Julie," she points out.

"Well, that's true, but we were a bit older than you when we became friends. And we've always had other friends, as well. I think that you can never have too many friends – as

78

long as they are real friends, of course," I add.

"Mum doesn't have any friends," Sophie says. "'Cept for me and Dad. And you," she adds, though she looks slightly unsure of this.

"Your mum is a very busy lady," I say, "and I am sure she's got lots of friends. But she does have a best friend, I'm sure of that."

"Who?"

"You!" I say. "And she is very lucky to have you for a best friend. My mum is one of my best friends, and she's a lot older than yours but do you know what? I can talk to her about anything and she always listens, and she always gives me good advice."

"What about your dad?"

I smile. "And my dad. He's one of my best friends, too."

"Do you miss him?"

"Yes, I do. And my mum. But I know that they love me, and they know I love them."

"Are they sad that you came down to Cornwall?"

"No," I say, "they're happy because I'm happy."

Sophie is quiet, thinking about this. "I want Dad to be happy."

"I know you do," I think I see tears forming in her eyes and I put my arm around her shoulders. "But the most important thing to him is that you are happy. You might think that's a bit strange because he's gone to Wales, but it was a difficult thing to do and the most difficult thing was leaving you."

"And you," she sniffs.

"Well," I say, "maybe it was difficult for Sam to leave me but I am telling you, Sophie, that the person he misses the most, by about a million, squillion, gazillion miles, is you."

"Gazillion isn't a real number."

We sip our drinks, then we have a poke around in the rockpools for a while. The sea is not too cold but the sharp wind is making us shiver so after a while we agree to wander back towards town, paddling through the shallows and holding hands. It feels good: Sophie's small, warm hand in mine; the sound and spray of the sea; the companionable way that Sam's daughter is talking to me, waxing lyrical about the seabirds which will be heading our way for the duration of winter.

"There's the grey phalarope, which you sometimes see in late summer. It's really pretty and not very big, but it's got a long beak and it likes to eat plankton so sometimes it's a way of spotting basking sharks." Sophie's enthusiasm, like Sam's, is catching. "And the Iceland gull, that comes here for the winter. It's beautiful, it's like snowy coloured. I know people don't like gulls, but... look, Alice!"

Sophie's eyes are shining and I follow her line of sight and her pointing finger to see a pod of shining, slippery-looking dolphins flipping and crashing through the waves; out beyond the surfers, many of whom have also turned to watch. The wet, dark skin of the dolphins looks almost black in the dull evening light but, as if magic itself is playing a part, at that very moment a few rays of sunshine push their way through the cloud, splashing onto the water, making me gasp. It is one of the most beautiful sights I have ever seen.

Sophie is mesmerised, too, and we stand there until the dolphins are out of sight, our bare feet growing cold in the water, legs splattered by mischievous waves taking advantage of our distraction.

After that, Sophie can't stop talking about them and she asks if we can phone Sam to tell him.

"Of course!" I say. "Let's just get to a more sheltered spot, where it's not so windy. It will be really hard to have a conversation here."

We walk the rest of the length of the beach and sit on a stone wall, tucked away behind the rocks. I hand Sophie my phone and she calls Sam.

"Dad!" she giggles, "It's me, Sophie. Don't call me that."

My cheeks flush; I wonder what he said. I hadn't thought this through. "Dad thinks you're sexy!" Sophie laughs, and my face grows redder still. She is not bothered, though; she has news to impart. She describes the scene beautifully to Sam and I can tell he's asking her questions, which she answers with a great deal of knowledge. "Short-beaked," she says; I start to hope she is talking about the dolphins and not me; "about twelve, I think." I relax, but I'm going to have to brush up on my wildlife knowledge again, if I'm going to have any chance with these two.

"OK…" I can tell that their conversation is drawing to a close, "I love you too, Daddy. Can you phone me later? Before bedtime? I love you, I love you," Sophie says, then hands the phone to me: "He wants to speak to you… *Sexy*," she says with an impudent smile.

"Hello?" I say, taking the phone from Sophie and giving her a mock-stern look. She grins and turns to look out to sea.

"You could have warned me!" Sam says and I think those sales courses were true: I can hear his smile down the phone line.

"What – phoned you first and said 'The next voice you hear will be… Sophie's'?"

"Yes, why not? It's nice to hear you two having so much fun together," he says. "I only wish I was there with you."

"I think we both wish that," I glance at Sophie, who is still turned away, maybe trying to glimpse those dolphins again.

"I'm so glad Sophie was here to tell me about the dolphins," I say, knowing she can hear me. "She knows more about all this stuff than you."

"She's brilliant, isn't she?" Sam says proudly.

"Yes," I say, "she is. Look, we're getting a bit cold out here. Why don't I speak to you later?" I have noticed something about Sophie, and I think I need to get off the phone.

"OK," Sam says, and I feel a physical ache for him. "I love you."

"I love you, too," I say, and end the call. I put my hand on Sophie's shoulder. She doesn't turn but I feel a little shudder in her.

"Soph?" I say softly. "Are you crying?"

The shoulder sinks a little and I edge up next to her, my buttocks and thighs stiff on the cold stone wall.

"You're missing him, aren't you?" I ask.

A sniff, and a nod.

"That's OK, in fact it would be weird if you weren't. It must be very hard for you."

Sophie leans into me then and huge sobs shake her. I put my arms around her and feel my own eyes well up. I may be missing Sam but it is nothing compared to what this little girl feels. I hold her until she stops crying, and looks at me with red-rimmed eyes.

"Don't tell Mum," she whispers.

"What? Well of course I won't, but I don't think she'd mind, you know."

"I don't want her thinking she's not enough," Sophie says and I feel a little crack split all the way up the side of my heart.

"She wouldn't think that, Sophie!" I say. "I know I don't know your mum really well but I do know that she wouldn't

82

want you to hide being upset from her. She will expect you to miss your dad, you know. In fact, even if you don't show her, she already knows you are missing him. Come on," I say, "let's go and get something to eat. I can make anything, from beans on toast to spaghetti on toast – maybe even a fried egg sandwich. How does that sound?"

"Good," she sniffs again and we walk slowly up the path which we had bounded down just an hour or so ago, Sam's daughter leaning into me as I wonder how either of us are going to cope with his absence.

When I drop Sophie off at her house, Kate is still in her Pilates gear. I can't help but admire her toned figure; tall and slender in slim-fitting jogging trousers and a vest top.

"Hi love!" she smiles at Sophie. "Did you have a good time?"

"Yes, it was good thanks," her daughter says. "We went to the beach and saw some dolphins."

"You'll be happy, then," Kate hugs her daughter.

"How was your class?" I ask her, unsure what to say.

"Yeah, good thanks," she echoes her daughter's words. I think that Sophie was playing things down so her mum didn't think she had too much fun while Kate is playing it down because she just doesn't like me. "Thanks for having her," she adds.

"It's my pleasure," I smile at Sophie. "Any time."

"Really?" Kate asks. "Only I was going to ask if you could have her next Monday, too."

I am slightly surprised by this, although I don't suppose I should be, given how she pretty much had me signed up to her Pilates class – filling in forms and agreeing to hand out fliers for her - within minutes of mentioning it, back when we first met.

"Sure, that should be fine," I smile at Sophie. "In fact, that will be great."

"Thanks," Kate says shortly then she smiles. "You'll be able to tell Alice all about our visit up to your dad's, won't you?"

The smile freezes on my face. Those words hurt. But I know it is so important to keep things positive and friendly, for Sophie's sake. I have nothing to fear from Kate, either, I remind myself. She and Sam are old news. But I hadn't thought until now of how it would work while Sophie is visiting; of course, Kate will be with her. She can't travel all that way alone. But Sam only has a small flat, with a bed settee. Where is Kate going to stay?

All these thoughts needle my mind but I keep my face smooth and expression neutral. "Great," I say. "Have a brilliant weekend, Sophie. Give my love to your dad, tell him I'll see him soon."

"Shall I tell him he's sexy, too?" Sophie asks and I feel my cheeks go red again.

"No, no, better not," I say, and I feel Kate's gaze boring in to me. "Right, better leave you two to it. See you next week, Sophie." She hugs me quickly and I return her embrace and smile at her.

"See you," I say vaguely to Kate.

"Thanks again," she says, "And I'm sorry your night with Sam was ruined the other week."

I bet you are, I think as I walk off down the street, the water in the bay glistening before me, in a last-bid attempt by the sun to make itself known before night folds in.

11

I have a long chat with Sam in the evening. He has just come off the phone to Sophie.

"Is she OK, do you think?" he asks me.

I am tempted to say yes, she's fine; I don't want to worry him. But I remind myself of the importance we have placed on being honest. A few weeks back, he confided in me that Sophie is not his biological daughter; a fact that only he, Kate, and now I, know. Besides, won't he think it's weird if Sophie is just fine with him being away?

"She's missing you," I tell him. "Of course she is, but she's also looking forward to coming to see you at the weekend."

Sam is quiet so I continue, "It's just going to take a while for this to become normal; there's no way it could be immediately after you've gone – and besides, wouldn't it be worse if she wasn't missing you?"

"For me, yes," I hear his breath as he considers the situation. "But actually, if she was happy, and I wasn't making her unhappy, then it would be better."

"You aren't making her unhappy, not really. Yes, she is a bit sad at the moment, but that's OK. Better to have feelings and acknowledge them."

"You should be a counsellor," Sam laughs.

"I don't know about that. I just know that life sometimes throws obstacles in your path, and you need to get over them, or past them. If everything was straightforward and easy, people would be boring, and lazy, and never develop.

So although this situation is making Sophie feel a bit sad at the moment, she knows full well how much you love her and that you are not abandoning her, even if you are living in a different place for the time being. Kids of service families cope," I am getting into my stride now, "and they don't get weekend visits when their parents are posted abroad."

"I guess," Sam says. "You're right, of course you are. Thank you, Alice."

"It's nothing."

"No, it's not nothing. And don't go thinking I am only missing Sophie, by the way. I miss you so much, I can't stop thinking about you. I want you, in my life, and in my bed."

My stomach flips but I laugh. "I am in your life. But no, not in your bed. Just two and a half weeks till you're back, though."

"I can't wait. I've booked that hotel, by the way."

"Have you really? That really is something to look forward to. I love spas."

"Oi! What about me?"

"Oh yeah, well, I suppose…"

"You'll pay for that," Sam says softly, and my stomach flips again.

On Wednesday, Julie is back when I return from work. My eyes are aching from staring at a computer screen all day; it feels a long time since I last did that – back at World of Stationery, a lifetime ago.

Bea has all sorts of spreadsheets set up, which I am trying to familiarise myself with. I have a meeting with the accountant coming up and, although I am sure Bea knows these documents inside out, and did go through them with me, it's taking me a while to get my head round it all. I am sure I can simplify things but I don't want to step on Bea's toes. I have made a note to bring this up on our next weekly Skype call.

"Hello down there!" Julie shouts from her room.

"Julie!" I am so happy to hear her voice. I bound up the stairs to find her chucking dirty clothes into the wash basket. "Look at you!" I exclaim, "so disgustingly happy and relaxed."

"Ha, sorry mate! What can I say? I've got myself a man of means!"

"Where is Luke?"

"He's had to go back to London today, he's got loads of meetings lined up tomorrow."

"Did you have a great time?"

"Er... yeah! The villa was beautiful, it had its own pool, and a gorgeous view. We hardly left the place."

"I bet." I feel that increasingly familiar tiny twinge of envy but remind myself that Sam and I are having a couple of days away in the not-too-distant future.

"Fancy tea out?" Julie asks. "My treat. I've got a month's work starting on Friday, at the Full Moon."

"That sounds perfect," I say, "let me just go and change."

I slip out of my smart trousers and top, and decide to have a quick shower. Having an en suite is the ultimate luxury – it's only small, compared to the main bathroom, but I love being able to walk naked into the shower and back into my room without worrying about being seen. Not that Julie would care, but I'd hate to accidentally bare myself to Luke if he's over.

Clean and refreshed, I slip on some old, faded jeans and a hoodie, leaving my feet bare for my sandals. It won't be long now till it's trainer weather, then it will be time for boots... I always find it hard to imagine that it can get so cold, but then, when winter sinks its teeth firmly into the year, I can't believe it is ever going to become hot again.

"Mainbrace?" Julie asks.

"Yes!"

We head down the hill towards the harbourside, Julie nattering on about Luke and Ibiza; me happy to listen.

"But how are you?" she asks suddenly. "Sorry, I know you probably don't need to hear me wittering on like this when you must be missing Sam like mad."

We are approaching the Mainbrace now and I spot a table outside being vacated. "I'll tell you in a sec," I say, speeding up so we can secure some seats in the fresh air.

"OK… I'll go and order, shall I? Chips and dips?"

"Yes! Thanks, Julie."

"No problem. I'll get us some crisps for a starter."

I laugh, and settle into my seat, watching the boats tethered in the harbour gently moving, up and down, as the waves push their way beneath them, the sea slowly creeping its way back to high tide. It won't be too long till it's dark but the air is warm on my skin.

Julie returns with a bucket holding a bottle of prosecco, three bags of crisps held firmly between her teeth.

"Prosecco?" I raise my eyebrows.

"Yeah, well I'm still in holiday mode. What I can't believe is that a few months back, coming here would have been a holiday. And it still does feel like one really, but now I get to have a holiday on top of a holiday."

"Well, I guess you deserve it," I say mock-grudgingly, "and I bet it did Luke the world of good. How is he?"

"He's great," Julie can't help smiling at the thought of the lovely Luke, "but we had a couple of wobbles while we were away. Not between us," she hastens to add, "but about his mum."

"I'm not surprised, it must still be so raw. I have no idea how long it takes to get over something like losing your mum. Or if it is even possible to ever get over it."

I think of my own mum, and my dad. Over the last few years they have both lost their parents. I wonder if it is made easier for them because my grandparents were all older; in their eighties. Or if it still hurts just as much. After all, they are still their parents. I can't bear to think of my own mum and dad dying. I cannot imagine life without them.

"No," Julie is thoughtful. "I must ring Mum, and see if she wants to come and visit. I haven't seen her since we've been down here."

"Do it!" I say, sipping my prosecco, feeling suddenly emotional. "She can come and stay with us."

"Yes!" Julie says. "I did think about inviting her for Christmas but I also want to spend it with Luke and I know he'll want to be with his dad and Marie."

"Well, she's welcome to stay here. I'm going to be at work anyway."

"Aw, that sucks. What's Sam going to be doing?"

I've already thought about this; I am gutted to think that we won't be able to spend our first Christmas together *together*, if you see what I mean.

"I don't know, I guess he'll want to be with Sophie."

"And do you mind that? It must be weird for you, with Kate around as well."

"It's not ideal," I admit, "but this is where we are now, I just have to get on with it."

The prosecco slips down all too easily as Julie and I sit chatting at our table and the sun too slips down, out of sight until the following day, making way for the moon and stars.

The chips and dips don't last long so I go inside and order more, plus another bottle. This is probably not a great idea, seeing as I'm working again tomorrow, but I'm enjoying myself.

As the evening grows colder, we move ourselves into the warm, welcoming pub and before long, Time is being rung.

"Oops!" I slur slightly, "I should be in bed by now."

"You'll be fine!" Julie says. "Anyway, isn't it worth it to spend some time with your old pal?"

"More than worth it," I confirm, and as we wander back up the dark streets, arm-in-arm, I feel happy. Sometimes there is nothing better than a night out with your best mate.

***

The weekend comes and goes. Although I shouldn't really be working, seeing as I did last weekend, on the Saturday I find myself at the Sail Loft, investigating entertainment options over the Christmas period and trying not to think about the fact that Kate is in North Wales with Sam – only because Sophie is, of course, but I still experience just a tiny grain of discomfort at the thought.

When Sam phones, I ask how everyone is. "Well it's just me and Soph, of course, Kate's at her mate's in Chester."

"Is she?"

"Yeah, you didn't think she'd be staying here, did you?" Sam laughs lightly.

"No, of course not!" I wonder why Kate didn't mention this before. What were her words last week? "You'll be able to tell Alice all about our visit up to your dad's." *Our* visit. I feel my hackles rise but I say nothing.

"Shit, Alice, did you actually think Kate would be staying here? Sorry, I never thought! I met them at Crewe, Sophie came back with me and Kate went on to her mate's."

Mixed with annoyance at Kate is a sense of relief, I realise.

I am going to have to stay determinedly strong through all this. Starting with not worrying about Sam and Kate.

After work on Monday, I pick Sophie up.

Kate greets me with a smile and a thank you for looking after Sophie again.

"It's my pleasure," I say, offering a smile in return. "Did you have a good time in Chester?"

"Oh, yeah." Am I imagining it or is there a sneakiness in Kate's smile?

"Great, it must be nice to get some time to yourself." I ensure that my own face is open, my smile as genuine as possible. "Are you ready, Sophie?"

"Yes! Bye, Mum. Have fun at Pilates." Sophie takes my hand in hers and we are straight off down the street, heading towards the sea.

At Sophie's insistence, we repeat our trip to the surf beach. She tells me about her weekend. I have already heard about it from Sam but I pretend it's all news to me, and Sophie describes his tiny flat, his piles of books and folders on his desk, how cold it was in the mornings... Sam slept on the settee and she had his bed. I know from Sam that Sophie got scared in the night and he ended up climbing in with her but I don't mention that.

There are no dolphins this week but it is sunnier and warmer and we spend an hour or so creating a sand village, with a moat around it. As the tide creeps closer, we dig faster, creating a town wall to protect our precious structures. We retreat to our rocky seats and watch as the water moves in; first falling into the moat, to the sound of our cheers, but gradually getting the upper hand and washing over the sand defences, first nibbling, then taking huge chunks from, the castles and houses we have constructed so that they crumble and dissolve.

I imagine the sand falling back into place under the waves; returning to its previous flat form but not quite the same as it was before.

This week we have pizza back at my house before I return Sophie to her mum.

"How was Pilates?" I feel myself stiffening as I talk to Kate but I must be polite, for Sophie's sake, and Sam's.

"Oh, good, thanks."

"Have you got many more people?"

It was very quiet when the classes first started up; I went to the first couple, then I hurt my ankle, then Sam came along and all friendship between Kate and I swiftly dissolved, like the sand castles in the sea.

"There's a few more," Kate seems to be talking more easily now. "A few regulars, then some that come and go. I'm knackered tonight, though, after all that train travel. That journey's a killer. I guess you'll find out for yourself soon enough."

Is she deliberately needling me? It's hard to tell.

"Yep, I guess. I'm glad Sam's coming down here soon, did he tell you we're going away for a couple of nights?" I can't help myself.

"No, he didn't say." I try to read Kate's expression then I kick myself as Sophie appears behind her mum.

"You're going away with Dad?"

Now I just feel bad. "Only for a night or two," I say, wondering why I feel the need to try and dilute the news. Why not just say two nights?

Kate fixes me with a look and I say goodbye, thinking that Sam is going to be annoyed now. "See you next week," I say but the door is already being closed.

12

Despite the lack of warmth between her mum and I, Sophie seems very happy spending Mondays with me and I have to admit I'm enjoying our time together, too. While there is still enough light left in the day, we spend time on the beach then come back to my place for something to eat. On the last Monday before Sam is due back, Julie is in and I see Sophie's eyes light up at the sight of my beautiful, glamorous friend; I also feel her retreat into herself a little. I put my arm around her, and wonder if I am starting to develop maternal feelings.

"Hey, Sophie!" Julie shares her wide smile with the girl. "Come and see what I've got on my iPad." That does it; Sophie is lost to me as she and Julie curl up on the settee, giggling at something on the screen. It makes me smile.

"That's not Uncle Luke!" Sophie exclaims.

"I'm afraid it is," Julie grins and looks at me. "I'm just showing Sophie what Luke looks like in a dress."

"Why on earth is Luke wearing a dress?" I ask, moving across the screen to peer at the phone. "And where did you manage to get one big enough?"

Sophie gasps, "Luke's not fat!"

"No," I laugh, "I didn't mean it like that! But he is six-foot-three and there aren't many women that size, so it can't have been easy."

"I made it," says Julie nonchalantly.

"But you can't sew!"

"No, if you look closely, you'll see that I can't! But I have been trying, I've been watching YouTube videos."

"Let's get back to why, shall we?" I ask.

"Ah, yes, well we're going to a massive party on Hallowe'en weekend. Luke's going as the mum from *The Goonies*; you know, the one with the Italian sons, and Sloth."

"And what are you going as?"

"Nothing!" Julie says. "But don't tell Luke. It's actually not a fancy dress party, but he doesn't know that."

Sophie collapses into giggles then looks concerned, "Won't he be upset?"

"I reckon he can take a joke," Julie says. "And then he's got his outfit sorted for New Year, too. So I'm doing him a favour, really."

"You're really mean," Sophie and I say at the same time and Julie makes us do a Jinx. I notice how quickly Sophie relaxes with Julie, and how reluctant she seems to go when it's time to get her back to Kate. I put it down to Julie's infectious sense of fun; ever since I've known her, people have been drawn to her. Above all else, she wants to enjoy life, and she wants everyone around her to, as well.

As we walk back towards Sophie's and Kate's flat, Sophie puts her hand in mine. I half-pull her up the hill, and she giggles. I realise how much I love it when she laughs.

"Can I have a sleepover with you and Julie sometime?" she asks.

"Of course!" I say, then, "If it's OK with your Mum. You'd be very welcome, but she may not feel happy about it."

"Why not?"

"Well, I suppose she doesn't really know me and Julie that well."

"But she does know you! And you're Dad's girlfriend.

And Julie's Uncle Luke's girlfriend. That means you're like family."

I can't help but smile at this. "That is a really lovely thing to say, Sophie. Let's hang on until after your dad's visit, then we'll see, shall we?"

Sophie smiles and hums to herself for the rest of the way home, her free arm swinging by her side.

Kate has the door open before we have a chance to ring the bell. "Hi, love!" she exclaims and Sophie steps into her embrace. "Thanks, Alice," she says, slightly less enthusiastically, but I think it may be the first time she's actually called me by my name since it all went wrong between us.

"It's really no trouble," I say, and chance a smile.

"Alice says I can have a sleepover with her and Julie," Sophie pipes up and I see a look cross Kate's face which I find difficult to read.

"Only if that's OK with you," I quickly add, "and I said we'd hang on till after next week, didn't I?" I look at Sophie, knowing that she just couldn't help herself. She shrugs prettily and wrinkles her nose.

"Oh yeah, next week, guess you can't have Sophie next Monday, can you? Isn't that when you're away?" Kate's tone is neutral.

After I had let the cat out of the bag the other week, I told Sam what I'd done and he had sounded annoyed.

"It's not you that I'm pissed off with," he'd said. "It's Kate. I told her what we're planning, I asked her to let Sophie know we were going to be away Sunday/Monday, and we went through the week together to work out when I can have Sophie – I thought it was better to spend the days with her seeing as she'll be off school, and get her back home

95

for bedtime, then I can have the evenings with you, when you're back from work. Would that be OK?"

"Of course," I said, "that sounds perfect." I loved the way he'd already been thinking these things through.

"I'll talk to Sophie," he said, "make sure she's OK with it."

"Great." I was relieved that I hadn't put my foot in it but I wondered why Kate hadn't told Sophie. Surely the more time she had to get used to the idea, the better? Also, maybe Sophie wants to spend some time with friends in the school holidays. It would make sense for her to do that while Sam's not around.

I rang Mum after I'd spoken to Sam, and she said, "It's not easy being a parent; kids can't be logical like we can — or at least like we should be able to. Maybe Kate had her reasons for not telling Sophie yet."

Why are you sticking up for her? I'd thought childishly but I took in what she said and I have tried to bear it in mind. Even so, that little seed of doubt about Kate and her motives started to take root.

"I can't next week, I'm sorry," I say to Kate now, "but won't your class be on hold for half-term anyway?"

"Oh. Yeah."

"And Sophie, I hope I'll get to see you some other time next week. And I know your dad is so excited about seeing you."

Sophie did a little jump at this and, to Kate's credit, her face broke into a wide smile at her daughter's happiness. I imagine it could be easy to feel put out about Sam's absence, and then Sophie's evident delight at the thought of seeing him again.

"Maybe you can have a break next week too, Kate." I'd

meant this kindly but I think it came out wrong as the smile dropped from Kate's face.

"I don't need a break from my own daughter," she snapped.

"No, I didn't mean…"

Before I'd finished my sentence, the all-too-familiar sight of the door being shut in my face.

***

The week passes unbelievably slowly, apart from the hours I'm at work. Julie's job means she is out most evenings so I get home to an empty house, make tea, have a chat with Sam, and try to fill the hours until bedtime.

I don't remember life being like this when I lived on my own in my flat but I suppose the difference now is that I have somebody to miss. There is a tangible absence in my life. No amount of phone calls can make it better, although I treasure the texts I receive, and usually find myself scrolling through them before I go to sleep.

Only a few days now! the most recent message reads, **I just CANNOT WAIT to see you.**

Hurry up and get down here, is my reply, **Can't you come now?**

I wish xxx

Inevitably, Friday does eventually come around and I wake up early, the kind of time I was getting up when I was waitressing. The difference is, it is dark now, and so much quieter than when summer was in full swing. I lie in bed for a while, thinking that this time tomorrow morning, Sam will be lying here with me. I hug myself at the thought, and smile.

I make a cup of tea and try to read my book but realise I am getting nowhere. Instead, I lean back against my pillows and just listen to the day getting started. Faint cries of gulls have started up as they rise up to meet the day, getting ready for a bit of fishing-boat-chasing or tourist-baiting. I know people hate them but I can't because whenever I hear them I experience a thrill to know I am here. We used to get them at home, of course; especially during the autumn and winter, when the weather was bad or, out in the countryside, when fields were freshly furrowed, and I'm not kidding when I say that the sound of their cries would make me ache for the sea.

I head into work early, determined to keep busy. Even when Sam's lectures are done, he still has hours of travelling. He won't be here till about nine at the earliest. Then we have what is left of the evening but I have to work tomorrow, and Sunday, before heading off to Devon.

Jonathan is busy getting everything ready for breakfast so I say hello and head into my office, checking for notes from Stefan. There are none so I guess he's had a quiet night but he will be just getting up now as well. It's strange doing the night shift; getting paid to sleep, in a house full of strangers. Bea's always done it, as the Sail Loft was her home, but she didn't want me to live in and she said it was because she couldn't guarantee who would be staying at the Sail Loft and didn't ever want me to feel like I was at risk of any danger. Rather sexistly, she knew she wanted a male night manager and actually we only had male candidates, anyway.

To be honest, it's not exactly cheap to stay at the Sail Loft, and the usual clientele are middle-aged and upwards; generally couples and occasionally families. I know this doesn't guarantee their trustworthiness any more than any other people but I've certainly never felt less than safe. At worst, the guests can be irritating. At best, they are funny and warm and just happy to be looked after.

I am glad, though, to have the differentiation between home and work. I have no idea how Bea managed to develop this place all on her own without crumbling to pieces but she says she needed it when she split up with her ex. It kept her sane.

A knock on the office door heralds Stefan, who comes in grinning, saying, "Today's the day!" His strawberry-blond hair is now complemented by a gingery beard, which really suits him. He has slightly scruffy hair but is always impeccably dressed. I wonder if he sleeps in his suit. I can't imagine him in pyjamas, somehow, but his clothes are always perfectly wrinkle-free. I wonder idly if he sleeps naked but realise he's giving me a strange look. He's asking me something.

"Erm… yes," I say vaguely, hopeful that this is the right answer.

"Really? You really think he will?" He looks so excited, I have to find out what I've just said.

"I'm sorry," I confess, "I wasn't listening." I can't tell him what I was actually thinking about.

"Ha! I knew it. I was asking if you thought Sam was going to proposition you at the hotel."

I'm taken aback at this direct line of questioning but maybe this is how they do it in Sweden. "Erm, I guess, yes," I say.

"That is so romantic!" he says, his eyes glowing.

"Is it?"

"Yes, getting engaged, to your childhood sweetheart, after ten years apart. Of course it is romantic."

"Engaged? Oh, did you mean *propose* to me? Is Sam going to propose to me?"

"Yes, exactly as I said."

"No, not exactly," I find myself brimming with laughter, till a few giggles bubble out. I explain the difference between 'proposition' and 'propose'.

"Oh," says Stefan, unfazed, "I see. Well, yes I see how that might not be romantic. It could be, though." He raises his eyebrows at me.

"Get away with you," I say. "Hadn't you better be getting home, anyway? Maybe you need to think about propositioning April."

"It's a bit late for that," he says, "as Reuben is testament."

Slight mix-ups aside, I marvel that Stefan's use of English is so much more eloquent than mine, or most of my friends'. I laugh. "I suppose so." I want to say that in that case maybe it's time he proposes but I know where to draw the line. We are becoming friends, I think, but first and foremost we are work colleagues. I can't suggest to him that he should be getting married, even if he has asked me if I think Sam will make a move on me while we're away. I should bloody hope he does.

Instead, we have a brief handover but there is nothing much to report. "OK, see you tonight," I say.

"Yes, and then it is off to your lovebird, don't worry if you are late in tomorrow morning. I would be disappointed if you are on time."

"Ha!" I say, "I'm British. Can't let a little thing like love get in the way of being on time for work."

"You will change your mind, I know it."

"We'll see."

The morning passes pleasantly. Lydia and Jonathan are both on good form and we have a real laugh together. I feel like we're becoming a proper team. It's a good feeling. I experience one of those moments I have when things are going well; that I am so happy, I feel things are almost too good, like I am too lucky. I remind myself that Sam is now living away and maybe that balances out how good things are at work.

After Lydia has gone off to college, I chat to Jonathan alone for a while, and help him clear up.

"You don't have to do that," I say.

"I know, but I don't mind. It's a quiet day today, till this afternoon anyway. We'll have a full house over the weekend," I remind him.

"Yeah, that's good news, isn't it?"

"Definitely," I say, "although it means harder work for us."

"And Lydia," he says.

"Yes," I agree, and think I see a little spark in his eyes when he mentions her name. *Uh-oh*, I think, although it would not be the first time I've seen a romance spring up in the workplace – it happened all the time at World of Stationery, but there were more people there, to dilute the effect, which was particularly useful if things went wrong.

I get the feeling he just wanted to mention Lydia's name. Oh well, we'll just have to cross that bridge if and when we come to it. She's quite a bit younger than Jonathan, though – and I hope he bears that in mind. Then again, she's at least as mature as him, if not more so.

After Jonathan's left for the afternoon, the phone goes.

"Hello, Sail Loft. Alice speaking."

"Oh hello there, I'm phoning from Kirsten Able Travel, and I'm enquiring about your Christmas package."

"Oh yes?" I reply eagerly, hoping that my enthusiasm comes across as exactly that.

"Yes, I'm trying to arrange a group tour of the South West, for eight – three couples and two singles – and I wondered if you have availability, and if you would be open to discounting your rates for a guaranteed group booking?"

"Which exact dates are you after?" I ask, tapping on my computer keyboard, watching nonsense appear on the screen in front of me. She tells me they would like three nights – Christmas Eve to the day after Boxing Day. "Yes, we have availability over that period, and if you can guarantee those dates, I can arrange a discount, but I'll need a deposit upfront and full payment two weeks prior to arrival. If you can give me your details, please, I'll email you some more info plus a link to some information about the hotel and the local area."

"Fantastic, thank you," she says, and reels off her details.

"Thanks so much for your call." I put the receiver down, grinning to myself.

I give it about thirty minutes before I send the email and I receive a reply within another thirty minutes, confirming that the group would like to book.

"Yes!" I exclaim. My first Christmas booking – and for eight! I have a tingly feeling of excitement at the prospect of running my first Christmas here, and I realise that it is nearly three o'clock, meaning that I have just six hours or so until I get to see Sam again. Today is a good day.

13

I practically skip home from work, I'm so excited. I ring Sam when I get in but he's in the car, his phone on hands-free. I keep it short. I hate talking to people when they're driving.

"I just wanted to say… I can't wait to see you!"

"Me too," he says.

"What, you can't wait to see you?"

"I knew you were going to say that, smart-arse."

I laugh. "I'm about 100 yards from home now. I'm going to get in, have a bath, tidy up… I will be ready and waiting for you."

"You'd better be. Is Julie at Luke's this weekend?"

"No, she's working at the Full Moon for the next month."

"She'll be out at work this evening, then? We'll have the place to ourselves?"

"Yes. Why?"

"Oh, no reason. Maybe you won't need to get dressed after that bath, that's all I'm thinking."

"Oh," I grin, my stomach doing gymnastics. "I see."

"Yes, you do. Now I've got something to think about on this loooong journey."

"Well hurry up," I say. "But also, drive carefully. Drive fast, but be careful. OK?"

"Got it! See you soon."

I have approximately four hours to kill till Sam gets here. It is such a long drive for him, he'll be shattered by the time he arrives. But not too shattered, I hope.

I decide to make a special effort for dinner. A salad with halloumi, and a chilli and lime dressing. Healthy, not too filling, and a kick from the chilli to help keep Sam awake. I also want to try to make bread rolls, and mini chocolate sponges for dessert. I don't know why, as I know I am just making life hard for myself, but I kind of want to kick this idea that I am a terrible cook. I pour myself a generous gin & tonic and set to work.

I prepare the salad; wash the lettuce and spinach - procured from Arnie, who supplies the Sail Loft with beautiful fresh local produce. I chop it roughly, then do the same with the tomatoes, cucumber, celery and onion. I peel and grate a carrot, chop a lemon and squeeze some of its juice over the thin orange curls. My eyes are watering from the onion but I keep on going. I know I have a few hours but I also want to tidy the house a bit, and of course have that bath. At least if I follow Sam's suggestion I don't have to waste time deciding what to wear. I grin to myself, take a slug of my drink, and turn on BBC Radio 6. There's some funky Friday night stuff going on and I dance back to my work station.

OK... what now? I know, I'll make the dressing. Or should I do the dough? I'll do that first, I'm sure it needs to prove or something before I form it into perfect little roll shapes and stick them in the oven.

I push the carrot peelings and onion skin to one side and give the surface a quick wipe, then dig out the bread recipe. Easy. Weigh the flour and tip it onto the surface, pile it up and make a well in the middle. I need to get some warm water, and yeast, and salt. I probably should have sorted that first. No worries, there's loads of time left. I check the clock. Wow, it's already nearly half-six. This is the best way to make the evening pass quickly. If I'd tried to sit and watch TV while I waited for Sam, I'd have been twitchy and agitated, I wouldn't have been able to concentrate on whatever was on. I take a gulp of my drink, put the kettle on and switch it off when I think the water will be warm, then I get a measuring jug. The kitchen is starting to look cluttered. I put all the salad into a big bowl and cover it, moving it onto the dining room table, being careful to put a mat down first. David is easy-going but I know he loves this table, which used to be his parents', and I would hate to damage it.

I mix the yeast with the water and add some oil, watching the different layers and bubbles form, then I slowly pour it into the well in the middle of the flour, pushing in my fingers and enjoying the feeling of warmth as I slowly create the dough. It seems quite dry so I add the rest of the liquid but now it seems ridiculously wet so I tip some more flour into the mix and roll it around until it becomes a bit more manageable. I go to the sink to clean my hands, which are covered in floury goo, and it's only then that I realise I've forgotten to add the salt. I flush. Does it matter? I suppose it does, otherwise the bread's not going to taste of much. I know, I'll put cheese on the top and make cheese rolls. Cheese is salty, isn't it? And we can add some butter, too. My mouth starts watering at the thought of freshly-baked rolls dripping with melting butter. I put the dough into the mixing bowl and cover it with a damp cloth. Great.

A quick time-check. It's nearly seven. I need to make the mixture for the chocolate puddings, and the dressing, and prepare the halloumi, which I can cook just before I add it to the salad. I consult the Mary Berry recipe. It says I should cook the pudding just before serving. Will it matter if I prepare it now? I'm sure that should be fine. Maybe I should tidy the rest of the stuff away first. No, that seems pointless. I put the bowl with the dough to one side, and clean the work surface again. I replenish my gin & tonic, which seems to have slipped down without me realising it, marvelling at Julie and Jonathan, who do this every day, for dozens of people, who all want different things. How the hell do they do it? I suppose they're not drinking gin & tonic, for one thing.

The chocolate pudding recipe is marked as easy, so that's good. I weigh out all the ingredients first, carefully, putting them in separate bowls as though I am on a baking show. Then I follow the recipe to the letter, even remembering to butter the ovenproof dish. I have to make the cake mixture first, then the chocolate sauce, which I pour over the top. I guess this is why I am then meant to bake it straight away, but instead I cover it and put it in the fridge. I'm sure it will be delicious.

The scene which greets me as I turn back from the fridge is unwelcome. There are vegetable peelings on the side; open bags of flour and sugar, and a spillage of cocoa powder which has made it onto the floor; a range of small bowls from my pudding preparation, and a scattering of flour from making the dough. I still have a dressing to make, plus dough to knead and form into balls. I glance at the clock. It's eight! I have an hour, which is both good and bad. Good because it really is just sixty minutes or so until I get to see Sam, and bad because I seem to have bitten off more than I can chew in terms of dinner preparation – and I haven't even begun to tidy the house or run my bath. Still, I am committed now, and the determined side of me really wants to impress Sam with a delicious meal when he gets here.

I grate some lime, chop some chilli and garlic, and get a bottle of olive oil. I find a bowl to mix it in, add some salt, have a quick taste, and cough at the strength of the chilli. I squeeze in some lime juice and brush some hair from my face, inadvertently rubbing chilli and lime juice into my eye. The pain is intense. I cry out and head to the sink, where I wash my hands and proceed to throw cold water at my face. I soak a piece of kitchen roll and hold it onto my eye for a while, until the pain subsides into a gentle throbbing.

8.15. Shit. Where is Julie when I need her? I get the bowl of dough and I scatter flour onto the work surface, throwing the dough down as I've seen done on TV and kneading it. I form rough ball shapes - let's call them rustic - then lay them on a baking tray, grating cheese over the top. I think I have to leave them for a few minutes again so I put the oven on and I begin the clear-up operation. My eye still hurts so I squint as I tidy, cursing myself for not being more organised. Just get on with it, I tell myself. All these things came from somewhere, so they all have places to go. I put the compostables into a biodegradable bag, ready to go in the neat bin at the end of the garden. Then I open the dishwasher. Dammit, it's full of clean things. I spend five minutes putting these away only to fill the machine straight up again. I put in a tablet and start a wash cycle, only then noticing I've left two bowls on the side. I put them in the sink, which I fill with hot, soapy water, and get a fresh cleaning cloth to wipe down the work surfaces. Through my good eye I can see things are starting to improve. I put the chilli and lime dressing in the fridge and realise I haven't chopped the halloumi. That will have to wait.

Bit by bit, I return the kitchen to the state it was in before I began this charade, but it is now 8.43pm. It is dark outside and I have approximately fifteen minutes before Sam gets here. I refresh my drink, to calm my nerves, and revise my plan for a long, leisurely bath to a quick shower. I put the rolls on their tray into the oven, setting the timer for twenty minutes.

Just as I put my foot on the first step, I hear somebody outside the front door. Oh my god. Is it him? Already? Or some charity fundraiser? I can't chance it. And I can just make out a familiar shape through the glass in the door as I approach. It's him! My stomach leaps for joy and I fling open the door just as he's about to put his key into the lock. And there he is, a bag on his shoulder and a wide smile on his face. It's only been four weeks but when I see him there in person before me, it feels like it's been years.

Sam's smile quickly turns to a look of concern. "Are you OK?" he asks. "Your eye…"

"My..? Oh, yes, slight chilli accident I'm afraid, nothing to worry about."

"Chilli? Have you been cooking?" he asks suspiciously, moving forwards and putting his bag on the floor so that he can snake his arms around my waist. "What have I told you about that?"

"That I'm endangering myself and others," I admit, feeling goose pimples parade up my back, over my shoulders and down my arms at his touch.

"Exactly," he smiles, "and I'd say that eye is proof. Are you sure you're OK?"

"Yes, I promise."

"Good, because I would hate anything to get in the way of this." Pushing the door gently to with his foot (don't tell David), Sam puts his lips on mine and kisses me gently, then presses them to me more urgently so that I open my mouth and his tongue finds mine.

I draw breath. "I haven't had a bath. Not even a shower."

"Don't care," Sam says, and intently he resumes the kiss, this time moving his mouth across to my earlobe, letting his tongue slide gently down my neck.

I push my hands under his top, feel his warmth and a slight shudder which passes through him. "Shall we go upstairs?"

"I thought you'd never ask."

I take his hand and lead him up to my bedroom, where the curtains are still open. I flick on my bedside light and hastily cover the windows, seeing Sam's reflection behind me just before I pull the curtains closed. His hands are on my waist again and he's pushing the hair away from the back of my neck, kissing me and saying my name. I haven't had a shower, I remind myself, but, like Sam, I don't care. I turn and peel the clothes from him, then he does the same to me. We are naked together and take a moment to look at each other; drinking the sight in. I feel a slight chill to my skin, and a ripple of anticipation. I walk forwards and press myself into him. "Alice,' he says again, and pulls me onto the bed.

It's only later, as we lie under the weight of the duvet, in the glow of the bedside lamp, that I remember the bread rolls.

14

Work passes slowly but I am aware I must be wandering around with a slightly moronic grin on my face. Some of the guests give me strange looks, Stefan teases me, and Jonathan, hearing him, rolls his eyes. He's been a bit off with me today, actually, but I put it down to having a chef's temperament. I'd never say that to Julie, of course.

Last night, folded up as I was in the rolls of duvet and the warmth of Sam, breathing sleepily and happily, I had a sudden shocking memory of those bloody bread rolls and, without explanation, I leapt out of bed. Sam, who I think probably had dropped off by that point, sat up and called after me but I was too busy running down the stairs, naked.

The air was smoky and all the more so when I opened the oven door. A cloud of bread smoke engulfed me and I started coughing, just as the smoke alarm began to go off. Sam arrived with a sheet wrapped around him, to find me naked save for some oven gloves, half-laughing and half-crying over what looked like a baking tray decorated with carefully lined-up lumps of coal.

"What..?" he asked, and opened the window, wafting the smoke outside with a tea towel. He got a chair and pressed the button to stop the smoke alarm. Then he fetched a coat from the hallway – it was Julie's but I didn't want to say anything – and wrapped it around me.

"Is this dinner?" he smirked and I couldn't control myself,

I collapsed with laughter. I pushed the tray into the sink, where it hissed in the cold water.

"They were," I tried to stop laughing to complete my sentence, "they were... bread rolls."

"Mmm, they look good."

"I'd forgotten to add any salt to the dough."

"So you decided to burn the shit out of them to disguise the blandness?"

"Exactly."

Sam put his arms around me, standing behind me and hugging me. "So is there anything else? I'm starving."

"We've got salad," I gestured towards the bowl on the table.

"Hmm. I've got to be honest, I don't think salad is going to cut it."

"I've got halloumi and stuff, too. And sliced bread in the bread bin. Oh, and a chocolate pudding which needs to go in the oven."

"Got any chips?" Sam asked.

"Of course."

"Great, let's make use of this pre-heated oven, and stick some chips in; have the salad for a starter, have the halloumi with the chips, and have chocolate pudding for afters. Sound like a plan?"

"Yes," I said, "sounds perfect."

We sat at the dining room table, drinking gin & tonic and eating happily. Luckily, the salad was good – if I'd messed that up, I'd be worried – and the halloumi and chips were saltily unhealthy but absolutely delicious. We wrapped them up in slices of white bread, just to add to the fully unwholesome meal. At least we'd started with salad. To complete the carb-fest we ate the chocolate pudding straight from the baking dish, but we did at least use spoons.

As we were starting to almost visibly expand, the front door opened and closed. "Hello-o?" I heard.

"Hi!" I said, "we're in here."

Julie came strolling in, "Something smells good… oh, Sam, you're just wearing a sheet. And Alice, is that my coat?" Oops. "I hope you're not naked undernea… you're not? Urgh. You'd better get that cleaned tomorrow, young lady."

"We've got chocolate pudding," I offered by way of an apology.

"So I see. You'll have to do better than that, though. Is that gin?"

"Yes. Do you want one?"

"Do I? Friday night at the Full Moon is not to be taken lightly. Bleeding hell, my feet ache. And that kitchen is so hot."

"Not as hot as this one was a while ago," Sam said, and I recounted my disastrous foray into baking.

Julie laughed, "Well at least you're not likely to nick my job. Now go and put some clothes on, please, both of you, I can't sit here and have a decent conversation with you looking like that."

We spent an hour or so chatting with Julie then made our excuses and headed up to bed. In the darkness, I lay in Sam's arms and listened to his breath, growing slower and deeper, until I fell asleep myself.

Before Jonathan leaves for the afternoon, I catch him chatting quietly with Lydia. She is gazing at him with shiny eyes and I think, oh no. I can see where this is heading, from her perspective at least. But maybe it will just be a harmless crush, and hopefully come to nothing. I have found myself feeling quite protective of Lydia. She works so hard, and she's so determined. I've told her she can come and study here sometimes, as her home is noisy with three younger siblings.

"Just check with me or Stefan first," I said, "but most days it should be fine. There's space in the office if you can put up with the occasional phone call interrupting your thoughts."

"Believe me, the occasional phone call is nothing! Thanks so much, Alice," Lydia gave me a hug.

"I can make you a snack, too, if you're here at the right time," Jonathan chipped in. "Brain food."

"Really? Thanks so much, Jon," there were those shiny eyes then, too – no hug, I noticed, but the 'Jon' didn't escape my attention. It reminded me that I'd half-noticed her call him that before and had wondered then if there was something going on between them.

Now, Lydia spots me and I am sure her cheeks flush slightly. Jonathan grins at me, and I wonder what's behind that smile.

"I'd better be off now," Lydia says, "I'll see you on Monday, Alice."

"You won't," Jonathan says, "she's off on a dirty weekend."

I shoot him a warning glance. "I am not, thank you, Jonathan. Sam and I are just going away for a couple of days, Lydia. I will be back on Wednesday morning."

"That sounds nice," she says cheerfully, "have a great time."

"Thanks, and you have a good break this weekend. Go out tonight and let your hair down! That's what being seventeen's all about."

"I will," Lydia grins.

As she trots happily off out of the door and down the stone

steps, I turn to Jonathan. I want to tell him he shouldn't speak to me like that and certainly not in front of Lydia, but he's already retreated. The door to the kitchen swings shut with a definite click.

I am too happy to stay annoyed for long. I retreat too, to my office. I love this time of day at the Sail Loft. Although guests can come and go as they please, most tend to go out for the day and return late afternoon so there is a pleasant peace about the place. Bea has a carriage clock on the mantelpiece of the office, which ticks satisfyingly and creates an air of a time long since past. The Sail Loft is an old building; built around 1800 for a local merchant. It would have been a grand house, perched up near the top of the town, allowing the owner and his family the chance to look down on the lesser mortals – those fishermen and other manual labourers who rose early, worked hard, paid for it with ill health and short life expectancy. When it is quiet like this, I feel the sense of history in this beautiful old building. I don't think it is haunted but there is a whisper of other lives and different times. Could those people ever have conceived that their charming home would end up as a hotel? Rooms paid for by the night – even the servants' quarters, in fact especially the servants' quarters, with their rooftop views across the town and beyond, to the sea. Sand tramped in and out of rooms, up and down the stairs. Loud voices echoing around the hallways as people return late at night after a few too many beers. I imagine that if there are any ghosts here, they stay quiet, backs pressed against the wall to let these loud strangers past; tutting and shaking their heads, aghast at the way life has gone.

I sit back for a moment in Bea's impressive chair, put my hands on my belly, and breathe deeply. I just want to give myself a moment to take everything in. I feel so happy.

Ping!

My phone alerts me to a text message. I pick it up from the desk, turn it over.

Sam Branvall (1)

My stomach performs its familiar little twist.

Just wanted to say hi. I can't wait to see you later. Sophie says hi too xxx

Hi, Sophie. And hi, Sam. Today is sooooooo loooooong. I hope you two are having fun, though. I should be back by 6 xxx

Great, I'll aim for the same xxxx

"Come on," I tell myself, "there's work to do." And there is. Running this place means one long to-do list, which never ends. I put my head down and get on with it.

***

It's getting windy as I walk back home. A storm has been forecast but I don't mind. I like storms by the sea, although I worry for people's safety. There's always somebody who wants to get a bit too close to those magnificent waves, without realising how much they are risking. Down by the harbour, when things really get going, the water crashes angrily against the walls, sending up huge shoots of foam, which come slapping back down onto the pavements. The open-sided gangway of the harbour; a great place to wander along on a calm, sunny day, becomes treacherous; the worn stone is slippery and the waves take no prisoners. One wrong move, one super-strength wave, and you're gone, washed away in the swirling sea, with little chance of getting out alive.

The town has a lifeboat and heroic crew, who risk their own lives to save others, but in a full-on storm, in the dark, the furious water swelling and seething, it is not easy to find a missing person.

I pull my coat around myself and hurry down the hill to the house, letting myself in. I have no great plans for cooking tonight, in fact I think we'll get a takeaway. I check my watch. It's 5.54pm. Not long now till Sam gets here. I put the kettle on and head upstairs. At six on the dot, just as I've turned on the shower, I hear the front door, then his footsteps as he leaps up the stairs, taking them two at a time. I meet him at the turn of the banister.

"Hello!" he grins and kisses me, putting his hand on the small of my back.

"Hi," I say, "how are you?"

"All the better for seeing you."

I kiss him now, putting my arms around his waist, and standing on my tiptoes to get to him. He feels warm, like he's rushed to get here. "I was just going to get changed," I say, "but I feel like a shower. Do you fancy joining me?"

"Let me think about that," his hands on my waist, he holds me at arm's length for a moment, his eyes running over me. "OK, if I have to." He starts to unbutton my shirt, tracing his fingers over the skin as it reveals itself.

I put my hands on his belt, slowly undo the buckle.

We move towards the bathroom, undressing as we go, shutting the door behind us so we have to find each other amidst all the steam.

15

The weather grew wild last night but inside the house, in the deep, dark bedroom, Sam and I were tucked up tight and warm. We'd eaten a takeaway then gone back to bed, where we lay together, listening to the wind rattling the windows as it tried to get in, and talking about our respective days. I told him about work; particularly the possible situation between Lydia and Jonathan.

"You're going to have to leave them to it," he said. "There's nothing you can do anyway, and whatever you say could just make things worse."

"Thanks very much!"

"You know what I mean. Nobody likes to be told what to do, especially when it comes to love. And Lydia sounds like she's got a strong head on her. You know what girls that age are like; if she thinks people disapprove, she's all the more likely to try and prove them wrong."

"Oh yeah? And what do you know about girls that age?" I'd asked, thinking I had been only a little bit older when I met him. But he was right; when people told me it was a fling, destined to be short-lived, it had made me all the more defiant and determined to make it work. As it happened, our initial relationship had been short-lived, but not for the reasons people thought.

It had been pure bad luck and subsequent misunderstandings that pushed us apart. So I know it's possible for it to be the 'real thing' when you're Lydia's age, but there is something about Jonathan which makes me want to keep her away from him. He is too self-assured, and at the same time too childish.

"I've been reading about teenage girls," Sam said. "No, that sounds wrong. I'm trying to prepare myself… for Sophie, I mean. She's ten next year; double figures. By the time I've finished my course, she'll be a teenager. I want to understand, be ready."

This is Sam all over and something I love so much about him. He wants to understand. Whether it's a marine mammal, or his growing daughter, he wants to learn as much as he can, to do the best that he can by them. I smiled and leant over to kiss him.

"What's that for?"

"Just for being the best… the best dad."

"Oh yeah? The best anything else as well?" He raised his eyebrows.

I spent a moment looking like I was thinking. "No, I think that's it."

"We'll see about that," he said, and turned me round to face him, kissing me deeply.

I try to tiptoe around as I get ready for work. He doesn't need to be up for another hour or two, when he's going to pick up Sophie from Kate's. They are going to see his Auntie Lou, who he lived with when his mum moved to Spain. Then Sam's taking Sophie to Sennen, to go for a long walk and talk wildlife.

I hear my phone buzz. It's Stefan.

Bad news, Stacy has called in sick.

Shit! I'll try and see if Lydia can come in, I'll just

give it an hour or so. Seems a bit mean on a Sunday morning.

That's not all. Jonathan sick too. Sorry, I did not want to break the bad news in one go.

Shit shit shit. OK, I'll sort it.

I must have cursed aloud as Sam stirs. "What's up?"

"Oh, nothing. We're just without a chef, and a breakfast waitress. On a Sunday morning. When we're fully booked up."

I am starting to panic. What would Bea do in this situation? I think. I know I have to text Lydia but I feel so bad doing that on her one day off.

Lydia, I am so, so sorry but we've got an emergency at SL. Any chance you can do today? I wouldn't ask if it wasn't urgent. Double time, and breakfast, and a day off during the week, I promise. A.

I'll just have to hope she gets the message. Otherwise, I'll be waitressing. Now I have to solve the chef problem. There is one obvious solution but she's not going to like it.

"Julie..." I knock softly on her door, a cup of tea in my other hand. No reply. "Julie." I try again, and knock a bit louder. There is a definite shuffling sound from within. I push the door open.

"Brgrgrff," or something like that.

"I'm sorry," I say, "I'm really sorry, but I've got no chef. Is there any way you can come and do breakfasts for us?"

"Offffsskk."

"Thanks, Julie, I knew I could count on you. You're such a great friend," I sing, putting the tea next to her and opening her curtains a little; revealing a thoroughly wet day outside. I know it's cruel, but she'd do the same to me. I leave her room, closing the door none-too-softly. Within minutes, she is heading to the bathroom.

"You owe me one!" she calls.

"I know. Thanks, Julie. Love you!"

Sam smiles at me. "You know how to pull it together in an emergency!"

"Well, yes, but only because I happen to live with a chef. Still no reply from Lydia, though," I tut, picking up my phone.

"I'll do it."

"What?"

"I'll be your breakfast waitress… waiter, I mean."

"Are you serious?"

"Yeah, sure, why not?"

"Have you done anything like this before?"

"Bloody hell, I didn't think you were going to interview me. No, I haven't, but how hard can it be?"

I smile knowingly. "Tell you what, we'll do it together."

Within twenty minutes, Julie, Sam and I are striding through the rain, on a cool Sunday morning, heading to the Sail Loft. I've sent word to Stefan to expect us, and texted Lydia again, telling her to ignore my previous message. I really hope I haven't woken her up. She deserves all the rest she can get. When I was seventeen, I was at college and I had a part-time job in a cafe but that was just Saturdays and holidays. And Mum and Dad gave me an allowance. I basically had it made, although I didn't realise it at the time.

Lydia is something else; she works so hard and is always so upbeat, and polite. I am sure that everything she is doing now will pay off for her.

Julie seems happy to get back into 'her' old kitchen and soon has things underway, as I make a pot of fresh coffee for us all.

"I'll leave you to it, then," Stefan grins at Sam, and he's away.

"See you this afternoon," I call from the doorway and he raises his hand then pulls his hoodless coat up over his head as he starts to jog off towards home.

I quickly fill Sam in on the breakfast menu, on how to take an order, and how to give it to Julie. So, he thinks it's easy... I have a little laugh to myself.

As the first guests come down, I send Sam in. "Small talk!" I hiss at him.

As it turns out, he's very good at small talk but not so good at remembering the breakfast options.

"Do you do poached eggs?" Mr Thompson asks.

"Erm..." Sam looks over to me in the doorway.

"Yes," I smile, "we can do poached, or scrambled, or fried. Or a combination of all three!"

Mr Thompson smiles back, "Just poached should be fine. As part of the Full English. But hold the tomatoes, and the beans, and the sausages."

"So that's..." Sam flounders.

"Poached eggs, bacon, hash browns, and beans. Is that right, Mr Thompson?"

"Yes, lovely, and can we have an extra round of toast?"

"Of course!" I say. "No problem."

Some places are very strict with their breakfasts; you may have fruit juice *or* cereal, and there is not a chance in hell of you getting an extra round of toast. But Bea likes to be generous, and accommodating. She says it helps mark the Sail Loft out as a hotel rather than a B&B, and that guests always comment on the brilliant breakfasts.

Sam smiles, and notes it down, then takes Mrs T's order, which is a bit more simple – scrambled eggs on toast.

"Do you want to take that through to Julie, Sam?" I prompt, then serve tea to Mrs Thompson and coffee to her husband.

Soon, the dining room is filling up and Sam is kept busy. I stay in the main space, answering questions when Sam is stuck and keeping the tea and coffee flowing. Normally, Lydia would be doing all this but it seems a bit mean to land it all on Sam.

I'm enjoying working with him, in fact, and he and Julie are having a laugh together, too. It gives me a warm feeling, us all pulling together, and I am touched that they have both helped me out. By the time Sam and I get to the hotel tonight, we're both going to be in need of that spa.

As the tide of holiday-makers starts to recede, I clear the tables of their breakfast detritus. Sam has been great at taking all the dirty crockery through to the kitchen; unfortunately, I think washing it is going to fall to me. I can't expect him to do it, nor Julie, who has to work again at the Full Moon over lunch and all evening.

I smile at the thanks of the last pair of guests, as they head off to their rooms, stomachs full, then I head into the kitchen. Sam is leaning against one of the industrial steel work surfaces, and Julie's just cleaning everything down. Almost all the plates, cups and cutlery have already been washed and put away.

"Who did the washing up?" I ask, delighted.

"Me," Sam says. "I felt a bit redundant out there; you had everything covered. Old habits die hard, I suppose."

"Still think it's easy?" I grin at him.

"No, I don't. I definitely don't. I need to go back to bed."

"You'd better hurry, though, you've got to pick Sophie up in twenty minutes. Julie, you should go, too. I'll finish off everything here. Thank you, both of you, so much, for helping out today. I genuinely don't know what I would have done without you."

"You'd have found a way," Sam says and kisses me.

"I'm glad you've got faith in me," I smile and I watch the pair of them head off into the rain-soaked morning. I smile to see them chatting together as they dash away. Two of my very, very favourite people in the world.

The clouds are dissipating, they are all cried out. A freshness has been left in the wake of the rain and it's still early, for a Sunday, so the town is quiet save for the ever-present sound of the gulls. Down in the heart of the town, the church bells begin to ring. I take a moment to just stand and listen, and look. Fat drops of rain are sitting proudly on the wide green leaves of the plants by the top of the Sail Loft's steps. Over the rooftops, I can see the bay, and the sea, which is calming now, along with the weather. A tiny crease of blue has appeared amongst the clouds. It looks like it is going to be a beautiful day.

***

At five o'clock, I begin to tidy my desk and make a note of the things I need to tell Stefan. Jonathan has called to say he can cover the evening shift as he is feeling much better. He turns up at the same time as Stefan, who is as reliable as ever. "Are you sure you're OK to work?" I ask Jonathan;

partly through concern for him but if I'm honest also because I don't want him passing germs to our guests and customers. However, we only have a few bookings this evening, luckily, and Jonathan does look fine.

"Oh yeah, just a bad headache really, I get them from time to time."

"Oh, OK, well as long as you're sure." Is it my imagination or does he look guilty? The main thing is, he's here. He slips away into the kitchen and Stefan and I go into the office.

"It wasn't a head this morning," Stefan says.

"What?" I ask, quickly jotting down a note about tomorrow's arrivals.

"Jonathan. He didn't say he had a bad head when he phoned earlier. He said it was a stomach bug."

"Are you sure?" I ask. I'm too busy whirling around - trying to suppress the excitement in my stomach and concentrate on what I have to do before I leave - to give much thought to Jonathan.

"Yes," Stefan says, "I remember because I always think how stupid the word 'bug' is for being sick."

"God, I hope he's not carrying germs," I say, but Jonathan isn't stupid. He wouldn't risk the health of his customers, or the wrath of Bea, for that matter. He must be better. The word *hangover* flashes across my mind but I am already gathering my notes up and sitting down to go through everything with Stefan so that I know I can leave this place safe in his hands and relax properly while Sam and I are away.

At six, I am trotting down the street, heading for home. I have half an hour to get changed and get to the car park, where Sam should be waiting for me.

I change my clothes, throw others into a bag. I run downstairs. I run back upstairs and get my bikini. I run downstairs again. I go to the back door to make sure it's locked; Julie won't be back from work till late and I feel extra aware of my responsibilities to David in looking after his house.

I pick up my coat, my phone, and my keys, and I'm out of the house. I have eight minutes to get to the car park but it only takes four. Sam is already there, his engine going and loud music muffled by the closed windows. I sneak up beside him and make him jump.

He opens his door. "You bugger!" Out he gets, and puts his arms around me. "I have been looking forward to this all day."

"Me too," I smile, feeling suddenly a tiny bit shy. "Come on, let's get going. Shotgun!" I bluff over the feeling, dashing round to the passenger side.

"I don't think that means much when you're the only passenger." Sam grins as he slides into the driver's seat.

"Well, I just wanted to be sure."

We are off, driving up and out of town, round the twisty coastal road then inland, following the A30 which snakes its way through the centre of the county, taking us upcountry. It seems an age since I last came this close to leaving Cornwall. I haven't been home since I came down in the summer. I must sort that out, soon.

"How was Sophie today?" I ask Sam. "Does she mind that we're going away?"

"No, she doesn't seem to. She's meant to be going to a mate's tomorrow, anyway. And Kate's got a job interview."

"Has she?"

"Yeah, some posh health centre near Penzance, they want a Pilates teacher. So she's taking Sophie to her mate's up on the moors, then going to the interview."

"Well that's really good," I say. I'm pleased for her, and also pleased for Sophie that she's got a day at a friend's. I've got the impression from her that while she does have friends, there is nobody in particular that she hangs out with, and that the other girls seem to have closer friendships.

"Yeah, it is good. I want her to be happy, you know."

"I know you do; of course you do. You're you."

"Ha!" Sam smiles. "It's not just for her, it's for Sophie, too. The happier her mum is, the happier she'll be. Stands to reason."

I think of Kate's drinking confession. I am sure for her it's a mixture of boredom and loneliness. Maybe a new job, meeting new people, will help.

We pass the huge wind turbines and I take in the place names I love. Indian Queens is one of my favourites. Before too long, we are at the Cornwall-Devon border then we are off and away, through the dark Devon night, along winding tree-lined lanes.

"Nearly there," says Sam, as I turn to look through the back windscreen into black nothingness.

"I remember reading about big cats round this neck of the woods," I say.

"Oh yeah, they'll be out there somewhere."

I shiver at the thought. Somewhere in that thick woodland could be a pair of keen amber eyes, watching and waiting.

"We should be safe enough in a spa hotel, though," Sam continues.

As we drive through the grand entrance, along the well-lit drive, and up to the car park, I feel excitement bubbling inside me. Glades Manor is huge and grand; uplighting casts shadows over the gothic masonry.

Sam pulls into a space and we get our bags from the boot, walking hand-in-hand through the enormous wood-and-glass doorway.

"Wow!" I look around the spacious entrance hall; polished-tile floor and ornate wooden panelling. There are plush settees and dark oak coffee tables set to either side, and a huge desk along the far wall. A smart-looking receptionist flashes us a smile and we walk over. Sam gives the details of the booking and hands over his card. Then our bags are whisked away and we follow the porter obediently, barely speaking to each other until he has left us in our beautiful bedroom, when we throw ourselves on the king-sized bed and laugh.

"This feels so grown-up," I say.

"Well, we're nearly thirty," says Sam. "About time we started behaving like adults."

He gets up and draws the thick curtains. Only a glow from the light in the en suite bathroom saves us from total darkness. He returns to me on the bed, puts his arms around me so that my head is resting on his shoulder. "We are going to have the best time."

***

We use the stairs when we head down to book a table for dinner; giggling like school kids as we fly down them, swinging around the corner and nearly knocking an older gentleman off his feet.

"Sorry!" I cry, full of joy, and luckily he gives a wide smile in return.

Table booked for the very last sitting, we head towards the spa. As we are handed soft white towels and robes, it feels to me like I really, properly begin to unwind. There is nobody else in the changing room and I breathe in the smell of expensive perfume; the only trace of a previous occupant. Folding my clothes into a locker, I push open the door to the pool area. It is beautiful. The old orangery of this grand old house has been transformed and, as it is night-time, the lighting is soft and low. Above, the clear glass ceiling allows a view of the night sky, stars shining bright and clear, and a delicate sliver of moon.

There are a couple of people talking quietly on the loungers but the pool is empty. I walk slowly, almost reverentially, down the steps, watching the water change shape with each movement of my legs. Then I take a breath and plunge in, deep, my arms and legs grazing the bottom of the pool as I propel myself along, reaching the other end before I come up for air. I love swimming underwater. The sudden isolation and removal from the noise above. The bubbles streaming from my nose and mouth, the satisfying feel of my muscles working before the relief of surfacing, breathing in, ready to do it all again.

But when I surface, I find Sam just a couple of metres away, wet hair, beautiful smile, moving towards me.

"Hi," I say.

"Hi."

I feel quite self-conscious, with that other couple nearby, and I don't think either of us are the type to canoodle, as my grandad would have said, in a hotel pool. Certainly not when other people are about, anyway.

I squeeze Sam's hand. "Shall we swim?"

"OK. Race you," he says, and he's away. Quite the opposite of canoodling. I imagine the other couple thinking how childish we are but I don't care. I'm not going to let him beat me.

I feel my back, arms and legs work as I front-crawl after

Sam, reaching his feet, and pulling them so that he tips up slightly, put off his stroke, then I plough on by. He is after me, I know it, but it's not a long pool. I reach the end before he catches up.

"I win," I grin.

"You'll pay," he says.

After a few lengths, we decide to have a sauna. We sit on the hard, hot, wooden benches, creating wet shapes of ourselves. I lie back, and Sam strokes my hair. We don't talk, we just breathe and I feel the heat soak into my body, soothing my muscles, burning away the tension.

When we return to the pool area, the others have gone and our voices echo in the empty space.

"This is just perfect, Sam," I say, and this time I kiss him, there being nobody to watch.

He returns my kiss. "Worth waiting for?"

"Yes, bloody hell, yes!"

"I'm so happy," he says. "I've been counting down the days since I booked it."

"Me too."

We step into the hot tub, pushing the switch and creating a loud whirring, which turns into a multitude of bubbles pushing their way ever more excitedly to the surface of the water. Sam slides his arm around my shoulders and I settle back, looking up at the night sky.

When it's time to leave, we do so reluctantly but I know we can come and do this all again in the morning. And I have to admit I am really hungry now.

I change quickly, drying my hair with a towel, and meet Sam in the waiting area outside the spa. Hand in hand, we walk back through the main hall of the hotel, smiling at the lady behind the reception desk, and up to our room. We have half an hour before our booking so decide to come back down and have a drink at the bar.

After opening the door to our room, I turn and kiss Sam, pulling him into the enveloping darkness, hearing the whoosh and the clunk of the door shutting. I can feel him, and hear his breathing, and just about make out his shape in front of me. His breath is hot on my neck and his hands are on me, urgently. He pulls my top off, and my bra. "You were going to get changed anyway, weren't you?"

I answer by pulling his t-shirt up and over his head, finding the buttons of his jeans. Our mouths meet and we are consumed by each other, the rest of the world lost to us.

Then from somewhere near our feet, his phone starts to ring.

"Mmmfff."

"Ignore it," I say.

"Don't worry, I'm going to," his hands are on me, and he is guiding me gently yet urgently through the darkness towards the bed. There is the beep of a message being left then it is just the two of us once more.

I am in the bathroom, getting myself ready for dinner.

"Bollocks," I hear from the bedroom. "Bollocks, bollocks, bollocks."

My stomach drops. I poke my head around the door. "What?" I feel a chill, a dread, wash through me. I think I know what's coming.

"That was Kate, on the phone. She's lost her keys, she can't get to her interview tomorrow, or get Sophie to her friend's."

"OK." This doesn't sound too bad. "Well surely she can get a friend to take them, or borrow a car. Get a taxi?" I suggest helpfully. "Why's she telling you anyway?"

"I don't know," he says. "She says I might have the keys. She gave them to me when Sophie asked me to get something from the car. I gave them back, I'm sure I did. I'm sure." He is grabbing his jacket, patting the pockets. His face falls. "Shit. They're here. I must be going mad. I'm sure I put them back on the stand in the hallway."

"How annoying," I say, "I don't suppose we can get a courier or something? Would that be cheaper than them getting a taxi?"

"I don't know," Sam says. He looks at me. Now I do know what's coming. "Alice. I'm going to have to take the keys back to them."

"No!" I exclaim. I can't help myself. This is our time.

"I have to," he says gently, "this is my fuck-up. I can't let Kate miss her interview, or spend loads of cash on a taxi to ship her about. And I know how much Soph was looking forward to going to her friend's. It doesn't happen often, you said so yourself."

I sit on the bed, utterly deflated. I want to cry but I know I mustn't.

"Look," he says, "it will take me four or five hours, tops. I'll drive down, chuck the keys at Kate, drive back. I promise. And we'll change that dinner booking to tomorrow. I'm so sorry, Alice."

He kisses me and draws back, looking worriedly into my eyes.

"It's OK," I sigh. I know that he's only doing what he has to do.

"I'll text Kate, and I'll get on my way, and I'll be thinking about you all the way there, and all the way back. I promise."

"Well, just take care, please. You did all that driving on Friday. In fact, do you want me to come? Shall I drive?"

131

"No, you just stay here and relax. Order room service, get into bed, and just veg out. I will be back as soon as I can and I'll make it up to you."

"You don't have to make anything up to me, just get back safely and we'll have all of tomorrow together."

"You're the best. I mean it. I love you, Alice." He pulls on his jacket, kisses me again and hurries off, out of the room. I call down to Reception and explain we need to cancel our booking, then I get the room service menu and choose the Thai green curry, with a glass of red wine, and pecan pie to finish. Then I switch on the TV, sit back against the wonderfully soft pillows, and try not to feel pissed off.

This is it, I tell myself; this is what happens if you're involved with a man who has a family. Or a kid. Whatever. Sam has ties which cannot, and should not, be broken. Sophie has to come first. Maybe not Kate – in fact, definitely not Kate – but if he's managed to come out with her keys then he has to be the one to fix things. This job interview will be important to her.

There is a thought which is threatening to surface. I do my best to hold it back but it has to come up for air and so it does. What if Kate did this deliberately? Sam did say that he remembered putting the keys on the stand. What if she slipped them into his jacket pocket before he left? She knows what a good man he is, that he wouldn't let her down. And because of my history with Kate – our friendship before we each realised who the other one was – I know she'd had thoughts of wanting to get back together with him.

No, I think. She wouldn't.

I try to push the thought back down but, like a life buoy, it refuses to sink and so it remains, bobbing about stubbornly, while I eat my tea, drink my wine, watch a film, brush my teeth, and, eventually, get into bed. I close my eyes, thinking that if I can sleep, Sam's return will feel much quicker. Every now and then, that little suspicion clashes against my consciousness, making my muscles tense and my jaw clench. But eventually I do fall asleep.

***

At the sound of that hotel-door click, I awake, seeing Sam's figure outlined in the glow of the soft light I left on in the doorway to the room.

"Sorry," he whispers, "go back to sleep."

I check the clock on the bedside table. It's 4.58am. "You've been gone ages!" I say. "Are you OK?"

"Yes, fine, just desperate to get into bed." He pulls off his clothes and moves under the duvet.

"You're freezing!"

"I know." I can tell by the sound of his voice that he's a bit fed up.

"What's wrong?"

"Oh, nothing. Well... Sophie."

"Is she OK?"

"Yeah, yeah, nothing like that. But she woke up when I got there – or she was still awake, I suspect, and I only went in to say goodnight to her but then she got so upset when I was leaving. I'm really sorry, Alice, but I couldn't just leave her."

Where was Kate? I want to ask. But I mustn't sound jealous. And I must be sensible about the relationship he has with his child.

"Poor Sophie," I say instead. "She really misses you."

"I know," he looks sad. "I'm only really realising that now. I suppose I thought that because she lives with Kate, although I knew she'd miss me, it's not like it would be if her mum went away."

"She's only nine. Of course she misses you. But she will get used to it, you know. Kids do get used to things. They're adaptable, that's what everyone says."

"Like it's that easy," he snaps. But he immediately apologises. "Sorry, I'm just so tired…"

"And worried about your daughter. I get it, Sam. I may not have kids, and I'm certainly far from an expert, but I remember a bit about what it's like to be Sophie's age. And I think the problem is that you're missing her, too."

"I am, so much. Do you know, when I'm having a crappy day but I know I'm going to see Soph, I know everything will be OK. But it's easy for me, being a part-time dad. Kate has to deal with most of the moods and the tantrums, and I just get to have the best bits. That smile when I pick her up. I love it. I mean, she's not always an angel when she's with me but I think I get a better deal than Kate. Or I did, when I was still living in town."

"But then you don't get to collect her from school, tuck her into bed. Kate gets those things." I feel very determined to stop him feeling sorry for Kate.

"True. And I don't get the arguments over staying up late, clothes, what she's allowed to watch on TV… Kate makes sure I know all of that alright."

I feel childishly pleased to hear this criticism of her. I kiss him. "Let's have a hot chocolate. And get some sleep. You did the right thing, taking those keys back. And Sophie was probably extra upset because she was tired. Don't worry. She knows you love her."

"Thank you, Alice." His tired eyes meet mine and I know he means it.

I turn to put the kettle on and busy myself making the

drinks. But I stop to look at him in the mirror and my beautiful, golden, exhausted Sam is already asleep.

***

In the morning, we are just in time for the last breakfast sitting. Sam can't stop yawning but a good blast of caffeine from the super-strong coffee picks him up.

"Let's spend the morning in the spa," I suggest, "then maybe we can go to bed this afternoon."

"Steady on," Sam grins and I kick him under the table.

We treat ourselves to hot stone massages, then lie side by side on the loungers in the orangery-spa. It's a wonderful, relaxing morning and we end up staying well into the afternoon. We both need this.

As time rubs on, however, a sense of sadness starts seeping into me. I try to ignore it but I think it's showing on my face as Sam asks me what's up.

"Oh nothing," I say but remember my vow to be honest with him. "Well, I guess I'm just thinking about how you're going to be gone again soon."

"I know," he says. "I seem to be upsetting all the people I care about. I do wonder if I'm just being stupid and selfish doing this course. And it's hard work, Alice. Really hard."

"But you are enjoying it?"

"Ye-es."

"And it's what you want to do?"

"Yes, but I'm aware of how much older I am than most of the others on the course. And because I'm being sponsored, I feel like I've really got to do my best – to make the sponsorship worthwhile."

"You will do your best, I know you will. And please don't worry about me and Sophie – well me, anyway. I shouldn't speak for her. But just remember, although she misses you, she's OK. And I get to see her every Monday so I can keep tabs on her, and pass on messages from you. Whatever you like. You've worked so hard to get to where you are, you can't give it up now. Three or four years sounds like a long time but I bet if you think back to four years ago, it doesn't seem long at all."

My speech makes Sam smile, and that smile makes me feel good. I just have to try to enjoy all the moments we have together, and put all sadness to one side.

"And you know what, Alice? You should be proud of what you're doing, at the hotel. You're working bloody hard."

"Thank you," I say, the thought of work skittering across my mind like a cloud above the sea. I don't want to focus on it now because the moment I do, it will niggle away at me, but for all its difficulties, I really am enjoying my job. My mission while Sam is away is to do brilliant things and to find out what I want from life. Yes, I want Sam, but I know a relationship is not everything. I want to spend my time doing something I love. And I think I may have found that thing.

We have a siesta in the afternoon. It does us both good. We stay in bed until it's nearly time for dinner, then head downstairs to the grand old dining room. Like the entrance hall and lobby, the room is wood-panelled. There are glittering but tasteful chandeliers suspended from the high, painted ceilings, and there are candles on all the tables. In the corner, a lady plays a piano. The other diners talk softly to each other. I look around, mentally conjuring an image of the Sail Loft dining room. This place is so much bigger; the two can't really be compared, but I try to take in all the details and wonder what I can learn.

We are shown to our table by a smart young man with an East European accent. He is friendly and efficient, taking drinks orders straight away then producing two thick leather-bound menus and handing them to us. A glass bottle of water is brought to us by a waitress and our drinks appear within just a couple of minutes. We are both having gin & tonic.

As I sip the cold, sharp drink, the ice cubes knock gently against the glass. I look around at our fellow guests. They are mainly a similar age to those we get at the Sail Loft. A very well-dressed couple are at the table closest to us (but this place is so spacious, they are still a good distance away). The waiter who saw us in comes to take their orders and I am not kidding, the man actually orders for her. "And the lady will have…" I look at Sam to see if he's clocked it but he's busy reading the menu. Suddenly, I feel a little bit out of place, and very young and – oh no – there's a giggle bubbling up my throat. I try to stifle it by pretending to cough. Sam looks surprised. "What's up with you?"

"Oh, nothing," I say, feeling my face growing red and trying to hide behind the menu. "Nothing." I can't help it. The laugh escapes. "It's just…" I can't get the words out. Sam is watching me with an amused expression on his face. I see the man at the nearby table cast a glance at me. My shoulders are shaking and the more I try not to laugh, the worse it gets. In the end, I have to excuse myself and go to the toilets, walking up and down until I have composed myself enough to return to the table.

"Alright?" Sam smiles at me. "What was that about?"

"Oh, nothing… I'll tell you later."

"The waiter came but I said you'd be back in a minute."

"You could have ordered for me."

137

We are too tired to do more than crawl happily into bed and into each other's arms but I have the best night's sleep I have had in some time, and I wake feeling refreshed, relaxed and happy. Even the slight niggling thought that Kate may be out to try and mess things up for us doesn't bother me right now. With Sam's arm lying heavily across me, his body warm next to mine, I know I am in the right place, with the right person.

We have a late-ish breakfast then head on down to the spa for another swim and sauna before we drive home. Sam is seeing Sophie this afternoon so we need to be back just after lunch. I don't have to be back at work until tomorrow.

"Want to come with us this afternoon?" he asks as we're heading back over the border into Cornwall. "I think we might just go to the cinema or something."

"Well, I will, but only if Sophie doesn't mind."

"I really don't think she will," he says, "but I'll ring her if you like, when we stop for fuel."

He does just that and says she's fine with the idea so after we've dumped our bags, the two of us head to Kate's to collect Sophie – who is waiting at the door so we don't actually see Kate. Hiding in shame? I push the thought away.

"How was your day at your friend's?" I ask Sophie when she's safely secured in the back seat.

"Oh, it was so good. Amber's new, ish, and I didn't know she lives on a farm. Well, a small one. She's got ducks and geese, and two dogs, and chickens, and a sheep. Her mum and dad grow all their own vegetables and Amber says they don't eat the animals. They keep the birds for the eggs and the sheep's their pet. They rescued her when she was a lamb. They're vegetarians. Like you, Alice."

"Really?" I say. My ears always prick up at the mention of other vegetarians round here; there are others, of course, but this is quite a rural community, and of course many people's livelihoods have depended on the fishing industry.

"Here we go," murmurs Sam.

"Yes, and I want to be vegetarian, too."

"Wow," I say, "that's great! I mean, of course, if that's OK with your mum and dad."

"Kate's not going to like this," Sam says quietly to me. To Sophie he says, "Let's have a chat with your mum later, shall we?"

"Fine," Sophie says, "but I'm not eating meat today, or fish. I'm surprised you're not vegetarian, Dad."

"Sometimes I'm surprised I'm not as well," he says. But he makes no further comment on the subject.

We have a lovely afternoon, watching a re-run of *Zootropolis* then going to Pizza Express for tea. Sophie can't stop talking about her friend, Amber. I'm really happy for her.

"Amber's got two older brothers, and she's got a cabin bed, and a camera set up in a bird box so she can see birds nesting in the spring."

"Amber's allowed to have her ears pierced."

"Amber says that when she grows up she's going to work for the RSPB. I want to do that. She says I know more about birds than she does, and the sea. She wants me to show her all the best rockpools."

"Sounds like you've found your soulmate," I say and Sophie slurps her drink happily.

It is only as we are heading back into our small town that she becomes quiet.

"Are you OK back there?" I ask, turning round, trying to read her expression in the irregular light provided by the occasional streetlight.

"Yes thank you," she answers politely but she looks sad.

"Sam," I say, "why don't you drop me here so I can get some milk and walk home, then you can drop Sophie off."

"Erm, OK," he says.

I just have the feeling Sophie needs some time with her dad. "See you on Monday, Sophie, shall I?"

"Yes please, Alice," her little voice is so despondent that it makes me want to cry.

"Look, come and hop in here next to your dad." I hold the door open for her as she slides across the back seat and then clambers into the front. "He'll like that, he wants to make the most of every minute he's got with you." I squeeze Sophie's shoulder then close the door, seeing Sam smile gratefully at me.

As I walk through the darkened streets, a light rain starts. It's feeling really autumnal now and soon it will be Bonfire Night. We're going to have a firework display at the Sail Loft. Stefan's quite into the whole idea of Guy Fawkes and thinks we shouldn't be burning an effigy of him but of an MP instead. "Any MP," he said, "they're all as… crooked as each other."

"Maybe not all of them," I replied, but I get where he's coming from and I like his healthy disregard for the establishment.

When I get home, it is to dark windows but a warm house. It's so cold outside that the heating has actually clicked on. I go around the house, closing curtains to keep the warmth in. It is cosy in here. I realise I've never been in Cornwall at this exact time of year before and I wonder how I will fare during the winter. Will I actually find out that everybody was right and it's just the lovely weather and the holiday feel of the summer that I want? I don't think so, somehow. I have already seen how this place has started to change with the turn of the season. It seems to have taken longer to get colder down here than in much of the rest of the country and flowers which by rights should have shed their petals and already hunkered down for the winter have still been in bloom. But now the colder weather is taking effect and the trees which have been changing colour for weeks are finally shedding their leaves.

It is different, but no less wonderful, being here in this muted time of year.

I think of Mum and Dad, and what it's like back home, then realise it's been a week since I last spoke to them so I decide to phone while Sam is still with Sophie. Hopefully he won't be too long.

"Hello, love!" Dad's voice is cheerful as ever. "How's life? What?" That is him talking to Mum. "Oh, oh yeah, Mum says how's Sam?"

"He's great, thanks," I grin as I picture the scene at the other end of the phone line. Dad will be trying to keep his eyes off the crossword as he knows that he should really be concentrating on the conversation with me. Mum, meanwhile, will be itching to get hold of the phone to catch up. But today, Dad wants to talk, for a change.

"Me and your mum were talking about you earlier, love."

"I should hope so, I should think you don't talk about anything else."

Dad chuckles. "Well yes, obviously. But we were thinking, I know you mentioned we could come down to Cornwall for Christmas but we were thinking we might... well... go away somewhere."

"Oh yeah? Where are you going?" I feel disappointed. It seems like ages since I've seen them. But I know I should make the effort to go back home, too.

"Well, on a cruise, actually."

"What?!" I exclaim. Mum and Dad really aren't cruise people. Or at least I thought they weren't.

"I know… I… hang on… OK love, here's your mum."

"Alice!" Mum says. "Are you OK?"

"I'm fine thanks, Mum," I do my phone-smile. "What's this about a cruise?"

"Oh, it looks lovely, Alice. And we really hope you don't mind. But you're going to be so busy at the hotel. And we know it's lovely there but, well, me and your dad fancied some winter sun."

"Of course I don't mind." Do I? "Winter sun does sound nice. Where are you going?"

"The Caribbean."

"No way!"

"Yes, it's a ten-day cruise, over Christmas and New Year."

"Really?" I hope the disappointment isn't too obvious in my voice. I've never had a Christmas without Mum and Dad before. "That sounds great, Mum, and you're right, I'll be really busy here. Maybe I can come and see you before Christmas."

"Of course! That was the other thing. We were wondering if you'd like to come up for a weekend at the end of November, and whether Sam might like to come, too? We need to meet this man!"

"I guess you do!" I laugh, cheered at the thought. "OK, let me talk to him, and Stefan, tomorrow, to arrange the time away. But that sounds great, Mum."

"We can have an early Christmas here."

"In November? That sounds a bit weird."

"Ha! Yes I suppose it does a bit. OK, maybe not an early

Christmas. But we'll have a lovely weekend."

"Sounds great," I say again. "Bye, Mum. I love you."

"I love you, too." I can hear my dad shouting 'love you' in the background, which makes me smile briefly, although after I've ended the call I find my eyes filling with tears. I really miss them, I realise. And I feel silly, because I'm nearly thirty, and I have to have a Christmas apart from them sometime, but I suppose I'm aware that Sam is going to be with Sophie and probably Kate much of the time. Julie and Luke are spending Christmas with Luke's dad and sister – it will be the first Christmas since Luke's mum died. Stefan will be with his family. But I'll be working, I remind myself, and bloody hard. At least this way I will be able to focus on making Christmas a success for the guests at the Sail Loft.

Sam turns up about twenty minutes later. Where I'd been hoping that he would cheer me up about not seeing my parents, he looks serious.

"What's up?" I ask him.

"Oh, just Sophie. Again. She got upset when I left. It makes me feel like a really awful dad."

"Oh, Sam. I'm sorry."

"Nothing for you to be sorry for," he says. "This is all my own making."

I know this is a problem which is not going to go away. I tell him about my call with my mum and dad, and how much I miss them. "So you miss your parents whatever age you are," I say. "Think about when your mum left to go to Spain."

"Yeah, it's weird," he says, "but I don't think I was that bothered. Maybe it was bravado. But I was sixteen and Mum was never that kind of mum anyway, you know?"

"I think so," I say, although I don't, not really. My mum

is definitely 'that kind of a mum' and my dad that kind of a dad. They are always, always, there for me. And although I'm their only child, they have been careful not to spoil me. Besides which, I've had to share them with Julie since we were eleven. Julie's mum is not 'that kind of a mum' either so Julie loved to find refuge at our house, where Mum would look after her and Dad taught us both things like how to fix a puncture on a bike wheel and, when we were older, how to change a tyre.

I put my arm around Sam. His shoulders sag, he puts his head on my shoulder. He feels deflated.

"Come on," I say. "You knew this wouldn't be easy. It's great that Sophie's got this new friend, though."

"You would say that, she sounds a proper hippy, like you," he grins.

"Well, of course. What more could you want from a friend?"

"I thought I'd let Soph break the news to Kate about being veggie," he grins again and a lightness comes back to his features.

I smile too. "Poor Kate."

16

I am up early in the morning, to get back to work. I leave Sam sleeping in the soft darkness of the bedroom, get dressed quietly downstairs, have a quick cup of tea and slice of toast, and head off into the morning. There is just the tiniest sliver of daylight at this time now. I'll have a brief reprieve next week once the clocks have changed but it won't last long. I love it, though; walking through this new day before it's really begun, hearing the sea further down the hill, hissing and sighing below the town.

When I get into the Sail Loft, I'm immediately hit by a wonderful warmth but I am also greeted by a Stefan with a grim face. This does not look good.

"Hi," I say, shrugging off my coat, trying to ignore the ominous feeling in my stomach. "What's up?"

"In here," he says, gesturing with his head towards the office.

In trepidation, I follow him in. Before I've even shut the door he says, "It's that idiot chef Jonathan, and Lydia."

Uh-oh. "What? Are they OK?"

"Oh they're fine, *he* is, at least. She not so."

I know what's coming.

"Want to know why he didn't come to work on Sunday? And why Lydia didn't get back to you?"

"I think I can guess."

"Yes," he says, "and now Jonathan's not interested and Lydia's not at work. She called in sick. And again. And again. Stacy's been filling in but she can't today and she was the one who saw them together too, on Saturday night. At the horrible club down near the harbour. I asked him on Monday about it and he said it was... what's that expression? One of those things."

Sadly, none of this surprises me. But I feel bad for Lydia. And so annoyed at Jonathan. Still, I must maintain a professional stance about all this.

***

"What the fuck were you thinking?"

"Good morning to you, too." I can just see an irritating little smile on Jonathan's face as he turns to carry on peeling potatoes for the hash browns.

"Don't give me that," I snap. "Where's Lydia?"

"I don't know. Called in sick, Stefan said. So I guess she's sick."

"And that has nothing to do with what happened between you and her at the weekend?"

Jonathan sighs. He walks to the coffee pots, plucks two mugs from the hooks above it, pours himself and me a drink and says, "Can we talk?"

"Erm, sure," I am slightly wrong-footed by this, having expected him to continue in his arrogant, smug manner. I follow him through the back door and out into the burgeoning light of day. Steam emanates from the coffee in this cold air, and the gulls are in full force now that the remnants of night have all but disappeared.

"Look, Alice, I'm sorry. I kind of don't want to say that because I think that what I, and Lydia, do outside work is our business. And I do like her, but I don't think we can have a relationship and work together."

"Have you told her that?"

"Yes, and she burst into tears, and I haven't seen her or heard from her since. I wish I hadn't, you know…"

"I know," I say. And, "Saturday night?"

"Yes, Saturday night."

"And you called in sick Sunday morning because of it?"

"Well, yes and no. I was genuinely sick. But," he looks shame-faced, "it was because of drink. I'd said I'd meet up with Lydia and her mates. Some of them I know from footie, they're a bit older than her. But when I got to the pub it was just her."

"Ah," I say.

"And she had a drink waiting for me, so I sat down, expecting the others to turn up. But they never did."

"Bloody hell, Jonathan. You still didn't have to…"

"No, I know. I know. It was stupid. But I really do like her. And we'd had a few. One thing led to another… my parents are away at the moment so we ended up back at my place."

"Shit," I say, my anger turned to concern now, and my brain ticking away, trying to come up with a solution to this problem. "OK, thanks for telling me, Jonathan. Go on back in, we'll talk once breakfast's cleared up. I guess I'm going to have to waitress today."

"Sorry," he says but he's already through the door, and I swear that he looks physically relieved. But whether that's from guilt about Lydia or having avoided a proper bollocking, I'm not sure.

I lean against the old stone wall of the hotel and sip my coffee as I watch the day set out its stall. The sun is already pushing itself forward, offering its services, and a small number of fishing craft are heading out to sea, bobbing up and down merrily across the waves. I don't suppose it will be hot today; it will be some long months now until we have a return to the glorious weather of summer but it looks like it might warm up enough for the holiday-makers to enjoy a drink outside one of the harbour cafés; coats on, sunglasses, too.

Sam is spending the day at Kate's today. Kate's waiting to hear about her job interview and apparently she's got a few errands to do, so Sam being there with Sophie will make things much easier.

"Do you mind?" Sam had asked me.

"No, not at all." And I don't, not really. I appreciate that Kate does not have a lot of time without Sophie. Unless you count those five days a week Sophie's in school, when Kate's, well, sitting around on her arse, I think bitchily but I know I'm wrong. I don't really think her life is like that at all. I am just still smarting from the idea that she might be trying to get in the way of me and Sam. But it's good for Sam and Sophie to have some time just chilling at home, not feeling like they always have to go off somewhere and spend lots of money. Sam says Sophie wants him to go through her shell collection with her, and she's got some film or other that she wants to watch with him.

"It sounds great," I said. "You can snuggle up on the settee together and maybe you could even talk to her about why she's so upset."

"I will definitely do that," Sam said. I kissed him. I love him. He is the best man I have ever met and the best dad – well, apart from my own, of course.

The coffee has cooled quickly. I tip the dregs into a plant pot then head indoors, straight through the kitchen without another word to Jonathan, who is busy getting things ready anyway. I push a smile onto my face and head into the dining room, ready to greet the guests. Inside me, a little voice is piping up, telling me I am well over halfway through Sam's visit. Well, I am just going to have to make the most of it.

When breakfast is over, I go into the office and I phone Lydia. She will be in lessons by now but I want her to know I've got in touch as soon as I can.

"Lydia? It's me, Alice. Look, there's no hurry to phone me back. I know you're in college at the moment, but we are missing you here and I really hope you can come back tomorrow morning. I know what's happened with… well, what's happened, and I want you to know that it's all going to be OK. You're an important part of the team here, Lydia. I don't think we can manage without you! Give me a call later when you can, OK? And have a good day."

Then I call Jonathan in. I tell him I've phoned Lydia.

"And I want you to do the same," I say. He goes to speak but I put my hand up. "Just a sec. Listen, your personal life is none of my business, I know that. But when it starts to interfere with work, you make it my business, to some extent. I would really like it if you would phone Lydia too, please, and tell her to come back, and that it's going to be fine working together. And then, when she comes back, you need to make sure that it is fine, you working together.

A petulant look has appeared on his face. "It wasn't just me, you know. She set me up anyway."

"'Set you up'? Jonathan, she's seventeen. She's clearly had a crush on you since she came to work here. You are her senior by six years, and also her senior at work. I know there's only a handful of us here, and I know we keep things pretty relaxed, but those rules still apply. You have a responsibility to her at work, as a junior colleague, and you need to make this right."

"Fine." His good-looking face is less so when he's sulking. "Great, now to the other thing. You called in sick because of a hangover. I appreciate that you can't possibly do your job if you're throwing up but you shouldn't have got into that state knowing that you had work the next day. So I'm going to give you a written warning."

"What?" I feel like I'm dealing with a teenage son now. "Oh, that's just great."

"Yes, well, like I say, we might be relaxed here but that is based on us all taking our jobs seriously. I don't feel like you were doing so at the weekend so I'm giving you a warning."

"Are you going to tell Bea?" he asks; the equivalent of 'don't tell my mum'.

"No," I say, "not this time. But if it happens again..."

"It won't." He is not contrite but I can see he's relieved that we are going to keep it between ourselves. He knows Bea could tell his parents. This only serves to reinforce my feeling that I am dealing with a schoolboy. Thank god he can cook.

***

The rest of the week at work is better. Lydia calls me back later on Wednesday evening and I leave Sam cooking while I talk to her.

"I think I love him," she says. I am tempted to say she's too young but I was only a few months older than her when I met Sam and I know full well that I have loved him ever since then. Jonathan is not Sam, though, and I really hope that Lydia is wrong and that she finds somebody more deserving of her.

"OK," I say. "Then I know this is going to be really difficult. But you need this job, and we need you. I really missed you today, and not just because Mrs Oswald kept asking me to change her order." I hear a little laugh and I'm relieved. "Seriously, three times I had to go back to the kitchen! But anyway, I think you're great, Lydia. I hope you'll come back to us and I hope you'll keep using the Sail Loft as a place to study when you need to. You're a very hard worker and you deserve to do really well."

"Thanks, Alice," she snivels, and I tell her to get a good sleep and I'll see her in the morning.

On Thursday, she is already in the kitchen with Jonathan and things seem OK between them, if a little strained. I can tell he's being especially nice to her; whether for her sake or for his, I don't know, but as long as she's happier again, I don't mind.

All the time now, though, that little voice is reminding me that I'm running out of time with Sam, that on Saturday he's going back to Wales. I've told him about Mum's offer and he's going to come to meet me in the Midlands the first weekend of December. It's only a month away but 'only a month' sounds so long. In the meantime, Sophie will be going up to see him again, and he says that she seems to be a little calmer about him going.

We're also making plans for Christmas so this should help carry me through and he'll be back for about three weeks then. If I look at it like I'm planning something for work: a month till I see Sam, another three weeks till he's back; three weeks with him back home, it begins to seem more manageable. "Then I've already done my first term," he says, "and really, I'm only ever going to be away for five or six weeks at a time. Think of the summer, too! Three months, though I'll have to get some work."

And I hope I'll have some work, I think. Bea's plan when she went out to the States was to be away for eight months so she's due back in May. It seemed ages at the time but now there are only six months or so left. I take a deep breath. I can't think like that. I push the thought into the recesses of my mind and concentrate on the here and now.

When Friday evening comes around, Sam arrives after having said goodbye to Sophie and Kate.

"How was it?" I ask as he comes through the door, bringing a small flurry of dry leaves in with him.

"Not so bad. Sophie had a few tears but she's got Amber coming over tomorrow so she's really excited about that, already planning where to take her, what to show her."

I smile. I hope that friendship lasts. It will do Sophie a lot of good to be able to help her new friend find her feet.

"That's good," I say and I kiss him, pulling his coat from his shoulders and leading him upstairs without another word.

There is no fancy meal tonight. This time last week, I was up to my eyes in flour and chilli. Tonight, Sam nips down to the Indian at the end of the street and comes back with food that smells so good it literally makes my mouth water. I put the cloth down on David's table and Sam lays out all the food. There is way too much for us both, really, but we pick at it all – crisp poppadoms piled high with chopped onion and coriander, drizzled with sweet mango chutney. Spicy paneer in a rich tomato-and-spinach sauce. Juicy Peshwari naan. Crunchy, warmly spiced vegetable samosas.

"Hey, you've gone all veggie," I say.

"Well, seeing as you and Sophie are, I thought I'd give it a try," he smiles. I lean forward and kiss him. Is it possible I could love this man more than I do right now?

In bed, I lie awake just thinking about the next few weeks, and how this week has been. I was surprised and pleased that there was no interruption from Kate tonight. Perhaps even she has decided to be generous to us. I think of Sophie, tucked up in her bed, excited about her friend's visit. It makes me smile. It also makes me think warmly towards Kate as I know Sophie says they rarely have friends over. It will do them both good, I think, and maybe Kate will become friendly with Amber's parents. But maybe I'm getting ahead of myself.

Next to me, Sam snores gently and I feel a small tear squeeze out of my right eye at the thought of how much I am going to miss him. I move closer to him and he murmurs, wrapping his arms around me. I move my head to get comfy then close my eyes, listening to Sam, and the sounds of David's house creaking and settling for the night, before I eventually drift off to sleep myself.

17

As autumn moves firmly in, it is taking no prisoners. There are two major storms, both of which summon enormous waves to lash the feet of the town, the sea advancing far enough to seep into some of the harbourside businesses.

Up in the Sail Loft, we are warm and dry, and all seems to have righted itself between Lydia and Jonathan. I still catch her looking at him with those eyes, occasionally, but my chef and waitress seem to be keeping a respectable, respectful distance from each other and have even relaxed enough to start having a laugh again. It's a relief.

The second of the storms hit just before this weekend, when Sophie was meant to go up to see Sam, damaging the train line so she was devastated to find out that she couldn't go. Kate, who got the job at the health centre where she had the interview when we were at Glades Manor, had made plans with some of her new work colleagues for Saturday night and I thought that I should show willing and offer to look after Sophie, so that Kate wouldn't have to cancel. This was not one hundred percent altruistic; I reasoned that if Kate's social life started to grow then she would have less of a problem with me and Sam. To be fair to Kate, she was very grateful and gave me what I think was her first proper smile since she discovered that Sam and I had started seeing each other.

She seems happier, these days, I think. When I pick

Sophie up on a Monday night, Kate seems calm and she looks different, somehow. I am sure that one night she wasn't wearing make-up, which I have never seen before.

So last night, as the wind howled around the rafters, Sophie, Julie and I had a girls' night in, watching *Clueless*, and eating pizza and a huge bar of Dairy Milk. Julie concocted some amazing alcohol-free cocktails and gave Sophie a facial. This is an area where I am always going to fall short, though I did stretch to painting Sophie's toenails. It was a lot of fun but I could tell Sophie was subdued. Sam, too, was miserable, when I spoke to him.

"I worked my arse off this week, so I could have the weekend with her. I can't tell you, Alice, how much I miss her. I miss you too, but…"

"But it's different?" I supplied. I am impressing myself with how understanding I'm being but it's difficult. Sam is my priority. Sophie is his. I understand but it's not easy.

Still, we made the best of it and we got Sam on Skype on my laptop, until a huge crack of lightning made us think we should turn everything off, including the wireless router.

I saw his face fall as we said we had to go but I was powerless to do anything. I was soon powerless in another way as the electricity went off. Plunged into darkness, I put a hand on Sophie's shoulder and checked that she was OK, then I called Stefan on his mobile but apparently all was well at the Sail Loft, with full power. A relief as I didn't fancy dragging myself through the stormy night to the hotel.

Julie and I lit candles, bringing inflatable mattresses and bedding into the lounge so we could all sleep there. I say sleep but in fact there was a lot more giggling and chatting going on than actual sleeping. I was returned to those days when Julie used to come and stay at my place – or, less often, I would go to hers. We used to have full weekends together and god knows what we used to talk about but we really did talk, well into the night, then all through breakfast, over lunch, into town, back again, and on again into the next night. Dad used to tease us about it but he says he loved it, hearing us have so much fun.

We told Sophie stories of when we were growing up but I was careful to cut them off at a certain point. I heard Julie mention Steven Wainthorpe – her first boyfriend – and I raised a warning eyebrow. Sophie is only nine. She doesn't need to know about this yet. And Sam, and possibly Kate, would kill me if she hears too much.

Outside, the storm threw huge tantrums, knocking over garden furniture and tossing the recycling about, but we stayed cosy and warm, safe under our duvets. I was touched to find Sophie wriggling closer to me. I put my arm around her. In time, Julie whispered, "Look." Sophie was fast asleep, her head on my shoulder and her clear child's skin smooth and wrinkle-free.

"Aaahhh," I whispered back. "I guess we should do the same."

All night, I slept with Sophie pushed up next to me. She flung her arm over me at one point, and talked and worried in her sleep. I wondered if it was the storm, or if she was always that way – it made me sad to think that she might be having internal struggles and worries at such a young age. I don't think I got more than a couple of hours' sleep but I didn't mind. I often forget that Sophie is not Sam's biological daughter. To me, she is a part of him and it felt an honour to have her trust me in such a way.

***

Sophie has come in to work with me this morning. We splashed through the puddles left by the storm, listening to the sound of water running down from high above the town, trickling and tinkling its way along gutters, taking shortcuts over paved driveways and down the steep steps, converging at the harbour, returning to the sea.

It's dark but not quite cold so that by the time we get to the Sail Loft we are both slightly too warm in our coats. We take them off and I hang them up in my office, making Sophie comfortable at my desk then heading into the kitchen to say good morning to Jonathan and Lydia.

"Good morning, Alice!" Jonathan says, handing me a coffee. Lydia passes the sugar jar and I stir a spoonful in.

"Morning!" I say. "Any chance of an extra breakfast today, Jonathan?" I explain about Sophie.

"Of course, no problem. Would she like pancakes? I can do Mickey Mouse ones."

Would Sophie like Mickey Mouse pancakes? Yes, probably, seeing as none of her friends are here to see.

"Thank you, Jonathan, that would be really nice."

"No problem."

"I'll bring them in to her," says Lydia.

I marvel at how quickly things have changed. I think Jonathan's written warning has made him think. Whether it's from loyalty to the Sail Loft, ambition, or fear of his parents finding out from Bea, something seems to have clicked with him. I've also noticed a change in his attitude to Lydia. More than once I've heard him asking how her studies are going, and whether he can help at all. I don't suppose he can; he is a fantastic chef but I don't know about his academic skills. Certainly his CV doesn't suggest he was that way inclined at school or college, but it's nice of him to be thinking of the things which matter to her.

Lydia, to her credit, does not seem to be letting what

happened between them bother her any longer – or at least she isn't showing it if it does.

I hum to myself as I walk back to the office, a cup of hot chocolate in hand for Sophie. Stefan comes in and we have a brief handover, but everything has gone swimmingly. There was no power cut at this end of town and no night-time disturbances for him.

Sophie sips her hot chocolate as I set her up at Stefan's desk, with a small spare TV I've swiped from the stock room.

"Alice?"

"Yes?" I am half distracted, already moving into work mode.

"I had a really good time last night. I like being with you and Julie."

"We had a great time, too," I smile at her and ruffle her hair. "You're great company and you reminded us what it was like being your age. We were only a little bit older than you when we met, you know."

"So me and Amber could be friends like you and Julie?"

"Yes, I really don't see why not! I had friends from primary school but lots of them went to a different secondary school and they weren't best friends, like Julie is."

"Do you think Julie is going to marry Luke?" she asks.

I laugh. "I think it might be a bit early for that, they haven't been together a very long time."

I suspect what she might really be asking is whether I might want to marry her dad.

"How long do you have to be with somebody before you get married?"

"Well, it varies. Some people get married after a couple of weeks! But most people take a lot longer than that. And lots of people want to live together first before they get married. That didn't used to happen very much but it's what lots of people do now."

"So if Julie and Luke got married they would live together first? Would they live in Cornwall or in London?"

"I don't know! You'd have to ask them that. But I think they'd be mad to live in London. Now I'm here, there is no way I'd want to live anywhere but Cornwall. If I can stay here, I will. And I know your dad wants to come back as soon as he can."

That answer seems to satisfy something in Sophie. She takes another slurp of her drink and spins round in the chair, ending up facing the TV. "I'll put CITV on," she says, and that's that.

It's a nice feeling, working with Sophie sitting on the other side of the room. Companionable. Every now and then something on the TV makes her chuckle, and once she lets out a helpless giggle, which I can't help but join in.

I text Sam.

Your daughter is sitting in my office, watching TV. She misses you. But she's having a good time. The same goes for me. Xxxx

It is just moments before a reply pings back.

God, I miss you both, too. I like thinking about you being together. I've just been working all weekend. Trying to get ahead of myself so I can have Sophie up here another weekend. I can't wait to see you at your parents' but I'm nervous xxxx

Don't be! They are lovely, and they will love you xxx

I hope so xxxx

When Lydia's shift is over, she comes and says bye to me and Sophie.

"Bye, Lydia," Sophie says. I see her looking at the older girl in admiration. Lydia has four earrings in her left ear, five in her right, and when she's not working she has a nose ring, which I see she's put back in. To a nine-year-old girl she must look pretty cool. To be fair, she looks pretty cool to me and I'm nearly thirty.

Jonathan is not far behind and Sophie looks at him with those same wide, adoring eyes. *Oh no, not her as well*, I think. What is it with Jonathan? David and Martin think he's gorgeous. Lydia clearly does, and so, it seems, does Sophie.

"Did you like the pancakes?" he asks Sophie.

"Yes thank you," she says shyly.

"Great, well any time."

"Really?" She is delighted but I bristle slightly. He can't say that to her; she can't just be here any time, and it's not his place to say that she can. While it's great having her here today it's not exactly practical to do it on a regular basis. Still, he is just trying to be nice.

"Course!" he says, slinging his rucksack over his shoulder. "See you later, Alice."

"Bye."

"You're so lucky to work here, Alice," Sophie says to me, swinging her chair round. "Can I come back another weekend?"

"Well, I'm sure… as long as it's OK with your mum and dad. You might get bored of it, though. There's not much to do really. Unless you fancy cleaning the guest bedrooms!"

"Can I?" she asks.

"That is the most enthusiastic response I've had to asking

somebody to clean for me!" I laugh. "But no, you can't. You're a bit young. You can come back sometime, though, we'll sort out another date, shall we?"

Sophie smiles and swings her chair back round to face the TV.

***

As soon as Stefan has come back in, I can walk Sophie home. It's been a long day for her but she has been great. She's been drawing, and writing, and to her credit she has just let me get on with all the things I've needed to do.

I've had a booking for Christmas – two couples wanting to come together – and a group of friends who want to come for New Year. It is filling up and I'm delighted but also nervous. This is the first real event planning I've done, and it's a lot on top of the existing workload. I think of Glades Manor and how much work it must be to keep that place running. Of course they have a huge team of staff, but even so... The thought fills me with dread. While Sophie sits and colours in a picture from some programme called *H2O* I make a list of what I need to do to make sure Christmas and New Year go swimmingly.

On Christmas Eve afternoon, we have a reception with mince pies and mulled wine, and a small local choir singing carols. In the evening, the bar will be open and Jonathan is laying on a buffet, rather than having table service. I want it to feel informal and relaxed.

Christmas morning is an extra-special breakfast, as designed by Julie. I need to get a personalised gift for each of the guests, to have beneath the tree which will be stationed by the bay window.

Tree, I write down. I must get that ordered for the start of

Advent. Which clashes with my weekend with Sam at my parents'.

Tell Stefan, I add.

I will open the bar at 11am, and we are doing Christmas dinner at 1pm. It is a lot of work for Jonathan and Lydia, but at least this way they will be free from late afternoon to enjoy Christmas with their families. I, meanwhile, will be staying on at the hotel. I've said Stefan can have Christmas off on the proviso that he is here for the time between Christmas and New Year. That's my time with Sam.

There will be Christmas films in the guest lounge after dinner. I have hired a proper projector and screen and I need to find out how to work them. I will be between the lounge and the bar but I hope that at least some of the guests will want to walk off their Christmas lunch and maybe others will enjoy a little nap.

From there on in, there is a cold buffet which Jonathan will have pre-prepared and which I will bring out early evening, for those who want it. I will keep the bar open for as long as required.

I also have to sort out festive music and a good sound system.

In between all this, I hope to fit in seeing Sam, but I have no idea how or when. Maybe between breakfast and the 11am bar opening. But in all likelihood, Sophie will want to be at home, opening her presents. I don't know. I'll have to ask him.

Writing things down does bring some order to the thoughts milling around my head but seeing the list grow longer and longer, and realising that I am leaving no time for myself, I can feel my chest begin to tighten.

It's just Christmas, I say to myself. I am off on Boxing Day, and have the whole of the following day off. Sam and

I can have our Christmas then.

It will be great, I know it. It's just an awful lot to think about.

***

When I walk Sophie home at the end of the day, it is in the orange glow of the streetlights. We have missed all the daylight that has been on offer and I feel bad for Sophie. She doesn't seem to mind, though.

"I've had the best day," she says to Kate, who meets us at the door. "And we had a power cut last night so I stayed up late with Alice and Julie."

"That does sound pretty great," Kate kisses her daughter and again she actually smiles at me. "Thank you, Alice. You really helped me out."

"Did you have a good time?" I ask. She looks happy, and relaxed.

"I did, thank you. I hope she wasn't too upset about not seeing Sam?"

"Well, I think she missed him, but we tried to distract her. He's been working all weekend to make sure he can rearrange."

I can't help myself asserting my position as his girlfriend but this is the longest conversation Kate and I have had in some time. Could it be the start of a truce?

"Oh yeah, he rang about that earlier. Have you spoken to him this afternoon?"

"No, not since this morning, I've been working," I say, feeling my hackles rise slightly. Is she trying a bit of retaliatory one-upmanship?

"Oh, right," I think she looks a bit uneasy. Or even... worried? Whatever it is, I am put on alert.

163

"I'll ring him when I get back. We normally speak in the evenings."

"OK," she says, calling Sophie to say goodbye to me. The girl runs up and gives me a hug. Kate meets my eyes before she shuts the door. "Thanks again, Alice. I mean it."

"No problem," I say before I turn and walk down the hill towards home, pondering the odd feeling I have been left with following that conversation.

18

"Alice?" I hear Sam's voice but my mind is stumbling through a variety of thoughts, trying to select the best response. "Are you still there?"

"Yes," I say, grateful for the chance of an easy answer.

"Did you hear what I said? About that weekend?"

"Yes," I say again.

"Say something, please."

Sam's begging doesn't make me feel any better. I just feel like a wave has come from behind me and knocked me down, from the back of my knees. It's melodramatic, I know, and it's not the end of the world – it never is – but my disappointment has come hard and heavy, and the niggling thought I've had about Kate for a few weeks is now throbbing at the forefront of my mind. It's her fault. She's done this on purpose. OK, she can't have conjured up the storm; she's not a witch, at least not as far as I know. But there's no way that the only alternative weekend for Sam and Sophie to get together is the one when he was meant to be coming to my parents' with me. And even if it is, why can't she rearrange her plans? Why is it us? Unless Sam wants this to happen. He said he was nervous. Maybe he's glad of the chance to get out of it.

These thoughts keep on coming afresh; as I sweep one aside, telling myself not to be ridiculous, a new one takes its place. "I'll call you back," I say.

I'm nearly home; after that exchange with Kate, I had decided to phone Sam on my way home through the quiet, dark streets, watching my shadow stretch ahead of me then shrink on the shiny wet pavement with each streetlamp I walk under.

I get my key into the lock and push my way into the dark house, pressing the light switch before the hot, angry tears find their way onto my skin.

I won't be seeing Sam till Christmas. And Christmas is going to be busy, ridiculously busy. And Mum and Dad are going to be disappointed. They'll think he can't be bothered. Maybe they're right. Even though Kate and Sam are long since finished, it seems that she holds the upper hand, has the final say, when it comes to how he spends his time.

I kick my bag angrily and the contents spill onto the floor. As I'm picking them up, muttering to myself, the door opens and in comes Julie.

"What are you up to... Alice? Are you OK? What's happened?" Her arm around me, she swiftly shepherds me into the lounge; sits me down; draws the curtains against the dark night.

And the whole sorry story comes tumbling out. Some of it she already knows but one part she didn't. And as soon as it's out of my mouth I feel bad because it is not my secret to tell. But I know Julie. I can trust her.

"So Sophie's not even Sam's daughter?"

"Well, she is, really – just not biologically." I feel protective of Sophie, and Sam, as I hear those words coming from Julie's mouth.

"All I can say is, Kate was extremely lucky to meet Sam when she did."

"Yes," I say, "it's almost like she planned it." I am feeling deeply, darkly cynical. I've never thought that about Kate before; these things happen and life gets jumbled up. But now, following our disastrous night before Sam went to Wales, then those keys turning up in his pocket during our trip away, topped off with this latest news, I am beginning to wonder.

"Bloody hell," Julie says, "Sam needs to sort himself out. He's your boyfriend, not hers."

"Yes, but he's Sophie's dad. And that comes first with him. And so it should."

"Do you have to be so reasonable, Alice?" Julie says. "Come on, let's get you a drink."

And so she does. She brings in a tray – with two glasses, a bottle of whisky, and a bottle of ginger ale.

"I had this with Luke at the weekend. It's perfect in the colder weather. Come on, let's just have one or two and talk this through. Yes, you need to phone Sam back but let him wait for a bit and think about what he's done!"

I smile at this and offer a silent prayer of thanks for having Julie in my life.

"It was never going to be easy, was it?" I say. "I've been telling myself all along that Sophie comes first, and I've been trying so hard to be good about it."

"You have been good about it," Julie says, "and Sophie clearly really likes you. Look at the way she was with you the other night. That was amazing."

"I know," I say. "And I really like having her around. But without having Sam around too, it's a bit weird. It's like I'm strengthening my relationship with her but ours – mine and his – is just dribbling along, with phone calls and texts. He's doing his course. I'm working my arse off at the Sail Loft and looking after his daughter from time to time. He gets back on 19th December – he'll have been away nearly three months and in that time I'll have seen him for just that week in October. And even that revolved around Sophie and Kate."

"Oh, Alice, he loves you, you know. It's so obvious, to anyone, and Luke says the same."

"I know he does – at least I think he does - but like with you and Gabe, is that enough? I remember you saying that when you two broke up. Is it enough to love somebody? Will that make a relationship a happy one? The right one?"

"It's the right one if it's the right person," Julie says. "I know that now. And every relationship is going to have its challenges. It's just a shame that you and Sam haven't had a few months of loved-up excitement before your challenges have been thrown at you."

After a couple of drinks, I feel OK to phone Sam. Retrieving my phone from my bag, I can see he's already tried to ring me back three times.

"Alice!" he says as he answers. I'd thought I could be cheerful, positive, but I find that on hearing his voice I feel miserable and negative and maybe even sulky. It's not going to be easy to hide that from him. But, I ask myself, why should I always be the one to be making everything OK? I'm always at the bottom of the pile, or so it seems to me in my self-pitying state. Sophie comes first – yes, I know that. It can't be any other way. But it seems like whenever Kate calls, he's at her side. Look at the way he left me at the Glades and drove all the way back here to bring her keys to her. I don't in honesty think he wants to be back with her, or anything like that, but I'd like to think I was somewhere on his list of priorities. Right now, though, I seem to be in fourth place – after his daughter, her mother, and his studies.

"Hi," I say, unable to lift my voice above 'glum' setting.

"I'm sorry, I'm so sorry. I was really looking forward to seeing you."

"Really?"

"Yes, of course I was. And meeting your mum and dad. I've bought a bottle of that whisky you said your dad likes. And I managed to find a copy of that Simon Armitage book that your mum wanted."

"*Walking Away*?"

"No, I'm not," he says. But I'm not in the mood for jokes.

"Look, I'll make it up to you at Christmas, I promise."

"I'm working at Christmas."

"Yes, but at *our* Christmas, the day after Boxing Day, isn't it? I promise nothing will get in the way of us spending the day together."

"Hmm." I am being childish, I know. But I don't want to give in to that part of me that feels sorry for Sam in his predicament. I don't want to be understanding again. And besides that, he can't promise not to let anything get in our way, not at Christmas or ever. He has a family; a daughter, who may need him to drop what he's doing at any time. There is no other way.

"I'm sorry, Alice," he says again, but I think I can sense a drop of annoyance in his voice now. "I don't know how many times or ways to say it. I want to be with you. I want to come to your parents'. I do not want to drive eight hours on Friday and eight hours on Sunday, and come back to do my exams."

"So that's the problem?" I know it's not.

"No," he sighs. "Look, you're annoyed. I get it. I am, too. And disappointed, like you wouldn't believe. But I have to see Sophie and this is the only way I can do it. I feel bad enough having left her; you know that. I have to be reliable

169

and make sure she knows I am. I have to make the sacrifice. I'm her dad."

"I know," I sigh now. "Yeah, let's talk tomorrow, shall we? I don't think I'm up to much conversation tonight."

"I love you, Alice," he says.

"I'll phone you tomorrow."

***

When I've had time to talk things through with Julie some more, and then time to reflect, I begin to accept the situation. Not that I have any choice in the matter. And I think that is the most frustrating thing about all this. It is all out of my hands. There is literally nothing I can do to change anything. I feel like I am at Sam's beck and call but I know it's not like that. He's not like that.

After Monday morning breakfast, I go into my office and phone Sam. The day has dawned bright and breezy and outside I see wisps of cloud sailing through the sky, the sunlight dancing on the wild, vast sea. The ginger cat from next door is rolling around on its back in the leaves which have collected by the garden wall. As I wait for Sam to answer, I take in the view, and enjoy the warmth of the sunshine, magnified through the glass of the window.

"Alice," he says, and he sounds pleased to hear from me.

"Hello," I say, "are you OK to talk?"

"Yes, just heading to the library between lectures. Are you OK?"

"I'm fine."

"Really?"

"Yes, I am, I promise. I mean, I'm disappointed, of course. But I'm not trying to make you feel bad about it by saying that. It would be worse if I wasn't disappointed, though."

"I guess," he laughs. "I'm disappointed, too. You have no idea."

"I do, I get it. I'm sorry I was so miserable last night."

"Don't be sorry. You've every right to be miserable. I keep mucking you about, letting you down."

The childish part of me wants to snivel at this and let him feel sorry for me but the truth is, we are in a difficult situation and I know he is trying to do the right thing. He wouldn't be Sam if he wasn't, and I wouldn't love him.

"Don't worry," I tell him. "Please don't. It's just the way it is. I don't suppose this was ever going to be easy, even if you were still living down here."

"No, I guess not."

"Let's just make sure we lock ourselves away from the world at Christmas, shall we? I'm coming home on Boxing Day, as soon as Stefan is back on shift. Let's get together then and not leave the house for two days."

"Sounds amazing," he says. "I'll see you before that, though, when I get back."

"Yeah, of course, but you know I'm going to be stressed out getting things ready for Christmas at the Sail Loft?"

"Then I'll have to look after you and give you lots of nice relaxing massages."

"That sounds good. I'm so nervous about it all."

"I bet. But it's going to be great. *You're* going to be great. And I'll have my first exams out of the way and be free to wait on you hand and foot, whenever I can."

"Now you're talking," I smile. "Look, I'd better get on, and so had you. I'll ring you later."

"OK, Alice Griffiths. I love you, you know."

"I love you, too."

***

A week or so later, I am in the car heading up to Mum and Dad's; driving through deepest Cornwall on a moody winter afternoon. At the same time, Sam is driving in the opposite direction. I imagine we've driven right past each other but this creates a physical ache within me. I want to see him so much. I could turn the car round, head back to town. He's staying at my place while he's back home. I can't bear to think of him in my bed without me, it's too weird. I have left him a note on the pillow, and left Julie instructions to look after him. I keep on driving. Sam may have his family to think about but I also have mine.

It is lovely to be back at my parents'; the house I grew up in. The fire is crackling away in the hearth, a bottle of red nearby, 'breathing'. As I shrug off my coat, Dad describes the wine to me. I haven't got a clue what he's talking about but I gratefully accept a glass. Mum brings in a tray with some tea for me: "Something light because it's so late." There are pitta bread strips, olives, houmous, and my favourite sweet chilli crisps.

I sit down gratefully, my body sinking into the familiar seat, and I listen to Mum and Dad's news, then look at their cruise brochures, while I crunch my way through my tea. Dad tops up my wine glass and then they look at each other, and then at me.

"What?" I say through a mouth full of crisps.

"Is everything OK, Alice? With Sam, I mean?"

"Yes." I feel defensive. Protective of him. But of course they have never met him. To them he could be the type of man to be messing his girlfriend about. I let my guard down.

"It is fine, but it's difficult."

I end up telling them the whole story, as I had with Julie, but missing out the expletives and the fact that Sophie isn't 'really' his daughter – because actually, she really is.

"Well, this Kate sounds like a pain in the arse," Dad huffs.

I laugh.

"Phil!" Mum says. "You don't know her. And actually, life's probably quite hard for her, being a single mum. I had you but god knows I felt like a single mum at times!"

Dad looks shamefaced.

"Not really," she says, "but you know what I mean. When you were away with work, it was just me and Alice. It was lovely. But it was hard work. On a practical level, and emotionally. Every day was like a rollercoaster, especially when hormones came into play. Sorry, love," she looks at me, "but it's true. And I expect I was the same with your grandma."

"I remember being an angel when I was a teenager," I grin.

"Pfft!" Mum smiles. "We had some rows, didn't we? At least when your dad was home I had somebody to bounce off. Kate doesn't have that, does she? And while Sam's off studying, she's got full responsibility for their daughter. And probably has to comfort her because her dad's not there. It won't be easy, I can tell you that."

I don't want to hear this sympathy for Kate but I know that Mum is right. I like to think that Dad is too, though. It feels like Kate's been trying to throw a spanner into the works of my relationship with Sam and I don't think that's right, no matter how hard it is being a single mum.

"Do you have to be so reasonable?" I ask with a laugh, aware that people seem to say the same thing to me.

"Yes, I'm afraid I do. Look, love, I can see how difficult it is for you. And I can also see how tired you are. That job's certainly taking its pound of flesh, isn't it? Maybe this relationship on top of everything else is just one thing too many. Like trying to balance one more pebble on a pile; it's too much, the whole thing will collapse."

"No," I say angrily. "It's not. You just don't know Sam, that's all."

Woah. It's like Mum mentioning my teenage self has summoned that person back into the room. I want to flounce off to bed, slamming the door behind me.

"Your mum's just looking out for you," Dad says. Now they're double-teaming me. I feel cornered. But at least the wine's good.

"I know. But I think that if… when… you meet Sam, you will understand why he is worth going through all of this. He is the best man I've ever met."

"Ahem," says Dad.

"Apart from you, of course."

The next day, I sleep in until well after ten, coming downstairs in my pyjamas to find Dad reading the paper and Mum doing the crossword.

"Morning, love," they both say at the same time. Dad rises to make us all some coffee and I sit down next to Mum. She puts her arm round me.

"I'm sorry for what I said about Sam."

"Don't be; I would think the same if I were you. You'll meet him soon, then you'll see what I mean."

"That would be lovely."

That is the end of the subject for the weekend. We go out onto the Malverns for a walk. I love being at the top of this long line of hills. Every way you turn, the landscape lays itself out before you; farmland and villages and occasional roads; miniature cars trundling along, the sun glinting off their windows. A reservoir glistens below and a kestrel hovers at eye-level, sight firmly fixed on an unwitting tasty morsel somewhere in the undergrowth.

The wind is bitter and strong and it is hard to hold a conversation but we push ourselves forward, headlong into it, feeling our cheeks grow cold and red. Walking back, further down the side of the range of hills, the wind is in our favour and helps us on our way. We pull off muddy boots in the car park then cross the road to the Malvern Hills Hotel, where we drink coffee and eat cake. Then it's back to Mum and Dad's for a different bottle of complex wine, accompanied by homity pie and salad. I go to bed full, and relaxed, and I don't think I wake once until the morning.

All too soon, it is time to return to Cornwall. I am looking forward to being back there but reluctant to leave my parents, and my childhood home. They each thrust a bag at me, and inside I can see a number of parcels wrapped in Christmas paper. I haven't even thought about their presents yet.

"Have these when you're with Sam," they say. "There's something in there for him, too."

"Oh wow, thank you," I feel my eyes fill with tears but I turn and put the bags in the boot of the car; I can't have my parents see my crying. They'll only worry. I quickly brush my eyes and then turn back, hugging each of them tightly in turn.

"Drive carefully," Dad says.

"Oh yeah, I hadn't thought of that," I tease him. "Of course I will. And I'll stop for a coffee near Exeter, and I'll let you know when I'm back. I promise."

I climb into my car and wind the window down so I can

shout bye to my parents before I drive away. Then I see them turn in unison, at the sound of a car which is clearly in a hurry, driving down their usually quiet street.

The next thing I know, the drive is blocked and there is Sam, pulling up, hurrying out of his car.

Mum and Dad look annoyed. "It's Sam!" I shout to them. "Sam's here!" A look of confusion crosses their faces, clearing from Mum's just before Dad's, as though she has passed her understanding on to him. Sam is rushing out of his car, saying, "Sorry, sorry!" and bearing a huge bunch of flowers, and a huge grin.

I scramble out. "What are you doing here?"

"That's a fine greeting!" he says, kissing me. "I've been on the road since breakfast time. I can't believe you were about to go!"

"Well I didn't know you were coming, did I?" I lean into him, so thoroughly happy. "Mum, Dad, this is Sam."

"Well, hello Sam, we've heard a lot about you," Mum hugs him and Dad shakes his hand.

"I'm really sorry for turning up unannounced, but I wanted to surprise you."

"You've certainly done that," Dad says, but he's smiling. He ushers us back through to the house and proceeds to put the kettle on while Mum mouths 'He's very good looking' to me. 'Dad?' I mouth back, and she nudges me.

I sit down next to Sam, and I can't take the smile off my face. To be fair, he looks pretty pleased with himself, too.

"How was your weekend? How was Sophie?" I ask. "Did she mind you leaving early?"

"No, she was OK, she understood."

I'm not convinced, from the way he says it, but I am so delighted that he's done what he's done – this detour must add about three hours to his journey.

"Have you had lunch, Sam?" asks Mum.

"No, well, I had a snack at…"

"I'll make you something."

"No, it's fine, I'll…"

"It's no bother, I can do a quick sandwich? Some crisps?"

"Just say yes please," I say, "it will be easier in the long run, believe me."

Sam smiles. "Yes please, that would be lovely."

Dad brings in a tray with tea and biscuits.

"Mum's doing Sam a sandwich," I say.

"Of course she is."

"So, Sam, how was your journey?"

"Oh, fine, thank you, Mr…"

"Phil!" I say. "You have to call him Phil. You can't call him 'Mr Griffiths'."

"Absolutely right," says Dad, "this isn't the 1950s." He then proceeds to grill Sam on the exact route he's taken, nodding in approval. In honesty, there are not that many options – A30, M5, then a few minor roads and you're here. Still, it makes Dad happy.

Mum returns with food and every time Sam takes a mouthful, she asks him a question.

"Mum!" I say.

"Sorry," she looks sheepish. "I'm just really happy to meet your Sam, that's all."

Argh. 'Your Sam'! I can't believe she's said that. Sam seems quite content munching away next to me, though.

We don't have long; both Sam and I still have long journeys to make, but I can tell my parents take to him immediately. I am so pleased. When it's time to go, even though we have only had a fraction of the time together that we were meant to, I feel like it's meant more than the whole weekend together would have done. For Mum and Dad, and for me, the fact that Sam went to so much effort to get to us speaks volumes.

As we walk out to the cars, Sam apologises again for turning up without warning.

"It's no bother," Mum says, hugging him. "It was a very unexpected pleasure. It's been so nice to meet you; I hope you'll come for the weekend soon."

"And we'll be sure to visit Cornwall when you're down there," Dad says. "I could quite fancy moving there myself."

"You'll never leave here!" I say.

"I don't know, I might surprise you," Dad says. "It's never too late for a cheetah to change its spots."

I don't correct him. I just give him a huge hug then he shakes Sam's hand. When Sam and I say our goodbyes, my parents turn away, unsubtly discussing the climbing rose that grows up their garage wall.

Sam and I giggle, then I put my hand on his cheek and I kiss him tenderly. "I can't believe you did this."

"It's nothing," he says. "I wanted to see you. So I was being selfish, really."

I look into his blue eyes and I don't want to let him go but I know that this last hour will keep me going now, until he's back for Christmas. "I love you so much."

"I love you, too. Now you drive safely, OK? And let me know when you're back."

"I will if you will. See you at Christmas."

"See you at Christmas," he agrees. He clambers into the car, blows me a kiss and toots his horn as he drives off.

"What will the neighbours say?" I ask Mum and Dad.

"Oh, stuff them," Dad says.

"He's just as lovely as you said," Mum smiles at me.

"I know!"

This time, as I get into my car, although I still feel sad at leaving Mum and Dad, my heart is pounding with happiness. As I drive away, my parents waving from the roadside, I marvel at how one short hour can turn a day around.

19

I try to carry that feeling with me through the rest of December, even though work is starting to get frantic as I endeavour to make sure we are all set for Christmas and New Year. I barely see daylight but it's not so bad because whenever I do set foot outside, it is into a town bedecked with sparkling, joyful Christmas lights and decorations. Festive music wafts from the shop fronts along Fore Street, and happy-looking shoppers pull their scarves and coats around them, clutching packages and bags, stopping every now and then to admire the beautifully designed shop windows. Even away from the main shopping area, there are strings of lights twinkling on houses, in trees, along the tops of hedges and fences, between lampposts. It is beautiful and magical. The harbour is dressed up, too, its decorations reflected on the ever-dancing water. Even some of the fishing boats are looking festive, with lights strewn haphazardly along their cabins and windows.

This is my first Christmas here; it will also be my first Christmas working, and my first Christmas without my parents, but I already love it.

Luke is staying with Julie and I much of the time. He tries to split his time between Julie and his dad, Jim, but since Luke's mum died in the summer, Jim has barely sat still. When he isn't working, he is involved with the artists' club which May used to belong to; working at a food bank, and helping get things organised for a homeless shelter's Christmas meal, over in Truro. He's roped Julie in to help prepare the food for this. Luke and his sister Marie are going to be there to serve food. This way, they will keep so busy over Christmas Day that they will barely notice May's absence. That is the general idea but I'm not sure anybody really believes it.

Anyway, it is fun having Luke around. Julie is busy working at two different places, and often out in the evenings so Luke and I are spending a bit more time together. On my Mondays with Sophie, I tend to just bring her back to our place now as it is so cold and dark early; even for me, the beaches don't hold a lot of appeal. And she's so tired; it seems like the lack of daylight, coupled with all the Christmas school activities, is taking its toll on her. She's normally just fit to flop on the settee and watch Christmas movies. This is fine by me as I am not good for much else, either. Sometimes Luke will join us, too, and occasionally Julie will have left us something delicious to eat – sometimes sweet things like cakes or brownies, and sometimes full meals: home-made pizza, or a vegetable lasagne filled with sweet, succulent vegetables bathed in a rich tomato sauce and topped with melted cheese.

The day after I got back from Mum and Dad's, I had picked Sophie up as usual. "I won't need you to do this in the New Year," Kate said bluntly.

"Oh, right," I replied, feeling slightly put out.

"I've got more hours at the centre, so I'm quitting Monday night Pilates."

"Oh, that's a shame," I said, not sure whether I meant for her or for me.

"Yeah, I know, I feel a bit bad, I've built up a regular little group, but I can't work all the time."

Or even most of the time, I thought, bitchily, but I held my tongue.

"Well, I'm still happy to have Sophie whenever."

As I was speaking, Sophie came to the door. "Oh yeah, Mum, I can still see Alice, can't I?"

"We'll see," said Kate, "It's a lot of bother for Alice, I'm sure."

"It's not, really," I said, and I meant it. "I enjoy our time together."

"Well, let's talk about it in the new year," Kate said, and smiled at me. Was it a real smile? I couldn't tell. I felt like my nose had been put slightly out of joint, like I was being pushed out.

Still, I put a smile on my own face, and my arm around Sophie's shoulder. "What do you say to pizza and *Miracle on 34th Street?*"

"I don't know what that is."

"It's like a round, flat bread, covered with tomato sauce and cheese…"

"I know what pizza is," Sophie giggled and hit me on the arm. "I meant Miracle on whatever."

"It's a classic Christmas film. Come on, Luke's waiting for us."

She took my hand and we skipped together down the hill, getting faster and faster, laughing until we had to stop just so that I could catch my breath.

I really don't want to give up my time with Sophie and it is not because of Sam, or to annoy Kate. It's because I enjoy being with Sophie and I feel like it does her good, too. When Sam can't be here, I like to think I can try to provide a bit of fun like I know he would.

On December 19th I am at work, humming to myself, knowing that when I get home, Sam will be there. We are not going to be able to see a huge amount of each other over the next week. He's got the school play to attend, which he is doing on both nights, as Sophie's asked him to. She and Amber both have bit parts and Sophie is very keen for Sam to go, and to meet her new friend.

"How could I refuse?" he said apologetically but it's fine because I have not had a chance to do any Christmas shopping yet. I'm planning to head over to Penzance for a late-night shop while he's at the play.

Stefan has also asked for some extra time as his parents are coming over from Sweden.

"How could I refuse?" I asked Sam, echoing his words.

"Bloody hell, between the two of us, we'll never see each other."

But we will, tonight; I'll make sure I leave the Sail Loft as soon as Stefan gets here then I'll pick up a bottle of wine and head home. Then it is just a week till we'll have our own Christmas together. A chance for a breather between the two main events of the Sail Loft's festive calendar. I swear that when I enter the house on 26th December, I will hang up my work worries along with my coat, and concentrate on Sam. Julie and Luke have decided to go away the day after, to Barcelona ("We might stay for New Year, we'll see how we feel" – oh to be young, free and loaded), so Sam and I will have the place to ourselves.

The Sail Loft is only half-full this week, which is fine and in fact a blessing, giving me a bit more time to get everything in order. Jonathan and Lydia are getting on like a house on fire these days and Jonathan's been a huge help to me making sure we've got everything ordered and double-checking the suppliers are definitely going to deliver what we need, when we need it.

"You've got enough going on, Alice," he said, "I'll do it. I've got the menu and I know how many people are coming. I'm sure this is part of my job, anyway."

It made me wonder if I'm turning into a bit of a control freak. He's responsible for the day-to-day ordering of supplies, and we manage the budget between us. I just can't bear the thought of anything going wrong here at Christmas and I know I will be worrying about it until it's all happened.

I am grateful for his help, though, and reluctantly I have handed over those reins to him.

Now, I'm happy I did. "Jonathan, I've got to get going," I say, wrapping my scarf around my neck. "Sam's back tonight."

"Oh yeah, have fun," he says distractedly.

"Thanks, I will!" I grin. "Shall we catch up in the morning? After breakfast?"

"Sure, if you like." He is rummaging in the freezer so I leave him to it and practically skip outside. A bad move, as it's starting to get icy. Grabbing the handrail just in time, before I cause myself a serious injury and mess Christmas up good and proper for us all, I walk the rest of the way in careful little steps, leaning back slightly as I go down the hill.

When I get to the house, I can see the curtains are drawn and there are lights on. My heart skips a beat, and the next thing I know the front door is being opened and I am swept up in a huge embrace.

"Happy Christmas!" Sam says, swinging me into the warmth.

"Happy Christmas!" I kiss him.

"You're cold!" he says. "Let me warm you up." He unwraps my scarf and unbuttons my coat, drawing me in for a kiss. I slip off my shoes and we walk slowly towards the

184

stairs, kissing all the while. I have my back to the staircase so Sam guides me up it, his hands firmly on my hips. When we reach the turn of the banister, he presses me against the wall and pulls my jumper over my head.

I shiver. "You're meant to be warming me up."

"Oh, I will," he says, and he kisses me again. I feel the cool Farrow & Ball-painted wall against my skin and wonder what David would say if he knew we were treating his lovingly-decorated house this way. The thought is fleeting, though, washed away by the feel of Sam's skin on mine as he tears off his own top and I am enveloped in his warmth. He nibbles my shoulder and gives a small laugh.

"Hungry?" I ask.

"For you," he laughs again. "How cheesy was that? *I must have you, Alice,*" he says with a mock-serious look on his face. Then he cups my chin in his hand and looks into my eyes. "But seriously, I must. Now."

He pulls me after him, into my bedroom. The door closed, the room lit only by the twinkling of Christmas lights outside, we fall together onto the bed.

20

And then Christmas is upon us. That first night with Sam was like a little haven of peace. A pause in the determined march of the season, which moves single-mindedly onwards. You must go with it, be crushed by it, or swept aside.

I decide to go with it, and so does Sam. While I head off to work and a barrage of messages to answer, from guests checking last-minute details or arranging just-thought-up surprises such as bottles of champagne, bouquets of flowers – even a miniature Christmas tree in one case – Sam heads for the shops then off to Sophie's school play.

"I've never missed one of her Christmas plays!" Sam says. "I was in tears the first year. And the one after. OK, for all of them."

"I don't hold out much hope for you today, either. Give her my love," I say and I kiss him.

Sam will be spending Christmas day with Kate and Sophie, at their place. "Are you sure you don't mind?" he asked me earnestly last night. "It's just, we've always done this. I get there in time for Sophie to open her presents, and we have dinner together. I usually leave them before she goes to bed."

"Of course I don't mind." And it's true. If I wasn't working then it might be different but I am so focused on what is happening at the Sail Loft, it would be extremely churlish of me to kick up a fuss about Sam being with his daughter. Besides, he'd only be on his own otherwise.

"Thank you," he said, "and I'll get to the Sail Loft as soon as I can – probably early evening. Don't worry, I won't make a nuisance of myself. I'll sit quietly at the bar like a good boy."

"Sounds perfect!"

When I get into work, I inhale the scent of the real Christmas tree, which we have had installed by the reception desk. There is a further, larger, tree in the dining room. We have had them both since the start of Advent. I was worried they'd be drooping and bare by this point but I'm pleased to see they're holding up nicely.

"Morning!" I say to Stefan, who is up and about.

He gives me a look, and gestures towards the kitchen.

"What?" I say, a fluttering of nerves in my stomach.

"In here," he whispers.

I follow him into the office and he shuts the door.

"I think Jonathan and Lydia are, you know…" he says.

"What..? No… are they? Why do you say that?"

"I've just seen them kissing in the kitchen."

My heart sinks. This can't be good news. "Shit."

"Yes, well, maybe. I mean, these things happen, don't they? Lots of marriages start in the workplace."

"True," I agree, but I am also privy to information that Jonathan had been seeing the barmaid from the Union. And, rumour has it, an older woman (OK, she's my age but she's older than him) who works at the holiday lettings place. I don't mention this to Stefan, though.

"OK, let's think about this. Do they know you saw them?"

"No, I was about to go in but that stopped me in my tracks."

187

"OK," I say, "then let's carry on like we know nothing about it. I just hope he doesn't mess her about."

"Or she could mess him about. It's not always the man, you know," Stefan grins.

"True," I say. But I think I have a fairly good idea of how Jonathan and Lydia see things. Oh well. There is nothing I can do. "OK, let's hope for the best. Now, you need to get back to your family! Anything else I need to know?"

"No, all quiet on the Western front."

"Good!"

All through breakfast, I am on the lookout for signs of something between my chef and my waitress but there is nothing to suggest they are anything more than colleagues who happen to get along very well.

I find Lydia before she leaves. It's her last day at college before the Christmas holidays. "This time next year you'll be coming back from uni!" I say.

She smiles shyly, "I hope so. Got to keep on saving, though. Do you think I'll be able to get some more work here in the summer? Maybe as receptionist? Jon says that's what you used to do."

"Oh, well, I don't know, to be honest. I guess Bea will be back here by then."

I can't even begin to think about next year but, come January, I'm going to have to. Were Lydia and I going to be vying for the two jobs? No, I can't see it, somehow. I can't go back now I've managed this place. I suppose what I'm hoping for is to make this Christmas and New Year a real success here and have something good to put on my CV and talk about in interviews. I can't think about that now, though. I have to focus.

"Oh, yeah, of course." She looks downhearted.

"You'll be fine, though, Lydia, one way or another. I'll talk to Bea about it, once we've got Christmas out of the way."

"Thanks, Alice!" she smiles brightly. "You're the best!"

"I don't know about that."

When she goes to get her coat, I hover around but she and Jonathan do nothing more than exchange pleasant goodbyes. I'm not convinced, though. Stefan can't have been imagining it, can he?

In the evening, I return home to find Sam, Julie and Luke sitting at the dining room table, drinking prosecco.

"She's back!" Julie says, and pours a glass for me. Luke stands to give me a hug and Sam gestures to the chair next to him.

"David and Martin are coming over, too," Julie says. "Let the fun commence!"

Julie's got a five-bean chilli simmering in the kitchen and there are bowls of nachos already out. I drink my wine then nip upstairs to get changed into jeans and a sweatshirt. When I get back downstairs, David and Martin are just coming into the hallway. I kiss them both on the cheek; their skin chilled by the cold night air. We eat and drink, and make merry, playing charades and Pictionary and the Logo game. Julie has made mini Christmas puddings ("This is just a warm-up," she says, "but I don't know when we're all going to see each other so let's make the most of it now. Hopefully this is the first of many such nights.") We soak them in brandy, switching the lights off and watching the blue flames glow and dance in the darkness. I am warm and content, from the wine and the food and the company.

"I had a nightmare at work today," I say.

"Don't tell me," David looks concerned. "Not Jonathan

and Lydia?"

"No, well that too, maybe," I can't remember having told him about them. Maybe Bea did. "No, one of the bookings for Christmas cancelled. Two doubles."

"Shit!" Julie says. "Had they paid their deposit?"

"Yes, of course, but it would have still left us out of pocket. I rang Tourist Info to let them know, in case they had any enquiries and by the end of the morning, I'd had two! The first one rang back, and they've booked both rooms! Two American couples. The only problem is, they're arriving Christmas Day. I'd really hoped to have everyone in on Christmas Eve, to save any disruption on the day itself. But they offered to pay the full package, and just stay two nights – they said they couldn't get to us any earlier."

"Rich Americans!" Luke laughed. "Paying for nights they're not even staying."

"I know, but maybe that means they'll tip well, too."

Julie and Luke talk about their plans for Christmas and David and Martin enthuse about what a great idea it is. "But being selfish buggers, we're spending Christmas Day being wined and dined – heading out in the late morning, and not getting back till the day after Boxing Day."

"That sounds amazing," I sigh, "can I join you?"

"Of course," David laughs. "Well, you could if that didn't mean my sister would absolutely kill me for stealing her fantastic manager. So what will you be doing while Alice is busy managing the Christmas Extravaganza at the Sail Loft, Sam?"

"I'm going to be up at Kate and Sophie's," Sam says, sounding slightly awkward.

"Of course," Martin smiles kindly, "Sophie must be so happy to have you back for Christmas."

"Yeah, and she's still excited about Father Christmas

190

coming so it's a proper magical time. May not be many more years of that."

"Christmas with kids must be extra-special," I see Martin smile at David over the top of his wine glass. David smiles back. I'm not sure anyone else notices, but I do.

"It is," Sam says, a faraway look in his eyes. I squeeze his hand.

"And he's coming to the Sail Loft later in the day, aren't you?" I say.

"Yep! Just for a drink or two. I don't want to get in the way!"

David and Martin stay over, in the room I had up at the top of the house. It feels weird, Sam and me going to what was David's room.

"I can't believe you're banishing us to the attic!" David laughs.

"It's no more than you deserve," I say and I kiss him goodnight.

In my bedroom, I look out of the window, watching my breath ebb and flow on the glass as I breathe in and out. I can't help but sigh to myself at the sight of this beautiful, sleepy town by the sea.

Sam laughs. Damn, I thought he was still in the bathroom. "Happy?" he asks, moving behind me and putting his arm around my waist, his mouth to my neck.

"Yes," I say, and right in that moment I really could not be happier.

21

Christmas Day dawns bright and breezy. I've been up for hours, and every now and then I peek out of the window at the town, lights aglow; being slowly lit by the rising sun which sends beatific rays onto the waters and glances gentle blows off windows. I see it all but I have no time to stop and admire it.

I spoke to Mum and Dad briefly on Skype last night, after the guests had vanished to their rooms. My parents look happy and tanned; cruising obviously suits them. Dad said he thinks he's found his true calling. Mum rolled her eyes and grinned.

"Have a great time," I said, "I love you. I miss you." For a moment, I felt myself well up.

We humans bring it on ourselves, this seasonal emotional overload. Fine if you're a loved and looked-after child or doting parent; romantic and heart-warming in a loving relationship (well, assuming that everything is straightforward and there are no exes or children from another relationship, ahem); fun and hedonistic with a group of close friends.

Terrible if you are on your own; recently bereaved; have just split up with someone; your ex has taken the children to their grandparents'.

Loneliness magnified and hammered in time and again by family films, TV programmes and adverts confirming that yes, you are alone on this endlessly long day when even the shops are shut and you have nothing to distract you from the fact that those who you love should be by your side.

But, that aside, happy Christmas!

Bea and Bob have left me a Skype message to pick up this morning. They look very merry, wrapped up warm as if they are going out somewhere, or have just got in. It's just a brief video, wishing me well for the day. I smile and put the screen of my laptop down. From now on, there will be no more screens. I am tackling Christmas head-on.

Jonathan and Lydia have arrived bang on time, bumping into each other on their way in. They both look fresh; cheeks pink and glowing from the cold morning air.

"Merry Christmas!" I say.

"Merry Christmas, Alice," Jonathan hugs me and kisses me on the cheek. Lydia does the same. I am filled with warmth and affection for them.

"Are you ready for this?" I ask.

"We're ready!" says Jonathan.

"Bring it on!" Lydia agrees.

And from that point until late morning, it is all systems go.

At about 10.37 (not that I'm clock-watching) there is time for a fifteen-minute break before I open the bar and am ready to go again. So far, so good. Everybody loved the breakfast, and most of the guests went for the Buck's Fizz as well, topping up their alcohol levels from last night when pretty much everyone had joined in with the carol singing, carrying on the impromptu seasonal karaoke long after the choir had left.

I have often wondered why people want to spend

Christmas in a hotel but now I get it. All they have to do is get dressed, roll down the stairs (none have literally rolled down them but there's plenty of time yet), be fed and entertained.

Carole, a lovely woman who insists I call her by her first name, said last night, conspiratorially, "It's been a revelation. I mean, don't get me wrong, I loved our family Christmases... *loved* them, but between the kids getting up at 3am and then being tired and fractious all day, his mum complaining about how they never used to eat dinner in the late afternoon, and never getting a chance to actually sit down, I was always glad when it was Boxing Day. D'you know what I mean?"

She actually said that, pretty much verbatim, three times. Each time, I nodded in agreement, although actually, no, I have never experienced a Christmas like that. This, really, is my first chance to host a Christmas and it is completely shattering but at least none of the guests were bouncing on my bed at an ungodly hour, and I am getting paid for this. I can only imagine how exhausting Christmas Day must be for overwrought parents.

Now, although it just feels like the most hectic work day ever, I have to remind myself to maintain a festive atmosphere. We have never done lunch here before; normally by mid-morning, it is time for a bit of a lull. Breakfasts are done, the kitchen is clean; the bedrooms are in the process of being made ready for new guests, or spruced up for the existing ones, if that's what they want. Some people prefer to just have their rooms left alone while they are staying. Today, though, it is time for a quick 'well done' to Jonathan and Lydia, a text to Julie to thank her for the excellent menu, and a slurp of coffee before the bar opens. I can already hear a murmuring of guest voices, even though it's not yet eleven. I leave Jonathan and Lydia in my office: "You two have a sit down for a bit, before you get going again."

"Thanks, Alice," Lydia says. "The boys were up at about four this morning and I was out till midnight so I've had pretty much no sleep."

"How the hell do you look so lovely, then?" I say, and she blushes. "If that was me, I'd have bags under my eyes and I'd look like a ghost."

Jonathan says something as I'm closing the door but I don't catch what it is. I do hear Lydia say, "Jon!" and giggle. I roll my eyes. He's either being horrible about me or he's flirting with her. Perhaps both. However, as Carole's husband, Pete, pops his head around the corner, saying, "Here she is!" I really don't have time to worry about it.

Every single one of the guests is in the bar by ten past eleven. The place is warm and noisy and I'm pleased to see people mingling with each other. Every time somebody buys a drink, they offer to get me one, but there is no way I can drink now. I have to keep my wits about me. Besides which, the Americans are due any minute.

I hand out the dinner menus to people, as a reminder of what they will be having – just in case any of them changes their mind. I want to be prepared for everything.

When all of them have their drinks in hand, I go back to the office. I push the door open and hear a slight scurrying noise, then see Jonathan sitting on my chair, Lydia perched on the edge of the desk, looking decidedly ruffled and red-faced. Shit.

I don't have time to worry about it now, either.

"Kitchen, please," I say. "It's half-past and we've got one and a half hours to make this the best Christmas dinner this lot have ever had."

Lydia looks at me, worried, as she goes past, but I just pat her arm and say, "Go on."

To Jonathan, sauntering past, I give a sterner look, but I know there is nothing I can do. Just hope for the best. He grins at me. He is infuriating. When is he going to grow up?

As I'm closing the office door, the front doorbell chimes. This must be our American guests. I put my best smile on, smooth down my trousers, and go to the door. It's David and Martin.

"Oh, thank God it's you two," I say, relieved and not that surprised to see them. "Wait till I tell you what I've just…"

The words are halted mid-sentence as, from the side of the doorway, steps Bea. Followed by a slightly apologetic-looking Bob.

"Oh my god!" I exclaim. "What are you doing here?"

Bea steps up, laughing, and hugs me. "I'm sorry, this is too cruel. But we're your Americans! We've come to stay the night. All four of us."

"You're..?" The truth dawns slowly.

"Blame these two," Martin says, kissing me. "Bob and I had nothing to do with it."

A train of thoughts runs double-speed through my mind. Is Bea here to check up on me? Is she going to approve? Has she decided to move back already?

"Happy Christmas, Alice," Bea says, letting me lead her inside. "And before you think anything of the sort, I am not here to check up on you. I know full well what a fantastic job you're doing here. If anything, we are here to help if you need it. And if you don't, we are here to relax and enjoy Christmas at the best hotel in Cornwall."

As David walks past he squeezes me and kisses me on the forehead. "Sorry!"

"Yeah, no problem, it's only my most stressful day ever," I kiss him back.

"This is for you, Alice," Bob says, handing me a distinctly bottle-shaped gift. "I think you'll be grateful for this later." He's very tall and dark, with a strong jaw. Even more handsome in real life than on Skype. Bea's done well.

"Thank you, Bob. It's nice to meet you." I remember my manners.

"That's very polite of you to say so, Alice," he laughs, "but I wouldn't blame you for cursing the lot of us at the moment."

"No, no, it's great to see you. Come on in, let's get you a drink before you get settled."

So in they come and before I know it they are mixing with the other guests. Bea doesn't let on to anybody that she is the owner and I am gratified to hear some of the other guests telling her what a treat she'd missed the night before.

I check everybody has drinks then I dash into the kitchen. It smells delicious; the huge pans of roasting vegetables and potatoes, giving off the aroma of caramelising garlic and the sweet smell of the soaked apricots which are going into the nut loaf. There is a turkey in one of the ovens, and a roasted marmalade ham, à la Jamie Oliver. The starter is a red lentil and red pepper soup with a drizzle of chilli oil, and a selection of artisan breads. What I am possibly most excited about are the puddings. A proper bread-and-butter pudding, a sticky toffee pudding, and a chocolate melt – which Lydia is making under Jonathan's guidance. I don't want to distract them but I watch for a moment, trying to read their body language. He steps behind her, putting his arms around her to help her fold in the chocolate. I groan inwardly.

"Everything OK in here?" I ask, more sharply than intended.

"Just swell," Jonathan gives me that grin again. I could throttle him.

"Great, thank you, Alice," Lydia says sweetly and she does look beautifully, unabashedly happy.

"Bea's here," I tell them. "She's the American! Well, Bob is, and Bea, David and Martin are the other three. They're staying as guests."

"No way!" Jonathan says. Lydia looks nervous. She has never met Bea.

"It's fine," I say, "she's really happy with how things are going. Bob's pretty good-looking in real life, too. Come and say hello when you've got a minute, Lydia."

I leave them to it, hoping to have annoyed Jonathan with the comment about Bob.

Back in the bar, there are gales of laughter. Bob, it seems, is quite the story-teller; he has most of the guests hanging on his every word as he recounts a story about a Christmas when he was a teenager and trying to get through the snow to some girl he had the hots for. "My car wasn't going anywhere so after dinner with my parents I hitched a lift in a truck and then walked about three miles in the dark, and when I got there her mum told me she was at her dad's, in the next state. She hadn't bothered to tell me. I ended up spending the night with her mom. Not like that," he says, at the sound of a snort from Carole's husband.

I take up position behind the bar and Bea comes up. "It's weird being on this side of things," she says, "but I think I like it."

"Really? You don't feel like pushing me out of the way?"

"Not at all!" she laughs. "You're doing a fantastic job, by the way. Everybody is speaking so highly of you. You're a great hotelier. And clearly you've got a bit of a thing for event planning, too. It sounds like that choir were great."

"Yes, I've got a surprise for after dinner too, though I don't suppose I should have told you that seeing as you're a guest!"

"Well, I won't mention anything to anyone else."

"Bob seems nice," I look at him, chatting to the Swannicks; two brothers and their wives, down from Leeds.

"He's a scream," she says. "But he is so kind, too. I can't believe I found him on a computer."

"You did very well."

"I did, didn't I?" I have never seen Bea look dreamy before but it's the only word I can think of to describe her expression. "And my little brother's done well, too." We both watch David and Martin, sitting quietly in the corner by the window, chatting intently. "Planning their wedding, I bet! It's only a year away," I say. "They should have it here."

"Well, maybe you should suggest that to them. Though they probably have their own ideas."

I can't really think about a year's time; the future is such an unknown. Bea will be back here in May and after that, who knows? Sam will be well into the second year of his course. I will be... well, I have no idea. *Leave it for January,* I tell myself. I check the time. "If you'll excuse me, I'd better go and make sure everything's ready for dinner."

"Let me know if I can help," Bea says.

"I wouldn't dream of it; you're a guest! But you're welcome to pop in to the kitchen and say hi to Jonathan and Lydia if you like."

Lydia, though, is putting the finishing touches to the dining room when I go through. The tables are arranged so that people are in the groups they booked with. The chairs are wrapped with gold bows and there are candles on each table, along with crackers and bottles of red and white wine. The Christmas tree seems more alive than ever, standing proudly by the window, its lights bright against the slightly grey backdrop.

"Thank you, Lydia," I say to her. "It looks amazing."

"It's no problem," she says, "I love doing this stuff." She comes closer to me. "And you don't have to worry," she says. "About… you know…"

She can only mean Jonathan. "Listen, it's none of my business, as long as it doesn't affect your work here."

She looks stung. "I don't mean that in a harsh way," I say. "What I mean is, I can't tell you what to do outside of work. I just hope you're happy and sensible, that's all." She blushes. Oh my god, it sounds like I'm talking about birth control. "I mean," I continue, wondering if I'm just digging myself into a bigger hole, "that you don't get hurt. That you look after yourself and you put your studies first. You work so hard, you deserve to do really well."

She looks relieved. I feel relieved. I hug her. "Happy Christmas, Lydia. Now, let's get this dinner going, shall we?"

Despite everything, running Christmas Day for twenty-four paying guests is an enormous buzz. It helps that they are, to a person, good-natured and appreciative of everything. They love the food, they love the drink, and they absolutely love the magician who I have organised for the after-dinner entertainment. He goes from table to table, wowing them with his magic skills. I'm pretty impressed, too, as he makes a card appear inside an empty champagne bottle.

I am still staying off the booze, drinking water and coffee alternately. I can't wait for later, though, to see Sam. I have hardly had a chance to think of him all day. After the magician has gone – disappointingly in a Fiat Punto rather than a puff of smoke – there is a distinct lull at the Sail Loft. The early drinking, the over-eating; they have taken their toll. I head into the sitting room and close the curtains – reluctantly as there is now a glow of emerging sunshine across the rooftops of the town, and over the sea – and get the screen and projector ready. First classic film: *It's a Wonderful Life*; followed by the original *Miracle on 34th Street* (which Sophie had loved when I showed it to her) and, if people can manage another, *The Muppet Christmas Carol*. That will take us well into the evening, when I will open the bar if there is anybody left standing, and hopefully Sam will be propping it up.

While Carole and Pete opt for a walk around the town, as do Bob and Bea, the other guests traipse into the sitting room. There are pots of coffee and plates of after-dinner mints on the side and as they help themselves and settle into their seats, I nip into the dining room where Lydia is clearing away and Jonathan is already making a start on laying out the buffet for later. "There are a few platters in the fridge," he says, "and the cheese is out on the worktop, warming up – without getting too warm, as it would out here."

"Thank you, Jonathan, you've done a bloody brilliant job today." And I really mean it. He's surpassed himself, and without getting childish or precious about the fact he's cooking another chef's menu. I hope all of that is behind us now.

He smiles widely, showing his beautifully straight white teeth. "It's been fun. Though I can't deny I'm looking forward to a break. You're going to be shattered, Alice. What a way to spend Christmas!"

"Ah, but my Christmas isn't for another couple of days. I

am just clinging on to that thought. And trying to ignore the fact we have to do all of this again, pretty much, for New Year."

"Don't remind me!" he says, but I can see he's happy. "You ready?" he asks Lydia as she comes through. He looks at me, as if daring me to say something.

All I say is, "Hang on, you two, you didn't think I'd forgotten you, did you?"

I rush into my office and pull out two carefully wrapped parcels. I push them into their hands. "Open them later, will you?"

Jonathan looks surprised and Lydia looks embarrassed, "Oh, but we didn't get you anything."

The 'we' is not lost on me.

"Don't worry," I say, "these are just a thank you from me for helping to make my job so much easier than it might be – and so much fun, too. Happy Christmas, you two. Now go and enjoy it."

I watch them walk down the steps. At the bottom, Jonathan takes Lydia's hand and they look at each other. If I'm not much mistaken, the look on his face mirrors hers. It gives me a warm feeling, seeing them like that. Love has to trump all. If anyone should know that, it's me. Now I just can't wait for Sam to get here.

By evening, many of the guests are or have been asleep. Carole and Pete, however, blow in with happy, rosy cheeks. "We've walked the length of the town. All three beaches!" she tells me. "This has got to be the best way to spend Christmas. Will you have us next year?"

Bea, just a short distance away, hears this and smiles at me.

"I hope so," I say, and I really do.

"I need to talk to you about that," Bea says quietly, brushing past my shoulder. My stomach sinks; I have come to love running this place but I know Bea's nearly halfway through her time in the States.

She raises her eyebrows at me, and grins. Maybe all is not lost.

While the film is on, I work my way through a plate of nut roast, vegetables and roast potatoes, and allow myself a small glass of champagne, which is only going to be wasted otherwise. I sit on one of the bar stools to eat, then pour a cup of coffee and take it to one of the armchairs, where I can sit back and let my muscles relax. I think through the day's events but I know that it is a long way from being over. There's a trace of a headache on my brow so I swallow a couple of paracetamols. As I'm glugging down some water, Bea spies me.

"There you are!" She comes and sits down. "Sorry, I don't want to interrupt your quiet time. God knows you must need it."

I smile at her. "I can't believe you were the American party! Do you know, you were lucky we had any spaces – there was a cancellation not long before you rang."

She looks slightly shamefaced.

"That was you too, wasn't it?"

"It was, it was. I'm so sorry, Alice. I just didn't want you guessing, somehow, if you knew that you had a booking from the States. But did you notice how soon afterwards we rang and booked? So you weren't stressing for long, I hope. Our intentions were good, I promise, though Bob has told me off. He says it looks like we were trying to trip you up."

"No, don't worry, I know you wouldn't do that to me," I say.

"I just thought it would be fun!" Bea smiles. "But I must admit I probably hadn't thought it through fully. David thought it was a great idea, though. He knows exactly how fantastic you're being here."

I could sit and listen to this kind of praise all day.

"And so I also wanted to ask you whether you'll stay on here, as manager? I've realised I've done my time, and I don't know whether I'll be here or in the States in the future – probably a bit of both – but I do know I don't want to be tied down to running a hotel anymore."

"Wow, really?"

"Yes, would you want to? Or is it too much? I know it's hard work, you know I do."

"Would Stefan be staying, too?"

"Yes, if he'd like to."

"I would love to! I really would."

"Oh that is a relief!" Bea hugs me. "I wasn't sure if you might be thinking eight months was quite long enough."

"No, I love it, I promise. And we've got a brilliant little team here." I decide not to mention anything about the fledgling romance in the kitchen.

"I can see that," Bea smiles. "Well, this deserves a drink, I'd say."

"It does," I agree, "but can it wait till later? I've just had a little champagne and I need to keep my wits about me. It's not over till the fat lady sings."

"You've organised entertainment for the evening, too?"

"No, I… oh yes, very amusing."

She laughs and stands up. "We will drink later, then."

"We will."

Shortly after this, Sam arrives. My heart pretty much leaps with joy at the sight of him, standing at the top of the Sail

Loft steps in the dark, the lights of the town glowing behind him.

"Happy Christmas," he smiles and kisses me. "Judging by the look on your face, all has gone well at the Sail Loft?"

"Yes!" I say. "Though you'll never guess who turned up unannounced. Well, sort of. They had booked in as guests."

I usher him in, shutting the door and telling him all about the day as he listens and laughs, and takes off his coat.

"I need to get the buffet laid out now," I say, "keep the guests topped up. Fancy lending a hand?"

"Of course!" In the kitchen, before I have a chance to switch the lights on, he sweeps his arm around me and kisses me. My top rides up and the cold steel of a work surface against my skin makes me jump. "I've been wanting to do this all day," he says.

"Not now!" I say, though I very much wish I didn't have to be so sensible.

"Not fair," he groans, but he allows me past him. The lights on, I issue instructions, which he follows good-naturedly. In the dining room, we lay out the bread and cheese, uncover the platters. Jonathan has already set out all the condiments; the pickled walnuts, dried fruits and chutneys. There are bottles of port and polished crystal tumblers. Fresh fruit juice and ice-cold water for those who maybe feel they have had enough booze. Home-cooked vegetable crisps and deep-fried broad beans. Olives and tiny sweet red peppers stuffed with cream cheese.

"Urgh, my stomach aches just looking at this," Sam says.

"Did you overdo things at Kate's?"

"Yeah, kind of! She had turkey, even though Soph and I aren't meant to be eating meat. I… I felt guilty and I ate some. To keep Kate happy. I'm sorry. She'd just gone to so much trouble."

"Did Sophie?" I ask.

"No, and she was very cross with me. So I had to say no to the pigs in blankets. It was difficult."

"The pigs will thank you," I say. "So did Kate eat them all?"

"Nope, that's the stupid thing, she hardly ate anything, as usual. She filled up on wine."

"Ah." I say nothing more about that. "Were they OK about you coming over here?"

"Yep, seemed to be. Well, Kate was... I'll tell you later."

Kate was what? I wonder but we're interrupted by David and Bea who come in and greet Sam.

"Your girlfriend is amazing!" Bea says.

"I know," says Sam, smiling at me.

I blush and make myself busy, straightening things up on the table. "Is the film nearly finished?"

"Yes," David says, "but take the compliment, will you? Today has been brilliant; all your guests are singing your praises. You've obviously found the right place."

"OK, I'm amazing," I say, "I always suspected as much."

"Modest, too," Bea laughs. "But you should feel proud, Alice."

The film over, the room soon fills up and is ringing once more with the sound of cutlery on plates, glasses clinking, and happy voices. I sit back and allow myself just a moment to take it all in. Inside this room there are people I barely know, people I am just beginning to know, and people I love very much. Outside the window, in that soft, dark night, the town I have come to call home is laid out in the darkness, carefully stepping its way down to the sea. I can hardly believe how much has changed in my life since I was last celebrating Christmas.

This time last year I was settled and secure; content but unwittingly bored. I had no idea any of this was coming and I'd have never imagined I'd be taking these risks: leaving a permanent, well-paid job I knew inside-out, for a short-term job with no foreseeable future. Finding Sam and renewing our relationship. Leaving the town where I'd grown up to become an outsider in a town I'd loved from afar.

Do you know what? I will take those compliments. I do feel proud.

22

Boxing Day heralds a late start and hangovers for many of the guests but the mood in the dining room seems to be one of quiet satisfaction. Jonathan's Full English goes down very well, and one by one the tables empty – some going back to their rooms for a comfortable nap, others heading intrepidly into the cold day which has dawned bright and clear, a frost twinkling on the slippery pavements and winter-length lawns.

David and Martin haven't even made it down to breakfast. "Any chance of room service?" they'd asked cheekily.

"No way!" I'd laughed. It is something we offer, but I've put a veto on it over the festive period. There are just too many other things to keep on top of and besides, I want this holiday to be sociable, not people holing themselves away in their rooms. They could be anywhere if they are going to do that. They could be at home.

"Well, Alice, this has been wonderful," Bob says. "I've heard so much about this place, and about you. I've been dying to meet you and I've got to say I haven't been disappointed."

His arm is draped around Bea's shoulders. She looks comfortable leaning into him. His handsome face is full of good humour. It's impossible not to like him.

"And how are you getting on with David?" I ask.

"Oh, he's just great. Exactly as Beatrice described."

"Don't call me that!" Bea nudges him.

"What not? It makes you sound like a princess."

"Well I don't want to sound like a princess, thank you very much. Billy-Bob."

"OK," Bob laughs easily, "point taken."

"David's missing you," I tell Bea.

"God, I miss him, too. I haven't told him yet, you know, about the plans for the future. Not that I really have any plans as such. I'm going to have a chat with him today. I need him and Martin to make a date for their wedding because that's one thing that I really do have to make sure I don't miss."

"Bloody hell, imagine that! I'm sure David will be happy." I wonder if he'll want to keep me on in his house, though. Maybe he'll want to sell up soon. He could certainly make a lot of money if he does. Much more than he's getting in rent from me.

"We're taking Bob to Land's End, and Cape Cornwall, that is if that lazy pair ever wake up."

"Leave it to me," I say. I go to the reception desk and dial David and Martin's room.

"'lo?" Says a sleepy voice.

"Oh good morning, this is Alice phoning from reception. I'm afraid you've missed breakfast but if you hurry I can ask our chef to knock you up an egg sandwich."

"You had me at 'knock you up'."

"Don't be disgusting, David," I hear Martin's voice.

"Yes, don't be disgusting," I say, "now you've got ten minutes before Jonathan goes so get a move on."

Sam stayed with me at the hotel last night, which he's never done before, but left this morning while breakfast was underway. He's taking Sophie to Luke's dad's house this morning then late afternoon, he and Sophie are going to the Lost Gardens of Heligan, to see the 'Heligan by Night' display. He did ask if I wanted to come, and a part of me really does but a far larger part is thinking of getting home, sinking into a long, hot bath, and getting my pyjamas on.

"I won't, if you don't mind, I think I'm going to be dead on my feet by this evening."

"Well, hopefully not too tired…"

We had both fallen into bed exhausted last night, and I don't know which of us fell asleep first. I think we just about managed a goodnight kiss.

"I'm sure I'll be rejuvenated by the time you get to me." I planted a long, tender kiss on his lips, turned and walked downstairs. I could just hear "Come back… pleeease…" from behind the door. I grinned to myself. Sam would have to wait.

I enjoy Boxing Day more than Christmas Day, but only because Christmas Day went so well. I honestly feel like every person here is happy, including Jonathan and Lydia. I don't mention anything to them about their blossoming relationship but I can see it now, the way they both look at each other. And, I think, as long as Jonathan is looking at her the way she looks at him, then things may just work out. God knows there have been enough successful relationships born from the workplace before; and it's got to be better than meeting somebody online. I am nervous, still, about if things go wrong, but we will cross that bridge when and if we come to it. In another few months, Lydia will be leaving for uni anyway. I am convinced she's going to get her grades, and she's told me she's putting most of her wages into savings – although she also footed the bill for the family Christmas. Knowing this, I'd spent quite a bit more on her than I'd meant to but it's going to be a tough year for her, working and revising, and sitting exams. I bought her some vouchers to use at the spa hotel which sits loftily on the clifftops. She can use the facilities once a month and choose a different treatment each time. When she came in this morning, she rushed to thank me. I felt a bit bad for Jonathan, for whom I had only got a bottle of whisky, but he seemed happy with that.

"Alice, I can't believe it! Thank you so much," Lydia's skin and eyes - pretty much everything about her - were glowing.

"It's a pleasure. Just make the most of it, OK? When things are getting tough, book yourself in and look after yourself. I am expecting great things of you this year!"

"I won't let you down, Alice."

"Hey, it's not about letting me down. Whatever you do, however you get on in your exams, as long as you've worked your hardest, you should be happy. But I have a feeling you're going to do brilliantly."

When the kitchen is clean, and the dining room ready for this evening, Lydia and Jonathan get ready to leave. I see him fastening her scarf around her neck, and I can't believe how different he seems. He sees me watching, and smiles. I smile back and head into the office. Then it's countdown time. There is relatively little to do today; all the guests are booked in until tomorrow, so there is nobody new to check in. The phone is quiet, and by dinner time Stefan will be here and I will be at home.

I take the opportunity to catch up on some paperwork then I get a cup of tea, and a sandwich, and I allow myself the luxury of sitting down in Bea's executive office chair, leaning back and eating at my leisure, just staring out of the window, watching the subtle colour changes of the sea;

noting the banks of clouds hanging low over the town; observing families and couples out walking, shaking off the excesses of Christmas. Kids on new bikes and scooters; one on foot, clutching a kite in one hand and the end of her mother's scarf in the other. Happy faces, wrapped-up bodies. Smiles and contentment. This is the face of Christmas which people want to see.

I wonder how Julie and Luke got on yesterday at the homeless shelter. I think of all those people who might want this time of year to be over. It's like the more effort we put into making something great, the further we have to fall when it isn't.

I think of Sam coming round tomorrow, of wrapping myself up in bed with him. A leisurely morning. A lie-in, a late brunch. Champagne. Chocolates. A crackling fire.

Right now, I tell myself, I have to accept this as a happy time for me, and just never forget how lucky I am.

***

When Stefan arrives, he is beaming.

"Merry Christmas!" he kisses me on the cheek.

"Merry Boxing Day!" I say, now brimming with excitement.

"I'm getting married!" he says, dancing me around. "I asked April last night, after Reuben had gone to bed – just in case she said no, you know? – and she said yes!"

"Of course she did!" I laugh. "That is wonderful news. We should celebrate."

"We should, for sure. But you know you and I are destined never to socialise, don't you? We're like ships which pass in the night."

"You're right," I say, "it's impossible! Let me get you a

coffee now, you can pretend it's something more exciting."

"Lovely." Stefan follows me into the kitchen, where Jonathan is back and busy prepping dinner. Adele, the waitress this evening, is chatting away to him but I can see his mind's elsewhere.

"Stefan's getting married!" I tell them. Jonathan looks up, smiling, while Adele merely says, "I thought you already were."

She is chewing gum. She'd better not be by the time she's waiting on. We've got a party coming tonight from town, non-guests. I know they're friends of Jonathan's parents so he really wants to impress them. Still, these are now Stefan's troubles. I pour him a coffee, we do a quick handover, and I am gone. I've said goodbye to my Christmas guests, who have all assured me that they will be back, and I've left a note for Bea as she, Bob, David and Martin are still out.

As I make my way through the quiet streets, I hum to myself. Most houses have their curtains drawn, or blinds down, carefully containing their precious family time. The odd one, however, is ablaze with light – I glimpse a family sitting at a table playing a board game, glasses and mugs and a bowl of sweets strewn around the room. In another house, a couple sit watching TV. I hug myself, knowing that will soon be me. The house is in darkness when I get in; Julie will be with Luke at his dad's. I go around shutting the curtains, switching on the lights on the tree, and gather a load of kindling to get a fire started. Upstairs, I get the bath running, then I run up to the top floor, taking a moment to gaze out of the uppermost window, in the room I used to rent. I can just make out the odd light on the sea, and the intermittent flash of the lighthouse across the bay. I open the window for a while, the cold seizing the opportunity to rush in. But I let it, feeling the wind – fresh from the sea –

on my skin. A little taste of the outside world before I settle in to enjoy a day or two's respite.

***

At about half past eight, I am sitting in the lounge, half-watching a game show Christmas special when my phone rings.

Sam Branvall

I experience a little shiver of delight. "Hello?"

"Hello my love," he says, "I was just phoning to say I miss you."

"I miss you too, so when are you getting here?"

"Sophie's just nipped to the loo, then we'll be on our way."

"Have you had a good day?"

"It's been… interesting. Julie and Luke weren't really talking to each other when we were up at Jim's, and Soph said she'd heard them having an argument."

"She can go a bit loopy at Christmas," I say. "I thought she'd be a bit calmer with Luke. She's been so happy lately."

"Must be something in the air, though; Soph's been a bit weird herself. Whereas Kate's happy as anything. She's got one of her new friends from work coming round tonight."

"Oh well, at least somebody's happy! I hope Sophie's OK, though."

"She's alright, in fact she's been wanting to hold my hand this evening and she hasn't done that for years."

"Make the most of it!"

"I will," Sam laughs. "And I'll be with you at about half nine, or just after."

"I cannot wait."

"Nor me."

He hangs up and I hug my knees to my chest. I kind of wish I'd seen the gardens in all their night-time glory but, hopefully, I might get to do it next year. I am still taking in what Bea's said. Without even looking for something, I get to stay in Cornwall, doing this brilliant job. I feel too lucky for words right now.

At just after nine-thirty, I hear a key in the front door and I rush into the hall. Sam sweeps in, a bottle of champagne in his gloved hand, and wraps his arms around me.

"Happy proper Christmas!" he says.

"Happy proper Christmas," I agree, and kiss him. He's grown some stubble this holiday and it suits him but it's bristly against my skin.

"Fancy a glass of this?" he lifts the champagne onto the sideboard. "Actually..." He kisses me for a little longer. I breathe him in; his warmth below his jacket against the cold of his cheeks. I unwind his scarf gently and kiss his neck. "Keep going," he says softly. I begin to unbutton his coat and nibble at his neck, making him moan quietly.

"We could take it upstairs," I suggest. "Or into the lounge. There's a roaring fire and Julie..."

It's like I've summoned her just by mentioning her name. The front door bursts open and my friend enters, her eyes red from tears.

"Julie!" I repeat, having been about to say that she was out for the evening. I hear Sam groan in my ear. I find his hand and squeeze it. "What's wrong?"

"Oh god, I'm sorry, I've ruined your Christmas..."

At that same moment, Sam's phone rings from somewhere inside his coat. "I'll get this," he says, looking at

215

me. "You sort her out. And I'll put *this*," he puts the bottle on the side while he retrieves his phone from his pocket, "in the fridge." He looks at his phone screen and mutters. "Oh bloody hell, what does she want?"

"Kate?" I ask, already shepherding Julie towards the lounge.

"Mm-hmm." His phone rings off. "I think she'd had a few drinks by the time I dropped Sophie off. Maybe I should have brought her here. Soph, I mean."

"She'll be OK. Call Kate back, though. But if she needs you to go and get her some booze, tell her to piss off!"

"I will!" Sam grins.

Julie is sobbing next to me. "Come on," I say. "What's up? Sam said he thought you and Luke had argued."

"Just a bit. I've made a right idiot of myself," she sobs.

"What have you done?" I sigh.

"I asked him to marry me."

"You..?"

"I know. What an idiot. He said no."

I take a moment to digest this information. "God, Julie, I had no idea. Why didn't you tell me you were going to..?"

"I hadn't planned it, not really. It had crossed my mind and then I was watching him yesterday, talking to one of those poor old blokes; he's so kind, so warm, so funny. I was looking at the back of him, thinking how much I loved him. And I want to spend the rest of my life with him."

"Wow," I say. "But he said no?"

"Yes. And he says it's because we've only been together a short while. But I don't think he trusts me. Because of what happened with Gabe."

"Julie," I say, "Luke is one of the most honest people we know. If he's told you that's why he's said no, you should believe him. And you have, really, only been together a

216

short while. What's the hurry?"

"Oh, I don't know. It all just felt so right. We had a lovely, lazy morning; breakfast in bed, the works. It felt so romantic. I felt so romantic. I just kind of… asked him."

"Well bloody hell," I say, then I hear Sam's voice in the hallway; loud and panicked. I stand up. "Hang on, Julie." I walk towards the door but he is already there.

"Sophie's missing," he says.

"She's..?" What's going on? I can hardly keep up with the night's events.

"That was Kate. She said Sophie had gone straight to her room, said she was going to watch something on her tablet. Then Kate went to see her and she'd gone."

"Shit." My heart is pounding. "Did she leave a note?"

"I don't know. Kate's pissed, and upset, and I can't make sense of what she's saying. Something about Sophie finding out I'm not her dad…" His voice is shaking and his face is a deathly white.

I put my hand on his arm. "Oh my god, we'd better get over there."

"I'll go," he says, "you stay, in case she comes here looking for me."

"OK, OK," I say, but I really want to be with him. Julie is in no state to deal with Sophie if she does turn up, though. "Get going, now," I parcel Sam into his coat. "See if she's left a clue about where she's gone. Maybe try Amber's place."

"I've already thought of that," he snaps but immediately apologises. "Sorry, I'm just worried."

"I know, I get it, don't worry. Just go."

I am worried for him, and worried for Sophie. I look at Julie and think I haven't got time for her problems right now. Why does she have to make a drama of everything?

Why couldn't she just be happy with what she already had?

As Sam leaves, she looks at me.

"What?" I ask, a creeping sense of dread coming over me.

"Bloody hell," she says, "I think it's my fault. It's my fault Sophie's run away."

23

As Julie spills out the whole, sorry tale, I feel an icy grip, squeezing my stomach, my heart, my chest.

"We've been getting at each other all day," she says; "Well, I've been getting at him, really. Throwing as many things as I can at him. I accused him of seeing other people while he's in London."

"Well, that's just stupid," I say, "but what's that got to do with Sophie?"

"No, no, that's not it… I'm just thinking about what I said to him, and when."

I hold my breath. I think I can see where this is going.

"He said he wouldn't cheat on me, and then he almost said something about Gabe, but he stopped himself. I saw red, though. I got mad at him."

"Was this while Sophie and Sam were there?"

"Yes, well, they were with Jim, he was showing Sophie the games room – he's done it up like May used to, with little lights everywhere. It's lovely." Julie looks at me, realises she's going off at a tangent. She keeps her eyes on mine as she says her next words. "Anyway, I thought Sophie had gone back inside the house, with Sam and Jim. Luke and I were going to the garden room to get some beers from the fridge. He was talking about you, and how hard it must be with Sam having a daughter, and being away, and I got annoyed, and told him you two weren't perfect, and I don't know why but I told him about Sophie, and Sam not being her... you know... real dad."

"You did what?" I have known this was coming but I am still shocked and now I'm so angry myself. I had told Julie that in strictest confidence but I feel guilty because I know full well that Sam had told me in strictest confidence. And it was not my secret to tell. I betrayed Sam's confidence, now Julie has done the same thing to me.

"I'm sorry, I'm sorry, I don't know why I did it. Luke went back inside but I went into the garden room, to get the beers, and then I saw Sophie. She was sitting on one of the chairs, with a blanket over her, reading a book. The radio was on, and she seemed fine. But what if she heard what I said?"

From the start of this conversation, I had known this was coming, but I had to hear it myself. I feel like a weight has dropped inside me. I sit forward, my head in my hands and my heart pounding.

"Shit, shit, shit, shit, shit."

Julie doesn't say anything but I can feel her eyes on me.

"So you don't know that she definitely heard you?" I'm ashamed at the tiny glimmer of hope that it may not be this which has caused Sophie to vanish. I know it's not the important thing right now. I look up at my friend but I can't meet her gaze. I can't bear to right now.

"I... don't know. I don't know. The weird thing was, Luke didn't seem all that shocked about it. I think he knew, or suspected something."

"I don't care about Luke!" I shout. "I need to know if Sophie heard what you said. This is bad. This is really bad. I need to tell Sam."

"You can't," Julie says. "He'll hate me."

"Oh my god, Julie, this isn't about you. And what do you think he'll think of me? But his nine-year-old daughter's gone missing and he needs to know why."

My hands are shaking as I pick up the phone. I select Sam's name and wonder if this is the last time I'll be able to ring him. There can be no way that he will want to be with me after this. But I can't think of that. Sophie is the important person here. It's cold out and god knows where she is.

"Is she there?" Sam's breathless, keen voice comes straightaway.

"No, she's…" I hear his sigh of disappointment. "Where are you?"

"On my way to her friend's… Amber's… I haven't been able to get in touch with them by phone. Kate's pissed, and hysterical. She keeps saying it's her fault."

"Sam…" I say.

"Yep?" he sounds like he's only half-listening.

"I've got to tell you something… about Sophie."

I've got his attention now. I tell him what Julie has told me. He makes no answer. I can hear the sound of the car so I guess he hasn't cut the call, but I can't hear him.

"Sam?" I say. "Are you still there?"

"Fucking hell, Alice, I can't believe you did this." I have never heard Sam's voice sound this way. "I trusted you. I have never told anybody else that but I wanted to tell you because I love you. And I didn't want there to be any secrets. Because you were so mad that I hadn't told you about her straight off. How could I be so fucking stupid? Now she's gone, she's run away, I don't know where she is, I…" Then there is just the sound of the car again.

"Sam?" my voice is panicked now.

The phone line goes dead. I sob, and run upstairs. I can hear Julie calling me but I can't answer. It's her fault, all this, I think, but even now I can hear a voice at the back of my head, telling me I've brought it all on myself.

I sit in my room by the window, not sure what else to do. I keep the curtains open, and just watch the street, in case Sophie should decide to come here. After all, she doesn't know it's my fault, does she? And she and I... we've grown close. I think of her small, warm body sleeping next to mine the night of the storm, and I can't describe how I feel at the thought of her being out on her own, in the dark. I feel physically sick, and desolate. If anything happens to her...

Kate crosses my mind, and I try to think how she must be feeling, and Sam. If I feel like this about Sophie, how must they be right now?

I don't know what to do. I just don't know. All I can do, though I know that really it is useless, is sit in the window and keep watch. Just in case.

My room is in darkness. Outside, those cheerful lights belie the stark reality of this night. From time to time, the street echoes with footsteps and voices; families, groups of friends, the odd lone figure striding along. I wish, I pray, that a small silhouette would appear under one of the streetlights, but it doesn't happen.

After some time, there is a gentle knock on my bedroom door. I don't answer but the handle turns and a small sliver of light falls across the bed and the floor, becoming wider and eventually allowing Julie in. I don't look at her, but I don't tell her to go away. She sits quietly on the bed and, despite everything, I find that I am glad she's there.

Time ticks on. Julie at some point fetches us some cups of tea, and some biscuits. I drink the tea but I can't imagine ever wanting to eat anything again, the way I feel right now. My phone is on the windowsill in front of me but it remains silent. As the night draws on, the street outside becomes increasingly quiet; passers-by now very few and far between. Finally, at about 3.20am, my phone beeps. My sore eyes take in the name that I want to see more than anything.

Sam Branvall (1)

I hardly dare open the message, for fear of what it might say. But I cannot be a coward. I must face whatever news there is.

We've found her. She's OK.

I let out a sob, and Julie comes to see for herself. "Thank god for that," she says, and I begin crying for real. Heaving shoulders, streaming tears. Relief, and anger, and sadness; mixed together and coursing out of me. Julie puts her arms around me and brings me over to the bed, sits me down.

"It's OK," she soothes. "They've found Sophie. She's OK. It's all fine."

But I know it's not.

24

I eventually fall asleep, Julie next to me, and when I wake up I can tell by the depth of the light streaming through the windows that it is late morning. I turn over, the events of the previous night hitting me one by one, as I wake up fully. Julie's confession. Sophie's running away. The end of my relationship with Sam.

Because how could it be anything else? I had given away his secret; the thing he had trusted me with, which meant more to him than anything else in the world.

I begin to cry all over again. I don't know that I have ever felt this bad. Eventually, I drag my sorry self out of bed. I need to use the bathroom and I need a drink of something.

I pull open my door. "Julie?" I say out loud but I can feel the house is empty and I am glad. I am not sure I want to see her right now. I need to straighten my head out about her. I might say something I regret if I see her at the moment.

The sunlight pours through the stairwell window, lighting the house with such determined brightness. I try to slip through it, unnoticed.

In the kitchen is a note from Julie:

Alice,
Please make sure you eat. I know what you are like. I am going to Luke's, I'm going to find out

what happened, and I am going to tell Sam that everything is my fault. I am going to make this OK. I promise.

J xxxx

I know she means well, but I also know Sam. Whatever she says to him, she can't make this right, because she can't undo the fact that I betrayed his trust.

I haven't heard from him since that message saying they'd found Sophie – and I don't expect to. I am grateful that he thought of me to let me know she is OK, but I don't imagine he has anything more to say to me now. He will be too busy looking after Sophie, and so he should be.

I think of her, and wonder how she is. What does it feel like, I wonder, to find out that the man you thought was your dad actually isn't? I mean, he is – in all the important ways. Sam is Sophie's dad, no matter who it was that Kate slept with when she became pregnant. But if you are nine years old, how do you sort out the important things like that in your mind? How do you make sense of it?

And Kate must be really angry, too. She must hate me. I've come along and ruined so many things for her; she'd wanted to get back together with Sam, only to discover that her new friend – me – was actually his ex, and also set on getting back together with him. Now I've managed to upset her daughter to the point of her running away. It must seem like I've done it on purpose.

I fill a glass of water from the tap; the bubbles frothing and fizzing over the sides. I drink it in one go then fill the glass again, to take upstairs. I may as well get dressed; create the appearance of some sort of normality.

When I spot the bottle of champagne on the sideboard, it breaks me. Thoughts of how last night should have gone flood my head; and what Sam and I should have been doing right now. We would probably have still been in bed; or maybe downstairs, opening the presents which lie under the tree. I go into the lounge and take in the scene. With the blinds closed and the lights off, the Christmas tree looks old and dark and worn. I can make out the shapes of the presents under its branches, including the one for Sam from Mum and Dad. The memory of him turning up at their house hits me. I begin to cry hard. I sit on the settee and put my glass on the floor, then allow myself to become wracked with grief. My parents had loved Sam, after just an hour. He had come all that way just to meet them. He really, truly loved me, but he can't do now. I am consumed by self-pity and, rather than go upstairs to put a brave face on it all, I lie on the settee in the darkened lounge, and cry and cry and cry, until I eventually wear myself out and fall asleep.

***

I am woken later, by the sound of the front door opening and closing.

"Alice?" It is Julie. I don't say anything at first. But then I grunt.

The light flicks on and my friend appears at the door, with Luke right behind her.

"Oh god, are you OK? You look awful."

"Thanks," I mutter, my eyes blinking at the stark brightness of the light.

"I'll put the kettle on," Luke says sensibly and I hear him head into the kitchen.

Julie sits next to me. "I've seen Sam," she says, "and Sophie. They're both fine. Sophie was hiding out in the garden room at Jim's place. Luke actually found her. She said she'd liked it so much when Jim had shown it to her. She'd fallen asleep in there but apparently she hadn't meant to be gone for long – she'd just wanted to get out of the house while Kate's mate was there. She didn't think anybody would notice she was gone."

"So she doesn't know..?" I allow a little spark of hope to ignite within me.

"No, she knows," Julie says gently. "But she's OK. I'm not going to say any more because Sam asked me to see whether you could go up there to see them."

My stomach sinks. I feel sick.

"Them..? At Kate's?"

"Yes, they're all there. Sam slept in Sophie's room last night, by the way."

"Oh!" My stomach contracts at the thought of this. My lovely Sam – always a brilliant dad. I think that Julie is trying to reassure me he didn't stay with Kate, but that thought had never even entered my head. I'm through with childish jealousy.

"Luke says Kate's really hanging this morning and she wouldn't talk to him. I dread to think what she'd do if she saw me right now."

"I don't think I can face her," I say.

"Alice, you didn't do anything. OK, you told me something Sam had told you, but you should have been able to do that and trust me to not say anything. I'm your best friend. You only told me about it because you were upset. It's been really hard for you since Sam went away."

"No. I shouldn't have told you," I say bleakly. "It's as simple as that. You've told Luke, but I've told you. We should both have kept our mouths shut."

"Well, get going. I know Sam wants to talk to you. So get yourself sorted, and get up there. It's all OK." Julie squeezes my arm and looks at me meaningfully.

"Alright." I get to my feet. "I'll have a shower and then I'll get going. I might as well face the music."

I feel sick as I shower, and find myself trembling. With exhaustion, or nerves, it's hard to know. Nevertheless, I wash my hair and I spend a little time drying it before I go. I rub moisturiser into my cheeks and pinch them, trying to bring a bit of colour to my otherwise pale skin. Julie calls up to me that there is coffee and toast and that I must eat it before I go or she will kill me. This brings a small smile to my face. I don't think I am angry at her any more. She's only done exactly what I did, after all. And she had no idea that Sophie would hear.

I head downstairs, to find Luke and Julie sitting in the dining room. Luke smiles sympathetically at me and raises his eyebrows, proffering the coffee.

"Yes, please," I say.

"There's sourdough toast here, too," Julie says, bringing a basket through. "Come on, eat up. It'll do you good. Never fight a battle on an empty stomach."

"It's hardly a battle, Julie," Luke says sternly.

"No, it's not, I know that. I'm sorry."

I force some toast down but I feel like it's going to stick in my throat so I wash it down with hot coffee. I don't sit.

"Alice, do you mind if we still go to Barcelona?" Julie asks, almost nervously. "I'll cancel if you want me to stay."

"No, of course. You go." In honesty, I'd forgotten all about it. "There's nothing more to do here, anyway. Sophie's fine. And I'll be back at work in a couple of days."

There is a small voice inside me thinking: *Great, everything's fine for you.* I marvel at how quickly they've got over their bust-up. It seemed like it was the end of the world when Julie burst in last night, but of course it wasn't the end of their world – just mine.

"Are you sure?" There is real concern on my friend's face, but what would be the point in them staying for my benefit? I think I just want to be alone anyway.

Before I leave the house, I send a message to Mum and Dad, which doesn't really say a lot more than that I hope they enjoy the rest of their trip and have a safe journey home. Then I pull on my coat and step out into the day, as bravely as I can.

25

I walk briskly through the cold air, up the hill to Kate's. There's a strong wind blowing over the rooftops, pushing pieces of litter and forgotten autumn leaves along the streets. Now that I am on my way, I just want to get this over with. As I ring the doorbell, I realise that I have never actually been inside. The only glimpses I've been allowed of Kate's home are into the hallway, when I've picked Sophie up or dropped her off.

Sam actually answers the door, and I'm glad. We look at each other almost shyly, and he goes to kiss my cheek. That in itself feels awful; a peck on the cheek. Like I'm an acquaintance.

"Hi," I say.

"Hi. Come in."

I take off my boots and follow him along the hallway, through the second door on the right. This turns out to be the kitchen; painted a lovely, soft terracotta and covered with Sophie's artwork. At the table by the window is Kate, nursing a cup of tea. She looks awful. I don't think I have seen her without make-up before but, more than that, she looks grey and washed-out.

"Kate's got a bit of a sore head," Sam says, and it seems to me that he's speaking through clenched teeth.

"I'm not surprised, you must have been up all night," I say sympathetically, trying to keep my teeth from chattering, I'm so nervous.

"It could be more to do with the wine and vodka," Sam says and Kate groans.

"I'm never going to drink again."

I stand in the doorway, not sure what to do or where to put myself. "Where's Sophie?" I ask.

"She's in her room," Sam says, "but I'll give her a shout. We all – all four of us – need to have a chat."

He passes me, politely saying, "Excuse me." Another dagger in my heart. I think I'd rather he was angry with me. Being civil is the worst thing ever.

"Do you want to sit down?" Kate speaks softly and I'm not sure I've heard her correctly but she pushes out a chair with her foot. Just as I'm sitting, unsure whether or not I should take off my coat, Sam and Sophie appear in the doorway.

"Hi Sophie," I smile at her but she doesn't meet my eye.

I don't know if I have ever felt this bad. However, I am here now, and just need to take whatever today dishes out to me.

Sam sits down next to me and Sophie pulls her chair closer to her mum.

For a moment, none of us speak. Then Sam says, "Shall I start?" As there is no answer, he goes ahead. "This is, has been, a nightmare," he looks at me, properly, for the first time since I arrived. I feel like crying. I will save that for the walk home, though.

"But at least now Sophie knows the truth and I feel – *we* feel -" he looks at Kate "- like we should have told her much earlier."

It's like they're closing ranks, as a family. "But I should also say, it wasn't anything to do with Julie, or you, Alice." Sam looks at me again. "It was... do you want to say, Kate?"

She looks daggers at him, then glares at her tea. "It was me. My fault. Sophie heard me talking to Isaac last night, didn't you, love?"

"Yes," Sophie's voice is almost inaudible. "But I wasn't running away. I just wanted to go out for a bit. I didn't think anyone would notice."

"Oh love," Kate says, "how could I not notice? I know I had my friend round but that doesn't mean I wasn't thinking about you. You know that, don't you?"

"Yes," Sophie says in that same small voice.

I don't know what to say. I'm shocked. I wait.

"So, you… you shouldn't feel bad," Sam says. "Neither should Julie. It wasn't anything to do with you."

But I still betrayed you, I want to say, but this is not the place. Instead, I say, "OK." I feel so awkward. If I was with any one of these three on their own – even Kate – I would find more words, but I am scared of saying the wrong thing in front of the others.

"Sophie also has something she wants to say," Sam says.

I look at her.

"I'm sorry," her eyes fill with tears.

"You don't have to apologise," I say, adding quickly, "not to me, at least. I'm just glad you're safe and sound and back home."

She looks down and a tear drops onto the shiny table-top. "It's not that. Well, not just that." She looks pleadingly at Sam.

"Do you want me to say it?" he asks. She nods.

"Well, what Sophie told me and Kate last night, we thought you should also know. She said she's been unhappy since I've been away. And because of that, she's done some things she's not very proud of. Like the night before I went away… the hospital trip. It wasn't, she wasn't…"

"I made it up," Sophie says, snivelling. "I said I was poorly because I didn't want Dad to go away."

I feel my own eyes pool with tears. "Oh, Sophie, that's OK. I know you've been missing your dad."

"That's not all," says Sam. He looks at his daughter and, keeping her eyes on his, like she is gaining strength from doing so, she speaks again. "I hid Mum's keys. I put them in Dad's pocket, when you went away to that hotel. I knew he'd bring them back. I'm sorry." She bursts into tears and flees the room. I am again lost for words, letting these revelations register.

"I know it looked like I was trying to mess things up," says Kate, looking at me. "And I know I've been a bit of a silly cow about things, but I wouldn't do that. I did think it might be Soph doing it on purpose but she always denied it and I had to believe her."

"God, no, I didn't think…"

"Yeah, you did! Well, I would have if I was you," Kate laughs and I feel an unexpected relief flow into me. "I definitely would have thought that."

I laugh as well, not exactly admitting that I had those thoughts, but no longer trying to deny them.

Sam looks from me to Kate and he smiles. At last. He looks shattered. They both do.

"So that was it, really," Sam said, his face more relaxed now. "We wanted to tell you what had happened, that you don't need to worry. And I am honestly really happy now that Sophie knows the truth. It's weird, she doesn't really seem that bothered. She says she's got loads of friends with much more complicated families."

She might say that now, I think, but I bet it hasn't hit her yet. And when she's a teenager, who knows how this might come out? Still, right now, everybody seems happy. Except

Sophie, that is, who I can hear sobbing in her room.

"Can I go and see her?" I ask.

"Sure," Kate says, "follow that weeping sound."

Sophie's door is adorned with a big painted snake, shaped like an S. I knock on the snake's head.

"Yeah?" I hear, and I gently push the door open. Sophie is sitting on the edge of her bed, crying and grasping a big fluffy bear tightly around its waist.

"Can I come in?"

"If you don't hate me."

"Hate you?" I say, walking towards her and perching next to her. "Of course I don't hate you. Why on earth would I?"

"'Cos I ruined things for you and Dad."

"No, you didn't. Not at all. You probably shouldn't have done those things, but I get why you did. You've had a tough time with your dad being away."

She looks at me now, and sniffs. I can't help but smile. She looks so young, and so earnest. I put my arm round her. "Sophie," I say, "do you know what? You are the most important person in your dad's life. Maybe it doesn't seem like it because he's gone away to study, and he's spent time with me when he could have been with you. But that's because he has to have his own life, too. He'd drop everything for you, though." I steer clear of the topic of whether he is her 'real' dad. I really hope that she always knows that he is.

"Do you really think so?"

"I know so." I kiss the top of her head. "Look, I'm going to go now. Everything's OK, though, I promise. I'll see you soon."

Sophie flings her arms around me and I squeeze her, until she laughs. "Take a couple of minutes and then get out

234

there and spend some time with your dad, and your mum. OK?"

"OK."

I find Sam in the kitchen, still sitting at the table. I don't know where Kate is.

"I'll get out of your hair now," I say.

"You're not in my hair," Sam stands and puts his arms around me. "Can I come round later?"

"Yes, of course you can." I'd been hoping he would but I wasn't sure that he would want to.

He kisses me. "See you later, then."

It's like nothing has happened. He's had the most traumatic night of his life but it's all now settled and, if anything, he looks happier than before. Kate even shouts bye to me when I'm leaving. I feel an unexpected warmth towards her.

As I walk back down the hill towards my home, I let the events of the last twenty-four hours spin through my mind. I think of Sam's anger, and worry, and how tired he and Kate look. Then I think of Sophie, and how sad she must have been to try and stop Sam and I being together; she's not a mean girl, or selfish so I can only think that she's been desperately sad about her dad being away. I have a sudden, strong feeling that I have been trespassing into a more adult world than I could ever imagine.

26

I sleep for a while that afternoon then, emotionally drained, I shove Christmas chocolates into my mouth and lie under the covers, watching *Love, Actually*, wondering when Sam will come and whether he might change his mind.

I cry very hard at the part of the film with the woman whose brother has mental health problems and who can't form a relationship because of it. Then at bloody Alan Rickman and Emma Thompson. Stupid man, letting that annoying woman in his office take his eyes off what's really important. Just as the finale is kicking off, with Hugh Grant and Martine McCutcheon revealed, ridiculously, kissing behind a curtain on the school stage, I hear the front door.

"I'm up here," I call, my heart thudding. I try to straighten the bed, hurriedly pushing chocolate wrappers into a pile in the hope that it will look like I haven't eaten so many. It doesn't work.

Sam appears in the doorway and I feel ill-prepared – lying in bed surrounded by chocolate wrappers, and looking, no doubt, like death warmed up. Why didn't I take a bath, get the Christmas tree lights on downstairs, and the fire going? "Hi," I say weakly.

"Hi," he says doubtfully, taking in the scene. "Are you ill?"

"What? Oh, no," I laugh. "Just stupid."

He laughs too then walks over, sits on the edge of the bed. All I want to do is kiss him but I feel disgusting, and I'm not sure of myself or Sam's feelings towards me. "How's Sophie?" I ask.

"She's… surprisingly OK, actually."

"Good." I really am pleased. At the centre of all this stuff; all us stupid semi-adults who seem to keep on making such a mess of things, is this lovely little girl.

"And how are you?"

"I'm OK too," he says, "and I'm sorry."

"Why are you sorry?"

"Well, firstly, for putting you in the position I did. I shouldn't have told you about Sophie. Well, really… Kate and I should have told Soph the truth a long time ago. I guess we thought what we were doing was for the best but really, it would have been much better to be open from the start. I thought I was doing the right thing by Kate. Protecting her reputation. Stupid, I know. When the important one was Sophie, all along."

"Yes, but you were young – you and Kate were both young – and what you did was a brilliant thing."

"Well, thank you. I think it's what most people would do, in that position."

"I'm not sure they would…" I can feel the conversation is going off on a different track and I don't want it to so I let my sentence trail away.

"I also owe you an apology," he says, "For taking it out on you. I was just so worried, you wouldn't believe." His brow creases at the memory. "And while I was beating myself up for telling you - the woman I've loved for ten years - about Sophie, there's Kate blabbing to some guy she's only known for ten minutes. And I really wouldn't be surprised if she's told other people over the years."

I look at him now and he takes my hand.

"I'm sorry, Alice. I was just so stressed last night."

"Well, of course you were."

"But despite it being an absolute fucking nightmare, it's actually done loads of good. All of it is out in the open now. I feel really relieved."

Sam looks at me; I know he wants me to smile. His beautiful eyes are on me, full of concern, willing it to be OK.

"Poor Sophie," I say.

"Well, yes, but she shouldn't have done those things. She's nearly ten years old."

"Nearly ten years old... she's only nine. That's so young."

"It is, I know it is. I didn't want to be too hard on her, I didn't have the energy, anyway." Sam moves next to me, puts his head on my shoulder. "I'm so tired, Alice. Can I just stay here with you?"

It's what I want more than anything in the world. "Of course you can," I say. I push the half-empty chocolate tub towards him and he takes one. I put the TV back on, and am happy to see it's *Die Hard*. Something we can laugh at. I am tired, and happy that Sam doesn't hate me, but I just can't feel that sense of relief he describes. My head is spinning, trying to make sense of everything.

Sam soon falls asleep next to me and, without him watching alongside me, I can't be bothered with the film. I switch off the TV and I lie there, thinking; listening to his deep, steady breathing; feeling his solid warmth against me; looking at his face in the darkness, taking in every detail.

27

I've always liked the start of a new year. There's something about the way people want to do things better, to make a fresh start. Granted, these good intentions often go to waste, but I love the energy while it lasts.

There is also something of a relief in the fact that Christmas is finally over. Love it as I do, it takes over everything, from November onwards, and by the time the decorations come down and trees are retired to back gardens and yards, or left out for the recycling trucks, I am glad to see things return to normal.

This year is no exception. After a very good New Year's Eve at the Sail Loft, with all the guests leaving happy and exhausted, the place is back to normal, and we are all enjoying a bit of a lull, as is normal for this time of year. It means that I can take stock, work with Stefan and Jonathan to review the last few months, and make plans for the next. It also means that, like now, I can occasionally grab a few rare and precious moments to just sit in the office, enjoy a cup of coffee, and gaze out of the window at the town and the sea.

After waking late, Sam and I did finally get to enjoy our Christmas together. I think we were both still shell-shocked from the events of the preceding day or two, but it was such a relief that Sophie was OK, and we were OK, together.

I had woken first so I'd crept downstairs, opened the

blinds in the lounge to let the sunshine flood the room; turned on the Christmas tree lights for one last-gasp chance at bringing some festive cheer into the house.

I made breakfast – toasted bagels with butter and spiced jam; a pot of coffee and a jug of warmed milk; fresh orange juice – and arranged it all on the largest tray I could find, then carried it up to my room. Sam was still breathing deeply in the warm darkness, so I placed the tray carefully on the table at the end of the bed and gently, slowly, opened the curtains just a little, bringing the bright day into this room, too. Sam stirred and I smiled as I watched him come round, although I was still slightly nervous that he might be angry at me. That the relief of having found Sophie may have been replaced by a reignited anger at my betraying his trust. But he blinked, looked at me, and smiled sleepily, stretching out a bare, beautiful arm for me to come back to him. I gladly did just that.

"You're cold!" he said, pulling me close and wrapping both of his arms around me. "Let me warm you up."

"I've been making breakfast," I said, my voice muffled into his chest.

"So I see. And I now realise I am starving!" Sam kissed the top of my head and released me, hopping out of bed to examine the breakfast tray. "This looks lush. But it's just a starter, right? I could eat a horse."

"Horses aren't on the menu, I'm afraid. But I'm pretty sure we've got eggs and sausages and hash browns downstairs."

"Yes!" he smiled, "Well, let's make a start on this, shall we? It might hold back my hunger for a while. I'm not sure I want to leave your bed just yet, you know."

He poured us both a coffee and brought the plate of bagels over. We munched through the lot of them, then

240

Sam put his arm around me and I leaned into him while I sipped my coffee. When my mug was empty, he carefully took it from me and put it on the bedside table, then with a gentle hand on my cheek, he turned my face to him. "I'm sorry I was so mad," he said.

"Don't be," I said, looking away, moving into the crook of his arm. "You had every right to be. And your daughter was missing. I'd have been more worried if you weren't angry."

"God, it was awful, she was only gone about three hours, but it felt like three days. It was Luke that found her, you know. I should have guessed she'd gone there. She's not stupid; she'd never have tried to get up to Amber's place on her own, in the dark, or even in the daytime. It's miles away and she knows how dangerous the moors can be. I could see when we were at Jim's how much she loved the garden room. Just like we always did. It's the perfect place when you're growing up – warm and dry, and tucked away so you don't feel like you're in somebody's garden. It's independence without any of the fear. Anyway, when Julie finally got through to Luke – he'd been deliberately not answering her calls because he was pissed off with her – she told him and he went straight up the garden. Said it was like a natural instinct; it was where he used to go in his teenage angst days. There Sophie was, tucked up under a blanket on that old settee, her earphones in and fast asleep."

I couldn't help smiling at the thought of this scene.

"I was so angry at her when I was going up to get her but as soon as I saw her, I could see she was scared, and upset, and all I could do was hold her. She was crying, I was crying, Kate was crying. I'm pretty sure I even saw Luke wiping a tear from his eye."

"I'm so sorry I told Julie, though, even if Sophie didn't

hear it from her. I had no right telling her something you'd trusted me with. And you can trust me, you know."

"I know. Of course I know. These past few months haven't been easy, have they? And I get it. You feel like you're at the bottom of my list – after Sophie, and my course, and sometimes even Kate. But I promise you, there is nothing between me and Kate, except that we share responsibility for Sophie."

"And I know that, really. I've just been selfish."

"No, you haven't. You need to make sure that you're doing the right thing. You've uprooted your life, taken a new job, got together with a bloke who's just fucked off up to Wales and can't be relied upon. You have to think of yourself, to make sure you're making the right decisions. There is nothing wrong with that."

I turned then and kissed him. And he kissed me. I felt his familiar warmth, the strength in his body as he pulled me down into the tangle of sheets and covers. I closed my eyes and breathed deeply as his mouth moved from mine, across my jawline, down to my shoulder, pulling my top away to reveal my bare skin. The stripe of sunshine from the partially opened curtains falling across both of us, we became lost together, all other thoughts banished from our minds.

We dozed in each other's arms till the early afternoon but then Sam insisted that we get up, eat, open the champagne and our presents. "It is Christmas, after all."

I dragged myself out of bed reluctantly, throwing on the previous day's clothes and pulling a comb through my hair. Sam got to work in the kitchen, making a very late breakfast. "The champagne's in the freezer, don't let me forget! I wanted it chilled fast." We ate at the dining room table, washing down our hash browns and beans with glasses of champagne, then we cleared up and moved into the lounge. While I lit the fire, Sam passed me a present. "I can't wait any longer," he said.

I could feel it was a small, hard box. My heart began to thud but I knew it couldn't be... could it? I opened it to reveal a beautiful pendant on a slender silver chain.

"You didn't think it was an engagement ring, did you?" he teased.

"No! Don't be daft. Of course not."

"It's a little bit soon for that kind of thing," he kissed me, "but I really wanted you to have something special, to wear while I'm away, to remind you that I'm thinking of you. Look, this stone is garnet. There's a little card that tells you what it means."

I unfolded the card which Sam handed to me:

Garnet is associated with romantic love and passion. It is thought to attract love and soul mates, to enhance self-esteem and encourage positive thinking.

Garnet is also known as a stone that can assist with success in one's career or business. It can be used to build self-confidence and to boost energy and creativity.

"Bloody hippy!" I said, kissing him and brushing a tear away with the back of my hand.

"I know! It just seemed perfect, though. Here, let me put it on you."

He moved behind me, pushing my hair to one side so that he could slink the chain around my neck, then he fastened the clasp and kissed my shoulder. His arms snaked around my waist and under my top.

"Hang on!" I laughed. "You've got a present to open, too."

I handed him a small, heavy box with a bow on it.

"It's not an engagement ring, is it?" He grinned.

"No!" I swiped at his arm.

He opened the box. I saw a huge smile spread across his face. "It's…"

"Yep. It's garnet. There's a little card which tells you what it means…"

"No way!" Sam laughed.

I had bought him a handmade garnet paperweight. "I wanted you to have something you might use, which would remind me of you while you're working."

"Well, doesn't that just tell you that we are meant to be?"

I smiled and kissed him.

The rest of the afternoon was as close to perfect as possible, given how tired we were. With Julie and Luke away, we had the house to ourselves all day and we made the most of it. After we finished the champagne, I ran us a deep bath and we sank together into the bubbles. I thought back to the bath we'd shared in the summer, the night Luke's mum had died.

"I love you, Alice," Sam said from behind me.

"I love you, too," I squeezed his hand, glad that he couldn't see my face.

In the evening we sat in the cosy lounge, blinds closed against the world.

"It's just me and you," Sam said. "At last." He kissed me deeply and I wanted to kiss him back but I knew that if I did I would never say what I knew I must.

"Sam," I said.

"Yes?" he was kissing my neck.

"I don't think we can do this."

"Why not? Julie's in Barcelona. Nobody's going to disturb us."

"No," I said firmly and he looked at me, concern writing itself quickly over his beautiful features. "What I mean is, I don't think that we can do this. Me and you, I mean. I don't think it can work."

Not now, I wanted to add, but that would have given some doubt to the situation. I knew that I had to be firm.

"Think about it," I continued. "From the moment we got back together, it's been one problem after another. It's like the world's trying to tell us something. And when I thought it was Kate, trying to make trouble, trying to split us up, I thought we could push through it. In fact, it made me even more determined. But it wasn't Kate, was it? It was Sophie. And she wasn't doing it to be malicious. She was doing it because she needs her dad. She already has to deal with you being away in Wales, and on top of that she now has to share you with me."

"But she really likes you…"

"Yes, I know," I smiled, "and I really like her. She is brilliant, and funny, and kind. And she is also a nine-year-old girl who needs her dad. She may not have run away properly the other night, and I am sure she didn't mean to cause so much trouble. But the fact that she did it seems so out of character for her. I think you need to be able to give her as much of yourself as you can."

Sam was looking down, his long eyelashes shading his eyes. I took hold of one of his hands.

"I wish it was different, Sam, you have no idea how much I wish that. Well, hopefully you do have some idea… but I just can't see it working between us. You have to prioritise your daughter, and your studies. You have to."

"I can't, we can't… we've only just got back together."

"I know," I said gently, "and I am so happy that we found each other again." Once more, I was tempted to say that things might be different in the future but I knew that if I did I would weaken my stance and I couldn't afford to do that.

"I think you know this is right, too, Sam. How can you give Sophie what she needs if you've always got to consider me, too? You have worked so hard to get on that course, and you need to give your best to that, and your best to your little girl. I can't expect you to be able to give your best to me, too. There's just not enough of you to go around, and you will end up worn out and not enjoying anything."

I saw a tear roll down his cheek, and I pulled his head to my chest, held it there firmly and willed myself not to cry.

"I've loved you since I was eighteen, Sam, and I'm not going to stop loving you."

"You are amazing, Alice," he said then, "I can't believe you're saying this, and I don't want to hear it, but I know you're right. You are."

He looked up then and kissed me fiercely. I knew I'd done it. I had said what I'd had to and he had listened. I kissed him back, and felt all of my passion and sadness and love for this man flood through me.

The next day, I was back at work. I threw myself into the New Year celebrations and tried not to think about Sam every second of the day. He took Sophie away for a few days, further up the coast, and sent me the odd message and picture. Kate spent New Year with her new man, Isaac, and I felt pleased for her. Now that I know she wasn't trying to sabotage my relationship with Sam, I feel a strange kind of warmth towards Kate. And a guilt that I ever suspected her.

New Year's Eve came and went. The guests were largely very drunk, bedecked in fancy dress and high spirits. They carried me through. Jonathan and Lydia were there throughout, and I went to bed at just after three, happily too tired to contemplate either the prior twelve months or the next. Julie sent me a message from Barcelona, as she and Luke had decided to stay on for a few more days. I sent back my love and wishes for a happy new year; telling her about Sam and me could wait till she got back home.

Now here I am. I just have to keep reminding myself that so much has changed since last January, who knows what may have happened by the next one? While I do love this time of year, I know it is also dark, and the weather can drown good spirits if you let it. Even so, I'm looking forward to seeing the winter out in this place.

Let the winds rock the seas and whistle through the streets; the cold bite my hands and sting my skin. Every day, the light seems to stretch a little further and I know that it can't be too long now until spring is on its way. I've just got to keep going, and push on through the darkness.

Thank you very much for taking the time to read *After the Sun*. If you've enjoyed this book, a positive review on Amazon or Goodreads would be much appreciated.

Coming Back to Cornwall

In the Coming Back to Cornwall series, Katharine E. Smith has found a subject, and a set of characters and places, which appeal to readers of all ages. With the glorious setting of Cornwall, and unforgettable, uplifting storylines, it is very easy to fall in love with these books.

All five books are available in print and Kindle editions, with audio versions being released in 2020.

A little taster of

As Boundless as the Sea:

Book Three of the

Coming Back to Cornwall series

It's hot in the club and the bassline of the music shudders through the floorboards as I sway almost imperceptibly in time with the beat, enjoying the feeling of hands on my hips, warm breath on my not-quite sunburned shoulders.

I lean back. His kiss slides along, from the straps of my sundress, up my neck, stopping just shy of my earlobe, where he whispers my name.

Just as he's moving his hands around my waist, the alarm begins to sound and I turn in a panic, to see beautiful, golden Sam.

"I'm so glad you're here," I say to him.

"I've missed you so much," he whispers into my ear but, just as in all good stories, I wake up to realise it's only a dream.

Sadly for me, I am no longer eighteen and my beautiful, golden Sam is long since lost to me.

But, as I start to come round, blinking sore eyes and cursing my alarm clock, I also take in the light – that special, unmistakable light, just beginning to help the day take shape – and the sounds from outside.

The seagulls calling from the roof.

The street sweeper, making its rounds, although the town is relatively quiet at the moment, tucked as it is somewhere in between the craziness of New Year and the more understated joy of the Easter holidays.

Garden birds and their songs add a sweetness to the morning; the early risers, unfailingly cheerful and seeming to sing for the sheer joy of another day dawning.

And just there, if I listen carefully – try to strain my hearing past this immediate cacophony – the constant, comforting – exciting – sound of the sea.

Sam may be gone but here I still am, in my beloved Cornwall, and I've survived my second winter here; one entirely without Sam, intact. This is the county that calls to me when I am away from it; rugged and wild, exciting and exotic. The place which makes me feel alive.

Julie, my best friend, my companion that first summer so long ago, is still here, too; tucked away in the room next to mine. These past two years have been eventful for us both. Now we are determined to build on these changes and move bravely forward into our new grown-up lives.

Besides which, the hard bit has been done, surely. It has to get easier from now on in.

Acknowledgements

I am very lucky to have a great team of supportive, honest beta readers and I would first like to say a huge thank you to all of you who have read *After the Sun* and offered your invaluable feedback, support and encouragement. In no particular order, thank you to: Helen Smith, Lucy Claire, Katie Copnall, Stella Leach, Janet Evans, Wendy Pompe, Claudia Baker, Jennifer Armytage, and my lovely dad, Ted Rogers.

As the second of a trilogy, I was inspired by the original *Star Wars* films to make this second book a bit of a 'down' ending. Life doesn't always go according to plan, and not every ending is happy – but there are still positive aspects as Alice develops her career (it's not all about having a man) and Kate proves to be a much better person than she may have first seemed. I didn't want her to be a jealous ex – it was too obvious and I don't want women to be portrayed that way!

While this is a book largely about people in their twenties, Sophie's presence brings a different dimension, reducing the freedom which Alice and Sam might otherwise have. Having two beautiful, wonderful, angelic (ahem) children myself, I guess this has affected the things I write about. We adults can't always put ourselves first when there are children involved, and Alice realises this.

I'm looking forward now to writing the final instalment of this series. Will there be a happy ending? You'll have to wait and see…

Writing the Town Read

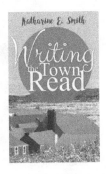

You can currently get an ebook of *Writing the Town Read* for FREE on Katharine's website: www.katharineesmith.com.

On July 7th 2005, terrorists attack London's transport network, striking Underground trains and a bus during the morning rush hour. In Cornwall, journalist Jamie Calder loses contact with her boyfriend Dave, in London that day for business.

The initial impact is followed by a slow but sure falling apart of the life Jamie believed was settled and secure. She finds she has to face a betrayal by her best friend, and the prospect of losing her job.

Writing the Town Read is full of intrigue, angst, excitement and humour. The evocative descriptions and convincing narrative voice instantly draw readers into Jamie's life as they experience her disappointments, emotions and triumphs alongside her.

Looking Past

Sarah Marchley is eleven years old when her mother dies. Completely unprepared and suffering an acute sense of loss, she and her father continue quietly, trying to live by the well-intentioned advice of friends, hoping that time really is a great healer and that they will, eventually, move on.

Life changes very little until Sarah leaves for university and begins her first serious relationship. Along with her new boyfriend comes his mother, the indomitable Hazel Poole. Despite some misgivings, Sarah finds herself drawn into the matriarchal Poole family and discovers that gaining a mother figure in her life brings mixed blessings.

Looking Past is a tale of family, friendship, love, life and death – not necessarily in that order.

Amongst Friends

Set in Bristol, Amongst Friends covers a period of over twenty years, from 2003 all the way back to 1981. The tone is set from the start, with a breathtaking act of revenge, and the story winds its way back through the key events which have led the characters to the end of an enduring friendship.

Both of Katharine's first two novels are written from a strong female first-person perspective. Amongst Friends takes her writing in a different direction, as the full range of characters' viewpoints are represented throughout the story.

How to Run a Free Kindle Promotion

on a Budget

Written primarily for other indie authors, this is a great guide to making the most of your 'free days' in the Kindle Direct Publishing KDP Select programme.

With BookBub deals hard to come by, not to mention pricey, *How to Run a Free Kindle Promotion on a Budget* takes you step-by-step through the process, from planning to record-keeping. It also includes real examples to illustrate the success or otherwise of the techniques described.

CPSIA information can be obtained
at www.ICGtesting.com
Printed in the USA
LVHW012019151220
674238LV00003B/373